Born in El Salvador, **Jorge Galán** is a poet and novelist. His works include *The Unending Day*, *Tuesday Afternoon* and *The Room at the End of the House*. He has been the recipient of several international literary prizes, among them the prestigious Premio Real Academia Española which he won for November in 2016.

Jason Wilson, Emeritus Professor at University College London, has written books on Octavio Paz, Jorge Luis Borges, Pablo Neruda, W. H. Hudson, Alexander von Humboldt and travel companions on Latin America, the Andes and Buenos Aires. He spends his time between London and Buenos Aires.

D1231222

November

A Novel

Jorge Galán

Translated from the Spanish
by Jason Wilson

CONSTABLE

CONSTABLE

First published in Great Britain in 2019 by Constable

This paperback edition published in 2020

1 3 5 7 9 10 8 6 4 2

Copyright © Jorge Galán, 2019

Translation copyright © Jason Wilson, 2019

The moral right of the author has been asserted.

A CIP catalogue record for this book is available from the British Library.

ISBN: 978-1-47212-535-4

Typeset in Caslon Pro by SX Composing DTP, Rayleigh, Essex
Printed and bound in Great Britain by Clays Ltd, Elcograf S.p.A.

Papers used by Constable are from well-managed forests
and other responsible sources.

Constable
An imprint of
Little, Brown Book Group
Carmelite House
50 Victoria Embankment
London EC4Y 0DZ

An Hachette UK Company
www.hachette.co.uk

www.littlebrown.co.uk

This story should begin in 1950 when a man in a poorly lit classroom asked if anyone wanted to volunteer for a trip to Central America. Sitting in their seats, the group of young men, none of them older than nineteen, listened to him in fascination. It was like listening to an adventure story. The man spoke of a place with cobbled streets in the foothills of a valley dominated by a volcano and surrounded by peaks, which were part of a mountain chain that stretched from Mexico into the heart of South America, interrupted only by the Panama Canal.

Despite their fascination, only one of the young seminarians raised his hand that morning. A little later, filled with a profound and growing happiness, he began his long journey to the other side of the world. He hoped that he would return a changed man. It didn't occur to him that he might not return, or that he'd return only to leave again. To truly return, we must belong, and that man came to understand that he no longer belonged to the place he'd left as a sixteen-year-old boy.

That's how this story should begin. With a young man in a black cassock descending the steps of a plane, the fierce tropical sun overhead, a warm breeze caressing his smooth face, simultaneously amazed and captivated by what he observes around him: the forest that stretches out from the airstrip, the peaks in the distance and the volcano that dominates the northern horizon. On reaching the ground, he closes his eyes and for a moment remains suspended in that strange stillness filled with aroma and light, and the distant cries of birds. Years later, we see the same man, his eyes closed once more, but there's no blazing sun overhead for instead of a summer morning in 1950 it's midnight in the winter of 1989.

In pitch-dark, lying on his bed, he opens his eyes. He thinks he hears voices, but can't be sure at first whether they are real. He's in his room in the Jesuit house of the UCA (the University of Central America, San Salvador), which has been his home for years. Despite the sound of violent clashes raging around the town, he had managed, at least for a few hours, to fall asleep – until the commotion wakes him up. Outside, there are men waiting for him and it takes a moment for this to sink in. He hears footsteps in the corridor; many footsteps. He sits up in bed, alert but not distressed. Someone is knocking on the door and he can make out the sound of metal on metal. Clearly it's not a friendly visit; the realisation fills him with sadness rather than despair. Had he been alone, he would have felt differently, but he is with his brothers. Himself included, there are six priests in the house.

Soon the whispers give way to raised voices as the men abandon the effort to conceal their presence. The first shot rings out. It comes from the back of the house, near the Centro Monsignor Romero. Ignacio Ellacuría gets up and reaches for his dressing gown. Though he isn't afraid, his hands tremble and it takes him a while to tie a knot in the strip of cloth that he uses as a belt around his waist. He runs a hand through his hair, a habitual gesture, and leaves his room. His fellow Jesuits are also awake. He tells them to remain calm. Some are praying. One of them asks: 'Are they coming to search us again?' Ellacuría doesn't respond and neither do the others. 'What's going on?' someone else asks, and again there is no reply. Once more he appeals for calm and says that he will go and find out what is happening. One of the others warns him to be careful. Ellacuría says, 'Don't worry.' What is the point in worrying when there's nothing you can do?

He walks towards the main entrance, stopping when he comes to a hammock; from there he can see them and they can see him. They're yelling and banging on the door. 'Don't get so excited, I'm going to open it,' Ellacuría pleads with them, and between that sentence and their entrance a few moments expand in time, not unlike that day when he delayed raising his hand in the classroom when a man asked for a volunteer to travel to Central America. It is as if he crosses over from deep night to an even deeper one, his thoughts no longer confined to that corridor or what is beyond that door but returning to his parents, his friends and the years of his youth. And as his trembling hand turns the lock and the door opens, the tepid breeze wafts in the smell of gunpowder and sweat – in its own way, an exhilarating smell. He feels strangely calm, like someone who has endured a long illness and knows they have come to the moment when it is time to rest. Suddenly it doesn't seem so frightening, and he is able to surrender himself to what will happen without caring what lies on the other side, even if there is no other side.

'Yes, I know why you're here,' Ellacuría tells them. While some of the men go to search the bedrooms, the lieutenant in charge orders an underling to take Ellacuría and the others to the garden. Perhaps if it had been a lone assassin, a single

3

gunman, he might have been able to talk to him and convince him, but there are so many of them that he knows it's pointless. Nevertheless, he gives it a try. 'You've come to get me, and here I am. You don't need to touch anyone else.' The lieutenant doesn't seem to hear him. 'Here I am. The others haven't done anything. I'm the one you want.' But the man doesn't even look at him. He walks a few steps with Ellacuría, as far as the garden. A soldier grabs the priest by the shoulder and forces him to the ground. Inside the house, the shouting of the soldiers drowns out the protests of the other priests. Ellacuría lies down on the damp grass. The crickets are making a din that goes unnoticed. The full moon, now at its zenith, illuminates the scene. In the windows of the surrounding houses, silhouettes appear and disappear in the darkness. They can't see inside the Fathers' house, but they can hear what is going on. One by one the other priests are dragged out by the soldiers and thrown on to the grass. 'I would have liked to say goodbye to my sister,' sobs Ignacio Martín-Baró. 'I talked to her today and said nothing.' Someone whispers to him: 'They mustn't see us crying.' Behind them, another says: 'This is an injustice.' Another twists his head towards the soldiers: 'You're a disgrace.' But soon they stop protesting and sobbing and one of them begins to recite the Lord's Prayer.

Later, witnesses in the neighbouring houses would tell of hearing a kind of 'rhythmic lament', but it wasn't a lament they heard, just the sound of the Lord's Prayer being intoned in unison. Having come to the country many years earlier as priests, they wished to leave in the only way they knew. After a few minutes, one of the soldiers took a step forward and opened fire. A priest tried to sit up but there wasn't time. Soon the 'rhythmic lament' ceased. Everything ceased. It was dawn, 16 November 1989.

PART ONE

1

The morning was cold, but not within the university grounds. Within a few metres of the entrance, he noticed the air was warmer here on campus. He could feel the warmth even in the area adjacent to the rectory, where the football pitch gave way to a shady border of pines. It was six in the morning. He followed the side street that runs along the back of the library and the laboratory buildings towards the Centro Monsignor Romero. It was even warmer inside. Without him being aware of it, his pace began to slow as if something was preventing him from moving forward, like a child wrapping himself around his feet to stop him going any further.

The door was open and the interior of the Centre was like a battlefield, with remains of cartridge cases strewn about. It was obvious that a fire had destroyed some of the rooms. He didn't enter any of them; instead his fresh footprints mingled with those already sketched in the ash as he made his way along the corridor and climbed the steps that led to the Jesuits' house. Then the Jesuits' corpses came into view. He walked around them without stopping to look, then bent down to touch Father

Martín-Baró. He placed his fingers on the priest's shoulder as if trying to wake him up, but he didn't react. A trail of blood led from the garden into the interior of the house. He felt as if a shadow had engulfed him, its weight unbearable. He had not come here in search of the priests. He had come for his wife and daughter, who lived in the same house.

Climbing the steps, he fought the urge to run to the room at the back where the two had spent the night. So long as he stayed with the assassinated Jesuits he could cling to the hope that he would hear his wife's voice telling him to leave all that and go into the bedroom, hurry and call an ambulance . . . but her voice did not materialise. He delayed a few minutes, gathering up the courage to leave the priests' bodies behind and face up to whatever awaited him in the bedroom at the back of the house. He didn't know when he covered his mouth with his hand. The silence told its own story. By the time he reached the door he was shaking. The door was open. Why hadn't his wife and daughter come out? Why wasn't he hearing them? He came to a halt in front of the door, feeling lost. A second later he looked in and saw them, one next to the other, sprawled on the ground, almost hugging each other. He sat down in the middle of the room, his hand still covering his mouth, but no longer looking because he did not want to see any more, did not want to think or feel. When he could finally stand up, he walked to the chapel, which was right next door, and sat down again, trying to summon up the strength to decide what to do next. Eventually, overcome with loneliness as much as horror, it occurred to him that he should tell the other Jesuits what he had seen. The moment he stood up, he was consumed by a sense of urgency, as if his arriving there faster could somehow make a difference. So he set off in the direction of the second Jesuit house, which was located at the end of a parallel street not far from the campus, practically running in his haste to spread the news, without being aware as he left that house that the morning was still just as cold.

2

José María Tojeira was on the patio, halfway through shaving his face, when Father Francisco Estrada appeared in the doorway.

'Obdulio just arrived — he says they've assassinated the Jesuits in the UCA as well as his wife and daughter.'

The ground under Tojeira's feet seemed to shift, as if he were in a pine forest where tangled roots lay concealed under a thick layer of needles, ready to trip the unwary. Feeling cold and light-headed, he struggled to make sense of what he had just been told, the news delivered in such a way that Estrada might as well have announced that breakfast was ready. He called another of the Jesuits to steady him while he finished shaving, as he felt he was about to fall over. When he was done, he went upstairs to his bedroom and got dressed. Whatever he was thinking in the meantime, he cannot remember; it has been lost forever.

He came down to find Obdulio sitting in the main room. The man seemed to have shrunk, like when an open hand becomes a fist. In silence, with a lost expression on his face, he sat with his head resting against the wall, apparently unable to hear what was being said to him. Standing next to Obdulio was a woman called Lucía who worked with the Fathers at the university. She had spent the night in a building next to the university that belonged to the Jesuits; they had put her up because she hadn't been able to return to her home, which was currently in the middle of a war zone. Lucía was accompanied by her daughter and husband. The minute she saw Tojeira appear, she rushed towards him and said:

'Father, I saw them, I saw them and I heard them. They were soldiers, Father.'

She had seen them leave the house, lit by moonlight, a light more radiant that night than any other night. Or perhaps the night had been lit by flares, thrown by the soldiers as they retreated. Tojeira and some of the priests spoke to Lucía. They asked her if she would be willing to testify. She did not hesitate. She swore she would do whatever was necessary. Fearing for her safety, they told her to return to her house and remain there. After cautioning her against talking to anyone or doing anything to attracting attention, they assured her that they would look after the rest.

Anxious to confirm the truth of the reports, the Fathers started getting ready to go out. 'And what will we do if the soldiers are still inside?' asked one. They began to quiz Obdulio, wanting to know whether he had seen anybody. He said he had not, there had been nobody around, or at least he had not seen anybody inside.

'What if they're hiding? It's still early, they could be waiting for us.'

'Obdulio, did you search the Fathers' house?'

'No, Father, I didn't,' the man answered. 'It was all I could do to go into my wife's room.'

'I think we must go and see what happened for ourselves,' suggested Tojeira. 'It would be worse if we didn't go. Does anyone want to stay here?'

Nobody spoke. Tojeira then divided them into two groups.

'You come with me,' he told the first group. 'We'll enter by the gate at the east side. The rest of you can go in via the pedestrian entrance. If you hear shots, run back to this house and call the international press. Don't go out.'

The house where Tojeira and the rest of the Jesuits lived was just a few metres from the pedestrian entrance to the university, at the back, in the same street. They could enter via the east entrance by going round the house and down an avenue that crossed from north to south, from Bulevar Los Próceres to Antiguo Cuscatlán. So Tojeira went that way, with the key to the door in his hand. He would have preferred not to hear the hinges squeaking as he opened the door, but it was unavoidable. From that entrance, the Centro Monsignor Romero was a few metres to the left as you walked up the internal street of the university.

UCA's Jesuit house stood opposite the Centro Monsignor Romero. It was possible to approach it from inside the Centre or via a door next to the chapel. On the left side of the street there were no buildings, just a long stretch of trees, grass and flowerbeds. On the right side there were a series of laboratory buildings occupied by the engineering department. Tojeira recalls walking under the shade of the tall trees that dominated that part of the campus; it was a luminous, cold day, with birdsong drowning all else. This made him think that what he had been told could not possibly have taken place, not on a day like this. It must all be some strange lie. This thought lodged with him even as he was entering the Centro Monsignor Romero through an unlocked door and caught the smell of tepid, bitter ash from the side rooms that had been burnt down. Still he persisted in telling himself it was all a mistake, a misunderstanding, as he climbed the steps to the Fathers' house, and he did not stop thinking it until, at the last moment, he saw first a hand tossed on the grass and then a whole body, followed by three bodies scattered like strange seed in the small garden.

They were lying face down, with their arms extended as if reaching out to something in front of them. Another body had one perfect bullet hole, assassinated with a coup de grâce. Tojeira and the rest of the Jesuits stood for a long time contemplating that unreal scene, perhaps trying to convince themselves that it was true. A few minutes later, Tojeira entered the priests' bedrooms and found Father Joaquín López y López in one of them, lying in a puddle of his own blood. Then he continued to the bedroom that Father Jon Sobrino usually used (he was on a trip outside the country); there he came across Father Juan Ramón Moreno's corpse, which appeared to have been dragged there. A little later, he left and went on to the bedroom that Obdulio's wife and daughter used.

'I wasn't crying,' Tojeira tells me.

'No tears, Father?'

'Not from Obdulio or me.'

Silent, fearful, so resigned and crushed by the weight of destiny that even sights like these do not elicit a sob – the reaction that Tojeira describes is typical of the people that live in this shadowy place. In a city and country like this one, resignation is the only option.

Obdulio's wife, Elba, was lying on top of Celina, his daughter; it was obvious she had wanted to protect her daughter and tried, until the last moment, to save her. The body and face of the mother were destroyed.

Tojeira speaks about that morning as if it was a month ago,

a week ago, a day ago, because the images of that dreadful moment, the things he had seen then with a glance hardened by circumstances, are not something that you can forget, even after many years have passed and even though all the years of his life have passed. When his final day arrives, this memory will stand out amongst the rest. As he speaks to me about the corpses of his fellow priests, he doesn't mention again the luminous morning, the riotous birdsong, the breeze, or the grass swaying around the bodies as if nothing had happened, as if death and fear were no more than a strange invention in the terrible world of men.

3

Five days earlier, on 11 November 1989, the military forces of the Frente Farabundo Martí for National Liberation launched their 'final offensive'. It was the most significant campaign of the entire civil war. Battles were fought throughout the country, but mainly in the capital, San Salvador, which had been spared from the fighting for most of the war. The sound of gunfire, near or far off, continued unceasingly and by the early morning of 16 November it had turned into a grim daily routine.

'We heard shots in the night,' Tojeira recalls, 'but we did not suspect anything, we thought it was another skirmish. One of many. For four or five days, it had been going on like that. The only thing that had alarmed us that morning was that everything was happening close by. It was twenty minutes of shooting, three grenades and a LAW anti-tank missile. An AK-47, which was the weapon favoured by the guerrillas, lots of army-issue M-16s, and one M-60, which they used to machine-gun the building. Lastly, they used a flamethrower to destroy the offices of the Centro Monsignor Romero. Of course, we heard that and thought it was a clash. What else could we think?'

I don't see how they could come to any other conclusion, but I'm not answering his question because in reality it is not a question but a lament. His eyes have dimmed as we speak, the way a room grows dark when a storm cloud passes over. We return to that morning, to the Fathers' bodies strewn in the grass and the horror that followed as they decided what had to be done and allocated tasks.

It was Tojeira who assigned the chores, like an elder brother speaking to the younger ones in their parents' absence, telling them what they had to do to stop the house falling apart. They have been abandoned, they are alone. And though they are men, some even older than those assassinated, the void is so deep that they understand they are alone, as if that were an absolute truth.

'You go to the archbishopric,' Tojeira ordered one of them, 'and tell the archbishop what has happened.'

'Wouldn't it be better to call?'

'Call him or go and see him, whatever you prefer. But he must be informed. And you, you must go to the Hotel Camino Real where the international press is billeted.'

'Are we going to stay here?' asked another one.

'What do you mean? Now?'

'Tonight. I mean tonight. Maybe it's not a good idea to remain in the house.'

'Perhaps it's dangerous to isolate ourselves,' ventured another, 'and we are very close to the university. We seminarians . . . '

'Fine,' Tojeira conceded, 'perhaps it would be best if we all stayed under one roof. We could all go to the Santa Tecla house, but let's see about that in a while. Our first priority is to work out what happened here.'

'We've got to leave this place. The Santa Tecla house is a good solution.'

'Yes, we'll do that. But in the meantime, what are we going to tell the press?' asked Tojeira. 'What conclusion do we draw from all this?'

'What Lucía told us, that's what we have to say, there's no other option.'

'Well, yes, but can we even say that? If we let on that a witness told us, it would be too dangerous.'

'What happened is obvious. The university is in a military zone. We are surrounded. Nobody but the army can enter.'

It's true. Opposite the university, across Boulevard Los Próceres, lies the Arce district, an exclusively military enclave. They are less than five hundred metres from the military school, the offices of the army's high command, the headquarters of both the armed forces and military intelligence. The entire area had been cordoned off by military personnel and soldiers had been deployed throughout the Jardines de Guadalupe district, surrounding the UCA. Even buildings belonging to the university had been occupied by military units. With that level of security it would have been impossible for a guerrilla patrol to enter the zone, let alone storm the campus and assassinate the Fathers. There is no need for the Jesuits to mention that Lucía witnessed soldiers leaving the scene.

'Then we're agreed: we tell them what we believe happened.'

'Yes. There's no other way.'

'We'll still be taking a risk in accusing the army. An army engaged in a military offensive. An army that has just assassinated our companions.'

'What else can we do?'

Though they had every reason to be afraid, they decided that they could not remain silent. At the end of that meeting, as each one left to carry out the task he had been allocated, they did not know what to make of the silence emanating from the surrounding houses. They saw no faces peering out of the windows. It was as if the occupants were unaware of what had happened, yet they saw them walking along the pavement, making their way like blind men through the ashes that covered the ground on that clear November morning. They felt the weight of the invisible burden that each man carried. They registered the terrible silence. And all this told them that something bad had happened at the university. No one waved, no one smiled or offered a greeting as they would have done normally; they had become faceless entities that came and went in the cold of dawn. It crossed the mind of some of the neighbours that there might have been an assassination, but they did not want to believe it. It seemed too far-fetched.

Tojeira made his way to his office. He needed to call Rome. Unaware of what he was doing, he dragged his feet, leaving a trail through the ash and pebbles and dried leaves, his mind oblivious to everything but the image of his fellow Jesuits sprawled in the grass, as if they had fainted. If there had been a chasm in the pavement, he would surely have fallen into it. He walked as if on autopilot, unaware of the prying eyes watching from the windows. Nor did he hear the whispers. The outside world had ceased to exist. He registered nothing beyond the thoughts in his head. In his mind's eye, he was still standing beside the bodies of his fallen companions, taking care not to touch them and not to let the soles of his shoes come into contact with their blood. Without realising it, he opened the door, went to his desk, looked up the number and dialled. While dialling he thought how awful it was to have to convey such news. What time would it be in Rome? The middle of the afternoon. Perhaps they would be having lunch. Or taking a siesta. Or drinking coffee. Perhaps one of their friends was about to tell a tale about Ellacuría or about Father Montes or about any of them. So far as the Jesuits in Rome were concerned, they were still alive. At this moment all their memories of their companions were good ones.

At the other end of the line a priest answered: *Buongiorno*. Tojeira felt as if his companions were dying all over again, breaking the news. But there was no way round it; he had a duty to explain what had happened and he did the best he could.

'But are you well?' asked the man on the other end of the line.

'Yes, yes, I am well,' Tojeira reassured him and carried on telling him what had happened. 'Do you understand what I've said? They've killed the UCA Jesuits, as well as two women who were at the house.'

'But you're OK?'

'They have assassinated Father Ellacuría, Father Segundo Montes, Nacho Martín-Baró, Amando López, Joaquín López y López, Father Juan Ramón Moreno . . .'

'But are you OK?' insisted the voice from Rome. Then Tojeira tells me he became angry, because at times like that you cannot think. It is impossible to gauge what impact your words have had. Perhaps the man on the other end of the line thought he had gone mad, that this was some insane and macabre fantasy. Perhaps he did momentarily suspect something of that nature, until he realised that his companion was distressed.

'But you are OK?' he repeated.

'Yes, well, yes, I'm OK,' Tojeira finally said, 'I'm OK . . . I am telling you this and talking to you, I'm OK . . .'

What Tojeira did not grasp was that his voice sounded different: higher, faltering, distorted by emotion.

4

The floor in the Pastoral Centre was covered in ash, while its walls, stained by shadows, were riddled with bullet holes, as were the filing cabinets and desks. They had finished off the place as if it was an enemy garrison's intelligence headquarters, not a Catholic university. The stench of gunpowder was unbearable. Tojeira came out and made his way to the garden where he had found the bodies of his companions. It was then that he realised Archbishop Arturo Rivera y Damas had arrived. He was dressed in black, with what appeared to be a gold cross on his chest. He was accompanied by a number of journalists who were firing questions at him. *Christians pray first and then give interviews*, he told them. And to some it seemed a frivolous response, but he had nothing else to say, at least not at that moment. If he could have avoided making any statements, he would have done, but this was out of the question so he made do with putting it off.

The archbishop approached Tojeira, offered his condolences and asked him to identify each one, for they were lying face down and in such a state that it would be impossible for anyone who did not know them well to identify them. Tojeira did as he asked, discreetly, hoping the journalists would not notice, but they were too close not to hear. Tojeira explained that inside, in the corridor and in the bedroom, there were two more bodies. Rivera y Damas asked for silence and said a prayer. The crowd respectfully kept quiet while he prayed.

When it was over, Tojeira accompanied the archbishop to the bedrooms, where they found the other two corpses. They walked in silence while they looked at the bodies. *What an outrage, and so much hate*, said Rivera y Damas when he saw Joaquín López y López's body. The Jesuit was wearing a shirt that did not seem appropriate for a cold November night, its cloth worn thin with use. He did not look like an academic. He was dressed with such simplicity that it was impossible to say what he did. Perhaps that image was a revelation for Rivera y Damas. A revelation of a life devoted to a purpose, a life of renunciation.

'We must convene in the Nunciature,' said Rivera y Damas. 'Let's say eleven o'clock. I'm going to see if I can arrange a meeting with President Cristiani.'

'You can count on me,' said Tojeira.

'That's good, Father,' said Rivera y Damas. 'We cannot stand by and do nothing.'

Tojeira nodded. And the archbishop, moving as slowly as the mist, walked away from the scene, and was met by the journalists, who once again surrounded him.

'Archbishop, who killed the Jesuit Fathers?'

'They were victims of the same hatred that killed Monsignor Romero,' answered Monsignor Rivera in what appeared to be an appropriate yet empty answer, but it was not. He had said what he wanted to say and so far as he was concerned it was the truth.

Soon after, it was Tojeira's turn to be questioned by the journalists. There were representatives from the newspapers as well as from the radio and some television channels, many of them foreigners who were in the country covering the latest developments in the offensive. He didn't say much, and no one expected him to, for they assumed he had only suspicions about what had happened. Gradually the crowd began to grow. Even some of the neighbours dared to emerge from their hiding places and to observe what was going on. Tojeira was still talking to the journalists when a man called Francisco Guerrero, an old politician and well known in the country, arrived on the scene. Guerrero seemed genuinely affected by the situation; he had known most of the assassinated Jesuits. Tojeira saw him enter through the door that led from the chapel. He hurried towards them and came to a halt by Ellacuría's body, without saying a word to anyone. Guerrero cried bitter tears, covering his mouth in an effort to muffle his sobs. Drying his eyes with a handkerchief, he stood there shaking his head. When Tojeira finished talking to the journalists, Guerrero approached him.

'Those bastards will pay for this,' Guerrero told him, his voice breaking with emotion. 'Those who have done this will pay, Father.'

'Yes, I know,' said Tojeira, trying to calm him down.

Guerrero put his arm around Tojeira's shoulders, forcing the priest to walk with him, leaving the journalists behind. Tojeira allowed himself to be led. Guerrero got closer to him as they moved away, leaning his head on the priest's shoulder.

'They really are going to pay for this Father,' Guerrero repeated in a very low voice.

'Indeed,' said Tojeira. 'There is always justice. Be it human or divine, there's always justice.'

'They will pay for it,' Guerrero insisted. 'And do you know why, Father? Because I have some recordings in my car. Recordings of military officers. I've got them on tape. That's the reason they're going to pay for this.'

'You should not talk about this here,' Tojeira pointed out, surprised that the politician would take him into his confidence. He knew the man, but only in a superficial way. They had never been friends.

'I don't care, Father.'

'Calm down, Francisco.'

'I'll hand these recordings over to you one day. I'm going to give them to you soon, you'll see. You'll see how these bastards will be screwed. You'll see, Father. They are going to pay for this. I swear on it.'

Tojeira never did get to hear the recordings. Twelve days later, Guerrero was assassinated while driving his car through the centre of San Salvador. A machine gun opened fire on him as he waited for a red light to change. Who took possession of these recordings and what was said on them will now never be known.

5

The morning was still warm and got warmer as midday approached. The murder scene was untouched, awaiting the arrival of the police. It was a picture in greens and reds under the sun, surrounded by journalists, friends and idle spectators. Suddenly, Tojeira discovered that there were flies on the corpses.

'I was furious,' he confesses.

'It made you angry?'

'Yes, when I saw the flies on the bodies I flew into a rage. It was humiliating. And I said to myself: "They've treated them like shit and now this."'

As he says this, he smiles ruefully. So many years have passed that now he can smile at the end of a sentence like that one.

Tojeira was the Jesuit Provincial for Central America. He was not one of the best-known priests at the university, not like Ellacuría or Segundo Montes, or even Martín-Baró, all of whom were invited to appear on television (especially Ellacuría), or were sought after by journalists and radio commentators because their opinions carried a lot of weight. Their influence had extended far beyond the university's classrooms, to the political, religious and social life of Salvador. Tojeira, on the other hand, was not influential in the universities nor in the work carried out by UCA. He had trained to work with ordinary people and if he had studied social anthropology on his own and liked mixing the gospel with reality, he always did so in the simplest way possible. At that time, the seminarians were his main concern, and he liked being their leader. He did not usually give interviews or was seldom asked to. He lived in comparative anonymity.

On the Saturday night when the offensive began, Tojeira could not get to his house because the whole street was cordoned off by soldiers. Earlier that afternoon there had been a skirmish between the army and some guerrilla fighters who were passing through the zone. Tojeira had gone to the cinema; by the time he returned it was dark and the military were refusing to allow anyone to enter the Jardines de Guadalupe quarter. So he took a roundabout route to a house occupied by some seminarians from his Order, intending to spend the night there.

Tojeira had known that something was about to happen; some of the priests associated with the guerrilla fighters, and they had been given advance warning. However, there had been many such warnings, and most of the guerrilla offensives consisted of an attack on a military post which was over no sooner than it had begun. Thus, on hearing the latest warning, Tojeira saw no reason to be alarmed or to change his routine. He went off to the cinema as he did every Saturday.

His near-anonymity came to an abrupt end on the morning of 16 November 1989 when he found the bodies of his assassinated companions. As a Jesuit Provincial, he realised it was his duty to provide leadership and take the consequences.

'If they killed those who were important and well known,

25

with international connections,' he says to me, 'why wouldn't they kill me? That was clear in my mind that morning. A Provincial works behind the scenes, assigns tasks and checks how well people do their job, nothing more. But I knew that it was my responsibility to step up.'

'I suppose there was no alternative.'

'None.'

At eleven a.m., Tojeira went to see Monsignor Rivera in the Nunciature and was told that they had an appointment with the president of the republic, Alfredo Cristiani, in an hour's time. There were many people in the Nunciature and it seemed more like a Sunday than a Thursday. Tojeira and Monsignor Rivera met in a small office where they were joined by another priest, a man named Gregorio Rosa Chávez. Tojeira delivered his analysis of what had occurred.

'There were twenty minutes of shooting,' he told them, 'a minimum of twenty minutes. I know that because we heard it. The place was overlooked by Democracy Tower.'

'Were there soldiers keeping watch up there?'

'They were on the lookout because guerrilla forces had attacked the Jardines de Guadalupe quarter five days earlier. So there were soldiers everywhere, including the Democracy Tower.'

The so-called Democracy Tower was a building to the east of the university, standing seventy-one metres high, with nineteen floors. When the killings took place, it was not yet in use and was not even finished, but it was in the final stages of construction so it was possible for the army to set up surveillance posts there. From the top floors and roof terrace you had a commanding view of the university, particularly the wing where the Jesuits lived.

'And it's obvious', Tojeira went on, 'that this killing couldn't have taken place without the army sanctioning it. The university lies just two hundred metres from the Arce quarter where many soldiers are stationed with their families. Military intelligence has their headquarters four hundred metres from the tower. The staff college is six hundred metres away. There was a curfew in force from six in the evening. It would be impossible to launch an attack that lasted twenty minutes without the army knowing about it.'

'It all seems very clear-cut,' said Monsignor Rosa Chávez.

'Everyone knows how the military operate,' Rivera went on, 'we've known it for a long time. Proving it is another matter.'

The three spoke a little more about what had happened, and argued over what they could or could not tell President Cristiani. Tojeira was then asked what steps the Company of Jesus had taken to ensure their safety. He told them they were thinking of moving into a Jesuit house located in the village of Santa Tecla.

'You would all live there?'

'For the moment, yes. It's a large house, and there would be about forty of us, so we'd have to share rooms. The crucial thing is to be together. I don't think that they can kill us all.'

A few minutes later, Tojeira and Monsignor Rivera left for their appointment with the president. The city centre was deserted, apart from soldiers patrolling the streets or standing sentry. From inside the Nunciature's car the two men watched them in silence. I ask Tojeira if, when he saw those soldiers, he felt frightened or angry, or if he wondered whether some of them had participated in the previous evening's atrocity. He tells me he can't remember. He has no recollection which route they took from the Nunciature to Cristiani's office, or what the weather was like. He can't recall whether he had eaten breakfast or what

27

time it was or who was with him or whether the people in the Nunciature that morning had greeted him or offered their condolences. One thing he does remember is that they had no difficulty getting in to the President's Palace. The building was surrounded by soldiers, standing guard along the pavement, between the bushes and under the trees. There was a tank right in the entrance, next to the metal gate, with soldiers armed with M-16 rifles on each side. Given that the palace had come under attack on the night the offensive began, the level of vigilance did not strike him as excessive. They entered the building without problem and parked under an enormous pine at the far end of the car park. When they got out, a military man saluted them and asked them to accompany him. At the entrance to the palace, the two soldiers on guard saluted them, stood to attention and touched their foreheads with the tips of their right hand. Tojeira was surprised that the secretaries were present as if it was a working day like any other. The visitors were not kept waiting for long; no sooner had they taken a seat in the reception area than a female employee ushered them in to see the president.

They entered the office and immediately noticed a drop in temperature; the air conditioner was operating at the highest setting. Tojeira tells me that when they took their seats opposite the president's desk, the covers of the chairs they sat on were cold. Even the floor beneath their feet was so cold he could feel it. Next to Cristiani stood a soldier, Colonel López Varela. They nodded to each other nervously and the president and the man next to him offered their condolences. Cristiani was noticeably contrite, but López Varela wore a steely expression that betrayed no emotion; it was as if he was playing that children's game where they stand opposite one other and stare, their faces smooth as the patina of a river frozen at night, and the first to laugh is the loser.

The atmosphere in the room was taut as a rope being pulled tight at both ends. Suddenly, Tojeira broke that rope and said:

'Mr President, I must tell you that it was the army that carried out these deeds.'

'But, Father, how can you say that?' said López Varela. 'Don't go making unsubstantiated accusations. This is a bad time to be indulging in that sort of thing.'

'The army is responsible for what happened,' insisted Tojeira, shouting now. And his facial expression was more implacable than the officer's.

'You cannot make unjustified allegations, Father.'

'I have justification.'

'If that's your attitude, I could just as easily lay the blame on the guerrilla forces,' said López Varela. 'And I have proof. They left graffiti all over the university.'

'Anyone could have painted those slogans,' Tojeira responded. 'We know it was the army. The university is close to army head-quarters and the district where military personnel are stationed. I saw from my own window soldiers patrolling the streets every night. We are surrounded. How can you stand there and claim that guerrilla forces slipped through the cordon and assassin-ated the priests. What do you take me for?'

'I repeat, Father: you cannot come here and talk to me like that. Who do you think you are?'

'I don't think I'm anyone. I'm just telling the truth. And the truth is that it was the army.'

Tojeira tells me that during those awful days, he was beside himself. To stand in the president's office and argue with an army colonel was not something that would have happened in normal circumstances. His reaction was excessive, although he had every reason to be upset. Thoughts of his dead companions preyed on his mind. He had taken a knockout blow, and although it hadn't floored him, he was hurt, on the ropes, on the verge of collapse, but he knew he could not let go. Fortunately, President Cristiani and the Monsignor intervened, bringing the heated exchange to an end. Tojeira pulled himself together and apologised for his ill-timed outburst.

'Regardless of who was responsible, the army or the guerrilla force,' Cristiani affirmed, 'we are going to investigate and bring the perpetrators to justice. You have my word that we will bring them to justice.'

This assurance from the president gave them some confidence. Calmer now, Tojeira delivered his analysis of what had happened. López Varela heard him out; not once did he raise his voice or contradict the Jesuit. At the end, Monsignor Rivera said he was in agreement with all that Tojeira had said and President Cristiani reiterated that he would bring the perpetrators to justice in the shortest time possible.

At the end of the meeting, when they had said their good-byes, Monsignor Rivera asked President Cristiani for military protection. Inwardly, Tojeira was seething at this: *What's the matter with this man – how can he ask for that after what has happened?*

'Yes, yes, don't mention it,' Cristiani replied. 'Colonel, can you attend to it?'

'We'll do that,' said López Varela.

'But only from six in the evening to six in the morning,' Monsignor specified, 'while curfew lasts.'

'Yes, yes,' said the president, 'as you wish.'

'You see,' Rivera continued, 'if the army is seen in the Nunciature during the day, nobody will want to come, and at times like these, people need to come and see us.'

'No problem,' said Cristiani.

'And I want to make it clear that the only reason I'm asking for protection is because, if they kill me, everyone will know who did it.'

Neither Tojeira, nor anybody else in that office, could believe what the Monsignor had said.

6

After their meeting with the president, Tojeira and Monsignor Rivera gave a press conference in which they explained their version of what happened. They spoke about the two hundred metres that separated UCA from the quarter where the military were stationed and the four hundred metres from the intelligence building and Democracy Tower with its surveillance posts. They also set out what would be their politics of action: truth, justice, pardon. These would be their objectives in the aftermath of the assassination of their Jesuit colleagues. Lastly, they announced that President Cristiani had promised to investigate the matter.

'Are you frightened, Father? Frightened that things might get worse?'

'We are no longer frightened,' answered Tojeira.

'You have just incriminated the army of the Republic. You're not worried they'll retaliate?'

'No.'

'Are there witnesses, Father?'

'No.'

'There are houses close by; the occupants wouldn't have been able to see what was happening inside, but they'd have been in a position to hear. Surely there must be witnesses who heard what went on?'

'So far there isn't a single witness.'

The press conference finished shortly before five in the afternoon. As curfew started at six, Tojeira had to hurry to return to his office. He already knew that they would be evacuating the house next to the university and moving to Santa Tecla, but first he had to drop by his office, for he had left early that morning, just after calling Rome to inform them. At that time the streets were silent, bar the occasional sound of soldiers making their way along the pavement or entering buildings. At one point, Tojeira came across a line of tanks driving in the opposite direction. They advanced slowly like a herd of very old elephants.

'Was there any interaction?' I ask.

'With the people in the tanks?'

'Yes.'

'I drew level with them and they continued to stare at me, but they did nothing, they made no attempt to stop me. Every so often I would glance at them out of the corner of my eye. But to tell you the truth, I was calm. I had come to terms with the situation.'

I ask him what he means by 'situation' and Tojeira repeats the answer he gave earlier:

'I thought that if they had killed those important, well-known men – men with international contacts – what was to stop them killing me? After all, who was I?'

'The Provincial.'

'Yes, but that isn't important. It's an internal position . . . '

'You were sure they were going to kill you?'

'Yes. At that time I believed it. I thought they were going to kill me. I had spoken out because I had to, because it was my duty. I thought I was as good as condemned once I did that, but I did it anyway, and I was fine with that.'

Tojeira travelled along San Salvador's streets at that late hour of the evening. The whole city was like a pressure cooker in danger of exploding. He carried on walking without thinking, only feeling, perceiving everything around him as part of what was happening, or at the centre of what was happening, and not only in the city of San Salvador in November 1989, but in the world, in a terrible and profound moment whose beginning did not have a true conclusion. Fulfilment took over, although he was not aware of it. He had accepted his destiny. The transcendence of that destiny. Just as, years before, Ellacuría had accepted his destiny when he decided to remain in a country that had threatened him and in which the university of which he was rector had suffered four attacks. In the end, everything happened because of Ellacuría, Tojeira tells me. They sought him out, not the others. Ellacuría was the beginning and end of this story. The others merely found themselves in a place where there could be no witnesses.

Tojeira entered his office without knowing quite what he was doing there. He did not have much time. By now it was twenty to six and he still had to drive to the house in Santa Tecla where he would join his companions to spend the night. He knew that at that hour they would be gathering and the door would be shut – not locked and bolted, because they would be waiting, but definitely shut. Perhaps they would be worrying about him, perhaps they would be praying that he might arrive without mishap. What was he doing in that office? Wasn't it foolhardy to be there? They could have been lying in wait for him, and he was offering them an easy target. Despite

34

all this he entered his office and immediately heard the sound of the telex machine. He walked up to it and realised that it had been left on all day.

'Do you know what a telex is?' he asks me.

'To be honest, I don't.'

'It's a machine that sends telegrams. I would write them on a machine with a ribbon and all you had to do was punch in the dots and send the dotted ribbon through the telex. You sent it and only at its destination would your message be printed out.'

'I get it.'

'I saw that machine must have been working all day. The messages were piling up – an immense outpouring of support – from France, from Italy, from Spain. They came from ministers, from students, from the Jesuit Institute. They came from parishes, too – I even got one from Japan – and from schoolchildren in Uruguay and universities in Europe, in Asia and Africa. There were messages from Mexico, from the United States, from England, from Argentina . . . it seemed like the whole world was writing to us, the whole world was on our side. At that moment I thought: *They cannot kill me!* When I left my office I was convinced they couldn't touch me.'

'You really thought that?'

'Yes. It wasn't that I was no longer scared, but my fear had ceased to matter.'

7

He reached the Santa Tecla house a few minutes before six. They had given up on him, assuming he was not coming, so they had double-locked the door. So there they were, forty men in a house lit by candles or gas lights because the electricity had been cut off that afternoon and not restored. Before the evening meal, Tojeira called on his companions to celebrate Mass. He went out to the patio. It was large, with flowerpots bulging with plants. He heard the low sound of a radio on nearby, but nothing else. For some reason you could not hear the gunfire or the exploding bombs dropped by the army's planes or the guerrilla force's anti-aircraft guns. All the sounds they had grown accustomed to over the last few days. Everything appeared to be calm. It was an unusual silence. It had density. Tension. Everything one associated with fear. That night, the sixth since the start of the offensive, the silence was greater because the fear was even greater.

Tojeira met with his companions and began the Mass. He does not recall which part of the New Testament he used, but he does remember the psalm because it was perfect for that moment.

'All the ends of the earth have seen the salvation of our God,' said Tojeira. That was the psalm. And he read it aloud one more time.

He thought it proper to inform everybody of the messages he had received in his office. He told them that hundreds, perhaps thousands of people around the world were speaking of their companions as martyrs. He told them there had been a tremendous reaction worldwide, though it would not be reported in their country's heavily censored newspapers. Far beyond San Salvador everyone was commenting on the assassination of the Jesuits, and saying that the government would collapse and they would lose the war if they harmed them. He said this in the crudest manner, as there was no other way of saying it. At the end, he added:

'These people who have written to us from so many countries have seen a victory in the death of our companions. And the psalm speaks for us, gathered here, it tells us: 'All the ends of the earth have seen the salvation of our God.'

Tojeira wanted to encourage his congregation and prevent them from feeling fear, and convince them that what had happened was an opportunity. That is why he said all that, but at the same time he firmly believed it.

That night, after Mass, they joined together for a meal and while they were eating Tojeira told some of his companions what had happened at the meeting with the president. He spoke about the army colonel with whom he had engaged in a shouting match, and about the archbishop's closing request, which caused a genuine shock. A little later, they retired for the night, telling each other to keep the faith and remain calm, for nothing would happen. They prayed fervently and then tried to fall asleep. At first they seemed to have succeeded in convincing themselves, but this conviction was short-lived; any

37

noise, however slight, woke them up and made them think that their enemies had come to finish off their business. A rat nudging a tin can on the roof, a door that opened or closed, a bathroom tap, the low hum of voices on the patio – the slightest noise made them hold their breath, sit up in bed, stand up, look furtively out of their doors. Many of them had to take pills to fall asleep or a Valium, which in those days could be bought from a chemist like aspirin. Some found themselves in the kitchen at two or three in the morning and made a coffee or some herb tea and spoke in whispers about what was happening.

One of them dedicated himself to praying and walked around the patio for hours while he meditated; another alternated his meditation with the Lord's Prayer or a Hail Mary and was constantly distracted by noises on the tiles or from the street. At three in the morning, nearly all of them were wandering about the house like shadows in a darkened theatre acting a tragedy where characters whisper sentences.

The car arrived. It wasn't yet four when they heard it stopping near the house. Tojeira, who had been awake for a while, clearly heard it and came to with a jolt and sat on the edge of his bed. The vehicle had stopped just outside his closed window. Before that, he had heard people whispering outside, not in the street but on the patio and in the corridors. He knew that everyone in the house had heard the car engine because the whispering had stopped. Tojeira approached his window and could hear nothing. A door was opened and then immediately closed. He heard a man's voice. It came clearly from whoever was in the car. *This is where those bastard priests are living*, one voice said. Tojeira could plainly hear what was said. The Santa Tecla house was large, with long corridors around a central patio. A house built at the beginning of the twentieth century. Tall columns made it impossible to climb on to the roof. And just one door to the house. It did not have a basement or an attic. If they came in, there was no hope for them. The men walked north, towards the entry door. Tojeira left his room and made his way to the entrance. Outside, everything was suspended. The shadows that were his companions were silent and paralysed as if part of a fantastic stage setting controlled by a mechanism that had run out of strings. It was a black-and-white photograph of a dark and serious moment, just before a tragedy. Tojeira walked to the door and waited. He waited for what seemed an endless moment of time for a voice to call him or shout for him to come out. He heard someone shout, but didn't understand what was said. Laughter. They were laughing. It was dawn on 17 November, a little before four in the morning. A cold, windy dawn in November, without a moon, with the electric street lights switched off, dark as the interior of a coffin when it is shut. The men outside were laughing. Tojeira then heard a sentence he understood: *What's up, sons of whores – your time is up.* He took a long time before realising that those men were not looking for them. They were soldiers or members of the National Guard and he did not know what they were doing at that hour in that street, but they were not looking for them. Not that night. A little later, you could hear farewells, an engine that started, car doors shutting and a car that moved off into the distance until it couldn't be heard any more. Someone sat down on the ground and cried bitterly. Others carried on doing what they were doing as if nothing had happened, as if the machine had started working again. At five, the community met to pray and prepare breakfast. That was the first night. After breakfast they were all tired, but there was also a sense of tranquillity, for with the arrival of daylight everything seemed less terrifying.

8

The day after the assassination, the activity was, if possible, more frantic. Early on, they received the news that the Spanish embassy would not admit the only witness to the assassination. The Jesuits had asked them to protect Lucía Cerna, her husband and their child and keep them safe, but the embassy had refused. It was a hard blow, a huge disappointment. Lucía and her family stayed hidden in the same house in which they had been all week, the same house from where she had seen the soldiers leave. They considered various options and they came to a decision, given there were no other possibilities. They would have to seek asylum at the United States embassy. That was the first decision of a hectic morning.

The second decision was to bury the Fathers in niches that would be prepared in the university chapel. Tojeira had the idea of burying them in accordance with the traditions of their homeland, Galicia, where the custom was to bury priests in front of a church door so that you literally had to step on their tombstones to enter. He outlined his idea and they all agreed that they ought to bury the priests in the chapel, but someone pointed out that this would mean trying to dig six graves in the middle of a military offensive, and they would struggle to find gravediggers to do the work. In the circumstances, they agreed it would be best to bury them in niches, which they would create by knocking down the wall that gave on to a side room in the chapel. That was the second decision taken: the preparation of niches.

The third decision, taken a little later, was to meet up with the family of the two women who had been killed, Elba and Celina. Tojeira explained to the relatives that his intention was to bury these women next to the Fathers. They refused. Apparently, it had been their mother's dying wish that Elba be buried next to her. Elba's siblings were adamant that she had been their mother's favourite and that she would have wanted to fulfil the old lady's last wish. Tojeira had no way of knowing if the story was true or if they were simply afraid and wanted to distance themselves from the Jesuits. He left them to bury the women as they wished.

The fourth decision was that the viewing of the bodies would take place in the university chapel and it would finish at five thirty in the evening, half an hour before curfew started. At this hour of the morning there was little movement, but after midday many more people would enter and leave the university chapel. Many were students or friends or neighbours, people close to Ellacuría or to Segundo Montes or to the other priests. There were heart-wrenching scenes of grief and uncontrollable weeping. There was also an inevitable tension in the air. A constant feeling that something could happen at any moment. But this did not stop people coming to pay their respects. Tojeira recalls how moving it was, in that context, in the midst of the fighting, to see people making the journey from the outskirts of San Salvador, some of them making a round trip of thirty-six or forty kilometres on foot, regardless of air-force bombing raids, or having to run the gauntlet of soldiers who watched their progress through the desolate streets. They were good people who came from very poor villages, from villages where Martín-Baró or Amando López had worked, who felt that they should show their solidarity and bravery because they had been looked after.

At some point, one of those good people said that he feared the assassins would return by night and steal the Jesuits' bodies or burn down the chapel with them inside. The rumour spread around all those present, leaving them overwhelmed with worry. Tojeira thought it was irrational, but then again, everything in the current situation was.

'And if they come at night and steal the bodies, Father?'

'It would be a good thing if they did,' answered Tojeira. 'If they were to do that, it would get those wretched people into even deeper trouble.'

Hearing this gave people some kind of consolation, although nobody was sure of anything. Some people wanted to spend the night there, but Tojeira and the other Jesuits refused; it would have been too irresponsible and risky to allow such a thing. Once again, all they could do was hope that nothing would happen. When the time came they locked the chapel doors and left. The next day, they confirmed that they had taken the best decision, for nothing had happened.

At a meeting before they left, they took the last decision of that day. It had to do with the burials. It was decided that weapons would not be permitted at Sunday's Mass; they didn't want armed people in the university. They took this decision because there was a niggling fear that something might happen. The wake had been a tense affair, and the burial ceremony was liable to be even worse. They were afraid that some envoys from the guerrilla forces might turn up, which would lead to an explosive situation. Thus they appealed for everyone to support them in establishing an atmosphere of absolute peace.

Their resolve was put to the test on Saturday afternoon when Tojeira received a visit from a couple of Cristiani's envoys. They turned up at his office in the middle of the day's preparations, a man named Pacas and another named Valdivieso, the minister and deputy minister of Foreign Affairs. They greeted him in a friendly manner, offered their condolences and told him the president had sent them to attend the burials, accompanied by their wives.

'We want you to reserve a seat for the president,' said Pacas, 'and we need to check the place to see where he is to sit.'

'The first two rows in the auditorium where the Mass will be held have been set aside for members of the diplomatic community,' said Tojeira. 'We can reserve seats for you there, but, please, no weapons. We don't want armed people.'

'But we are talking about the president of the country!'

'I don't want to cause offence, but it doesn't matter whether it's the president of the republic or the pope, we have taken that decision and will not go back on our word.'

'What do you mean by "it doesn't matter"?' Valdivieso was alarmed. 'Look, Father, I don't want to cause offence either, but let me remind you that you are a foreigner. And I'll remind you also that in this country, you cannot order people around – least of all the president. Given the situation we are in, you cannot expect him to attend without his bodyguards.'

'Mr Pacas,' said Tojeira, 'you can do what you like – it's obvious that I cannot stop you. But I must warn you: if I see weapons in the auditorium, I swear that I will refuse to say Mass or go ahead with the burial of the Jesuits until the armed men have left the hall. TV cameras will be present and people will be watching the spectacle live. So I leave it for you to decide.'

'So you don't want the president to turn up?' asked Valdivieso. 'Because, that's what your attitude seems to imply.'

'I did not say that. Don't put words into my mouth. If he wants to come, he can come, but under the conditions that I've stated.'

'You cannot dictate conditions, Father. Who do you think you are?'

'I do not think I am anyone. As to whether I can impose conditions, all I will say is let's wait and see.'

Tojeira tells me that all the images of that period rush by more rapidly than any other time, as if the film of those days was running ever faster, perhaps driven by the surge of adrenaline.

'So what are you proposing?' asked the minister.

'If you want to be completely certain about his safety, then he and his wife can stay on the platform where there will only be priests. So if someone wants to shoot the president, he'll have to kill quite a few priests. Do you like that idea?'

'We'll have a word with him,' said the minister.

They said their goodbyes and left. Tojeira told me, twenty-five years later, that such things would never have been said before or after. During that time, diplomacy did not exist; rage, pain, resignation – these raw emotions stripped everyone of their finery. And although he thought that such harshness was a little extreme, he is still convinced that it fitted the moment and he said exactly what he should have said.

9

'What happened during the Mass and the burials?' I ask.
'The president and his wife sat with us.'

'What did the president look like?'

'Serious, very serious.'

'Did he talk to anybody?'

'Just his wife.'

'He didn't exchange any words with you?'

'He offered his condolences. Very briefly and very formally.
I talked more with the Under Secretary of the Spanish Foreign
Ministry, a conversation that was to have an impact on the
witness.'

'In what way?'

'It was only then that I understood why the embassy had
refused to grant asylum to the sole witness.'

The Under Secretary of Foreign Affairs for Spain, Inocencia
Arias, arrived in San Salvador the day before the burials, but
he was early, so he showed up in the buildings of the university
a little before the ceremony. He came accompanied by the
ambassador, a man named Francisco Cádiz. Tojeira was outside

the auditorium with the other Jesuits when Arias approached, greeted him, offered his condolences and said:

'Father Tojeira, the Spanish embassy will do whatever you want.'

This friendly, perhaps genuine offer was not well received by one of the Jesuits who accompanied Tojeira at that moment.

'Don't lie to us, Mr Under Secretary,' said a priest called Rogelio Pedraz. Mr Arias looked to Tojeira for an explanation.

'Perhaps you should tell the Under Secretary what makes you say such a thing,' said Tojeira.

'Because that man,' answered Pedraz, pointing at the ambassador with a finger, 'said to my Provincial that the Spanish embassy could not accept a witness who came from Salvador. So you should not say to Father Tojeira, "do as you wish".'

'Is that right?' the Under Secretary asked Mr Cádiz.

'Those were the instructions I received from Madrid,' answered Cádiz. 'That we could give asylum to Spaniards but not to Salvadorians.'

'Well, accept the witness,' the Under Secretary said.

This conversation took place shortly before Mass, which began without setbacks, with the president and his wife on the platform, seated amongst the priests.

That day the auditorium was packed to bursting point. Politicians, ambassadors, members of the Evangelical and Lutheran churches, businessmen, people from villages in the interior of the country came together to celebrate Mass . . . And all this on an afternoon when bullets were flying on the eighth day of the guerrilla forces' offensive in a city taken over by the armies on both sides. Many people could not get in and had to follow the Mass outside, leaning on the outer walls or at the back.

There were three brief homilies: one from the Nuncio, another from Archbishop Rivera and the third from Tojeira himself. Up until then, Tojeira had not shed a tear for his companions. Such was the tension he had had to endure that he had become cut off from his emotions. But he had to hold his tears back at one unexpected moment of his homily. His contribution lasted eight minutes, perhaps a bit longer, and towards the end he said:

'While gangsters killed Jesuits, young people who were in the Chacra district collected corpses from both sides so that they could bury them with dignity and not leave them lying in the street. Although they killed Jesuits they have not been able to kill the Company of Jesus, nor the UCA, they haven't killed it . . . '

He spoke passionately. His aim was not to provoke a reaction but to say what he genuinely believed. The final sentence of his speech, *they haven't killed it*, was not written down; it had occurred to him as he was delivering the homily. That emphatic sentence made everyone in the auditorium stand up and applaud. Tojeira was so overawed by this spontaneous act that he took it as a gesture of solidarity. He felt tears surging up but managed to stifle them and return to his speech, which he read as best he could.

'And what happened after that, Father?' I ask him.

Tojeira tells me that a few minutes before the end, Rubén Zamora, a member of the political arm of the guerrilla forces, turned up. The presence of this man drew applause from everyone. He was not meant to be in the auditorium, he was not even meant to be in the country. He was a political exile, on the run, and that he could be counted on as one of those who attended was both an act of valour and folly at the same time. When he came in, he walked the length of the auditorium up to the platform, where the bodies of the priests lay, and embraced Father Ellacuría's coffin. The emotional applause wrapped him like a shawl.

'And what about the president, Father?'

'Cristiani had just left. They didn't meet. I'm guessing that he was in control of everything, that he entered when it was convenient for him, and he stayed to the end and helped carry Ellacuría's coffin to the chapel, without anyone being aware, and then disappeared.'

Inside the chapel, to the left of an altar decorated with unorthodox figures recalling peasants dressed in colourful clothes, are the six niches, bordered by candles and adorned with roses and white flowers in jars on the ground. On the day of the burials the coffins were placed in the niches while the archbishop said a few words and led everyone in a final prayer. The ground under them was covered in bits of cement and white flowers.

'After the archbishop's prayer the niches were sealed and we began saying goodbye to the mourners.'

'And nothing happened?'

'Nothing.'

'Nothing that day?'

'Nothing, at least for that day. What came after was a very great struggle.'

'A struggle against who?'

'Against darkness. Against what's hidden in shadows. Against evil.'

PART TWO

1

There was a screening at six thirty, so they must have left the cinema some twenty minutes before that time. The bus stopped just opposite. They stood on the pavement to wait for it and while waiting commented on the film they had just seen. They also talked about a report that had appeared in that morning's newspaper, about a ship that had run aground. Unfortunately there was no photograph, only a brief account of the incident.

'It only just happened. I'm sure tomorrow they'll have more details about it.'

'Well, it doesn't matter in any case – tomorrow we'll take our own photos. What a pity we didn't realise sooner. You could have got your father to take you there today.'

'He couldn't have gone. He had to work.'

They were sixteen years old. That afternoon, while they were looking up the cinema screening times, they had come across a report about a 'ghost ship' that had run aground near Acajutla harbour, in the west of the country. To them the report held the promise of adventure: a mysterious ship without a crew, and according to the reporter it was old, possibly dating back to the Second World War and crewed by spies. The article ended with a promise that further information would appear in tomorrow's edition. To pursue a phantom ship was an opportunity not to be missed. They were engaged in an animated discussion about it when they heard the first shots. The sound seemed to be coming from the south of the city, which is where they were heading. 'What's going on?' one asked the other. The second boy wasn't in the least concerned. 'It will be over soon,' he said. They were used to hearing sporadic gunfire and skirmishes that were over before they had begun. Minutes later, the bus arrived, they climbed on and continued talking about the ghost ship, wondering what might be aboard: a map or a letter or corpses of German sailors. The journalist had said that nobody had been permitted to board the ship. They were waiting for the authorities to check it out because it could be dangerous. The boys did not believe that for a moment; they reckoned it was just a ploy to scare off thieves.

It would have been ten or twenty to seven when they reached the Santa Clara district, where they lived. Neither of them paid any attention to the shots and they were not scared. Someone on the bus said that whatever was going on, it was in San Marcos and that was on the other side of the San Jacinto peak from where the boys lived. He did not see any reason to get alarmed. It would soon be over. Or so they thought.

Mario, whose father said he would take him to the ship the following day, told Miguel that he would let him know at what time they would leave for Acajutla.

'Tomorrow we'll confirm the time, but be ready by eight.'

'At seven thirty I'll be waiting.'

They were neighbours. They lived opposite each other and had known each other since they were children.

When they were ready to leave, they didn't ring each other, but let the other know by a whistle, which was the special language of the boys who lived in the area, a cul-de-sac of thirty houses, fifteen on each side, that bordered a hill.

On television there was a variety show, and Miguel ate his dinner watching a clown act. He lived with his mother and paternal grandmother. Sometimes, his mother's sister would stay at the house as her husband had left months back for the United States, like Miguel's dad, who shared his son's name, and had been out there for over ten years, from the start of the 1979 war. Miguel's mother was called Edith, and her sister was called Margarita. Margarita did not have any children. She worked in a secondary school and last year had been the worst year of her life. She feared her husband would renege on his promise to send for her once he had established himself. Being childless made her feel unprotected, lacking any real bond that united them – or at least, that is what she told her sister. Edith, far from consoling her, informed her that having children did not make the slightest difference, or at least it had not to her husband, Miguel, who had abandoned her and Miguel Junior for a Dominican whore after only one year abroad. She did not want her sister to suffer like she had, so she warned her that, where men were concerned, it was better not to entertain any expectations.

Despite being separated, Edith still lived with her mother-in-law, Eunice. The old lady had lost three sons in 1978, all in a single night. Miguel's brothers had been massacred while at a party with university friends. According to the official version of events, someone in the building where the party was being held had opened fire on some soldiers with high-calibre weapons and they had fired back in self-defence. You could

53

never get to the truth of these events, Eunice said, and besides, what did it matter? Nothing would change the fact that her three sons were dead.

When Miguel rang to tell Edith that he wanted to separate, Eunice begged her daughter-in-law not to move out. She could not be left without her grandson, especially when she had no family left, her miserable sod of a husband having died from cirrhosis of the liver two years earlier. She believed the old adage that nobody who leaves the country returns, and she had given up hope of ever seeing her son again. What would be the point in Edith moving away and paying rent when they could go on sharing this house? In the end, Edith had said she would stay for a while. Ten years had passed since then.

After his television programme, Miguel went to his room and looked through some magazines about paranormal phenomena. He amused himself reading an article about a building in the centre of Madrid that was overrun with ghosts. He was struck by two unfocused photos where he could make out a girl. While he read, he could not avoid hearing the distant explosions, but did not yet attach any importance to them. When, around ten, he turned out his light to go to sleep, he realised that nothing that was happening was normal. The war did not take place in the city, but in the country's interior. When there was some clash in San Salvador, it was sporadic and lasted a few minutes. At times bombs went off or there was some assault or a kidnapping or an assassination in which a car drove off in a hurry, but that exchange of fire had been going on for hours. He got out of bed and walked to the dining room. The patio door was open and the lights were on. He went out and found his mother and grandmother talking in low voices. He approached them.

'It still hasn't stopped.'

54

'They said on the radio that it was very serious,' answered his mother.

'But it's in San Marcos, isn't it?'

'And in Santa Marta as well. It seems something is happening. They asked us not to leave our houses.'

'I hope it's nothing serious.'

'Better get inside,' Edith warned them, 'it could be dangerous with stray bullets.'

'Miguel, you shouldn't sleep in the bedroom overlooking the street,' Eunice ordered. 'I'll help you move your mattress to my bedroom. And tomorrow you'll phone your sister, Edith, call her while it's still early. I don't know why she insists on remaining on her own in that house of hers, as if her husband still matters.'

'Yes, I'll call her in the morning.'

It was Saturday 11 November, 1989. The greatest offensive in the Salvadorian civil war had begun.

2

Edith was used to getting fresh bread every morning. If it was a Sunday, she left after eight, as she did that day. When she woke up, it was a little after seven and you could still hear some gunfire, but nothing compared with the intensity of the day before. She prepared her coffee and drank one cup. While she was doing this she called her sister, but did not get an answer. Then suddenly she realised that the shootings had ceased, so she took this opportunity to go out. She left the house and went uphill towards the street at the end of the cul-de-sac, which ended in the hill. Nearly there, she saw a column of what she first took for soldiers because of the high-calibre weapons they were carrying. Then she understood they were members of the guerrilla forces because they were not wearing uniforms. She had never seen a guerrilla column and never imagined she would see such a thing in the city. Quickening her pace, she walked to the bakery while calculating what provisions they had in the house. Their supplies were running low; she had not been to the market in three or four days. She would go that morning, she told herself, though she thought it unlikely she would be able to. In fact, it was unlikely the market would be open. Instead of going to the bakery, she went to a small store to buy some eggs, two litres of milk and coffee. It was not far off, just at the beginning of the same street.

Santa Clara was a district divided into cul-de-sacs of some twenty-eight to thirty houses. It was crossed by a wide street from which all the cul-de-sacs branched out, heading uphill as the district was built in the foothills of San Jacinto mountain. The third street, Flor de Loto, was the only one that wasn't a cul-de-sac but a street, which led uphill to the peak, first along a tarred road, and then along a narrow dirt track that wound its way up the hill until it came to the coffee plantation. Miguel, his mother and grandmother lived at 20 Flor de Loto, on the left, as houses with even numbers were on this side and the uneven ones were on the other side. Mario lived opposite, at number 21. The bakery was number 2, on the corner with the main street. The store was number 6. When Edith reached it, there were few people shopping and everyone seemed to be in a mad rush. She asked for the few items she could afford, as she didn't have much money on her, but the woman serving her took ages.

'That woman doesn't understand that we are in a hurry,' said a neighbour, who was also waiting.

'I don't know why she can't serve someone else,' complained Edith.

The neighbour, who was about seventy years old, lived next door to the store. She was called Sara and had recently moved in. She lived alone. Edith had chatted a few times with her, very few, three or four times at most, when she bumped into her on the bus or at the baker's.

'You should buy some candles,' Sara suggested. 'I heard it on the radio.'

'Good idea, I hadn't thought of that,' said Edith, and asked for candles and matches.

As she was paying, they heard and saw a helicopter coming from the east. Edith grabbed her bag and left in a hurry. Sara did the same and as she walked up the street, she watched the helicopter hovering above them. It fired a missile towards the hills. Everything shook. The women huddled against a low wall. Edith thought of the column of guerrilla fighters that she had seen ten or fifteen minutes earlier. She hoped they wouldn't return fire, but they did. Sara suggested that they run to her house, a few metres away. They did so, and she opened her door with difficulty as her hands were trembling. They got in and threw themselves to the ground as outside the helicopter launched more missiles and the guerrilla forces returned fire from the hills.

'This is very worrying,' said Sara.

Edith nodded. 'My son is alone with his grandmother.'

'Nothing is going to happen to them. At least they're at home. My son is in the barracks.'

'And where is that?'

'He's in the Atlacatl Battalion, so you can imagine how I feel.'

'May God protect him.'

'I phoned him this morning and was told that nobody could take calls. Can you believe that? They wouldn't even say whether he was in the barracks or had gone out to fight.'

'Unbelievable,' said Sara.

When the helicopter moved on, a few minutes later, Edith said she had to go. She cautiously peered out of the door that gave on to the street and looked up the hill. Nothing out of the ordinary was going on. There was no one about, apart from some neighbours doing the same as her, poking their heads out of doors or windows.

'Be very careful,' said Sara.

'You take care too and I hope your son phones you back,' Edith replied. She heard the woman sigh behind her, but she didn't turn around because she was already running up the street.

3

Miguel's head was poking out of the window, looking down the street, when his mother appeared. He'd wanted to go and fetch her but did not dare leave the house. His grandmother stood behind him, telling him to stop doing that and close the window before someone mistook him for a guerrilla fighter and shot him. His mother rushed into the house and immediately dropped the shopping on the dining-room table, grabbed the telephone and rang her sister again. Once more, there was no answer.

'From where she lives, she probably can't even hear the gunfire,' Edith complained. 'I don't understand why she's not answering.'

Margarita lived in the northern area of the city, but San Salvador is not that big, not a city where shooting in the south could not be heard in the north.

'Perhaps she's with her boyfriend,' said Miguel.

'If only she had a boyfriend,' answered Edith, 'but no such luck.'

An hour later she called again, but still there was no reply.

By then the bombing had begun again and the radio announced that a guerrilla offensive was under way all over the country. They were listening to the latest news when the doorbell rang. The three of them rushed to open the door, hoping it would be Margarita. But instead it was Mario.

'What are you doing here, young man?' Edith scolded.

'Nothing's going on,' answered Mario.

'Something was going on earlier. Didn't you see the helicopter?'

'Yes, I saw it, but it flew off. Nothing else is going on here. My father says it's all happening in Santa Marta, in Soyapango and in San Marcos.'

'But we're surrounded,' Eunice pointed out.

'What's going on?' asked Miguel.

'Nothing,' sighed Mario. 'My father says there's no way he'll take us to the boat.'

'What boat?' asked Edith.

'The boat that's run aground near Acajutla.'

'There was no crew,' Miguel added enthusiastically. 'It just drifted in with the mist early on Friday morning.'

'Where did you hear about that?' asked Eunice.

'It was in yesterday's paper.'

'I didn't see it. When I was a child we would go with my father to see the ships passing close to the beach. Did you know that I lived near the harbour, Mario?'

'Yes, I did.'

'I lived there as a child. And we often saw ships, but not like today's ships. These were huge and made of wood. My father used to tell us they were pirates.'

'Pirates in ghost ships?'

'That's what my father said. And you could see drowned men walking on the beach. It's a well-known fact.'

'I didn't know,' said Miguel.

'Had you lived on the beach, you would've known. There, everyone sees them.'

'The thing is,' said Mario, 'my father won't take us, so that's put paid to all our plans.'

'Even if your father could have taken you,' Edith told Miguel, '*I* would have put paid to all your plans. No way would I let you go.'

'If all this finishes today, maybe tomorrow . . . '

'This is not going to finish today,' said Eunice.

'Listen, Eu,' said Edith urgently. 'Listen.'

Outside, the battle had started up again. The gunfire seemed to go on and on, and there was a new urgency to it. In ten years of war they'd never heard anything like it.

Sitting together in the front room, the four of them remained silent for a few moments. None of them fully understood the dire situation they were in. The boys fretted over the disappointment of not being able to see the ghost ship. They lived in an area that until now had remained untouched by the fighting; no one there had any thought of escaping, or tying a white shirt to a pole and braving the bullets to wave it as a flag of truce – something that in other parts of the city people were already doing. The smell of blood hadn't reached them and could not affect them. The distant war was like a bad dream. They didn't begin to seriously worry until around noon, when Edith tried to phone her sister for the fifth or sixth time, even though she knew no one would answer. She let the phone ring for a long time, waiting for Margarita to pick up, but she didn't. Edith hung up and dialled again, and again nothing. She tried three more times and still no answer. She could not understand it. Margarita did not stay out overnight for fear of the neighbours gossiping. As a married woman, the last thing she wanted was for someone to tell her husband that she had been carrying on while his back was turned.

'Still no answer?' asked Miguel.

'No.'

'I'm sure she's fine,' said Eunice. 'We'll have to pray to God.'

'Why doesn't she pick up the phone? It's driving me mad with worry. I don't feel like praying to God – I want to go and see that she's all right.'

'Don't be a fool, Edith.'

'I'm scared.'

'We're all scared.'

When it got dark, Edith told Miguel that they would all sleep in granny's bedroom. She asked him to take the mattresses from their beds and get everything ready while she got on with cooking dinner. Miguel did as she had asked and collected the two mattresses then placed them side by side on the floor, so that the small room was turned into one large bed. Then he stretched two duvets over the mattresses and placed two pillows on top. Once he had finished, he lay down on his grandmother's bed and started looking at the photos on her wall. They were old, from when she was a little girl with young parents. She had stored all the photos of her children and husband in a trunk, because looking at them made her sad. However, those black-and-white photos from her childhood brought back a time when life was good, and looking at them always cheered her up. Miguel especially liked the one where his grandmother was standing on the steps of a train. She had told him that it was a private train that belonged to a rich family, plantation owners, and they had a railway line that ran from the west, where they grew coffee, to the east, where they grew sugar cane, and then dropped down south to the ports in Puerto El Triunfo, Usulután and Acajutla, in Sonsonate. His grandmother recalled how the train took them through the mountains and slowed down at prehistoric caves where you could see cave paintings lit up by torches stuck in the ground, showing great red and yellow birds and tigers with enormous teeth like sabres and animals that resembled horses but with hairy legs and backs painted with stripes like zebras, but only halfway up. There had also been human figures, all of them exceptionally tall. Her friends, Julia Colt and Eva Colt, were fellow students at the Normal España, an institution where, in the first half of the twentieth century, teachers received their training. Their uncle, Erick Colt, owned the train as well as the coffee and sugar cane plantations. When one of his nieces celebrated a birthday, Uncle Erick would throw a party that lasted two or three days. It was during one of these celebrations that they boarded the train at a station in San Salvador and began the journey west. When they reached the owner's house in the Agua Blanca farm in the mountains of Ahuachapán, where the coffee bushes grew, they attended a ball, and the next day, in the port of Acujutla, they attended another. Those were the days, Eunice would sigh. And they clearly were. Another photo showed the arrival of Eunice's brother-in-law, as a child, next to a wooden raft on the banks of the river Acelhuate. In this image he was surrounded by many people while being embraced by a man with a huge moustache in the shape of an M. Another photo showed Calle Arce, in the centre of town, with old-fashioned cars parked next to clean pavements and pruned bushes and trees that Eunice said were maquilishants which had yellow and white flowers that turned the street into something from a Japanese painting.

Miguel got to his feet to take down one of the photos where his grandmother was holding his father. They were on a beach and it was the only colour photo. They were laughing. His father must have been three or four years old. As he looked at it, he tried to work out how long it had been since they had visited the beach. If only they could go and see the ghost ship that had run aground. He wondered whether the train his grandmother talked about was still running. If it was, you could climb aboard and leave the city, maybe even go as far as Acajutla, and visit the mysterious ship.

4

On Monday morning the government announced that the country was undergoing its worst ever security crisis and from that day a curfew was being imposed that would prohibit any civilian leaving his house from six in the evening to six in the morning the following day. There would also be cuts in electricity and the water supply that would last several hours a day until further notice. The public were advised not to leave their houses. The guerrilla offensive had spread all over the country, but the government expected to have everything back under control within a matter of hours.

At midday, Edith turned the radio off because listening to the news was only making her anxiety worse. She went out to the patio and cleaned the barbecue that she sometimes used to cook meat. She looked for some coal and lit the fire. She grilled some pieces of chicken and some plantains. When everything was ready, they ate in silence, listening to the distant gunfire. As soon as she finished eating, she thought of phoning Margarita, but stopped herself because she knew it would be useless; with everything that was happening she would have to call when she could. Eunice suggested that she try saying the rosary, as that always helped. Both women then shut themselves in Eunice's room to pray, while Miguel went to his room to get on with his latest project.

They couldn't afford a proper table football set, so Miguel had made his own. Whenever he wanted to make a new team, he'd asked a carpenter to sell him twenty-two bits of wood a centimetre thick and three centimetres high, with a hole on one side to put a screw in. If the bits of wood were leftovers, the carpenter would often let him have them for nothing. Miguel would then paint each piece with his favourite team's colours: a greenish yellow for Brazil, blue and white for the El Salvador national team, or white for Alianza, which was his team. He could also paint them the sky blue of Maradona's Naples or the black and red of Van Basten's Milan, his two idols from abroad. When he had painted the players, he screwed them to his table, which he had already painted as a football pitch in green with white lines. Once the teams were in place, he'd surround his diminutive pitch with black thread and his table football was ready. Then, he and his friends would play, using wooden handles a centimetre thick and a marble as a ball. They would usually play their tournaments at night, getting together in his house or in the house of one his friends.

In the afternoon they preferred playing football in the street, with plastic balls. They would use stones to mark out the narrow goals. Those games were five against five or six against six, without goalkeepers because the goals were not wider than four paces, perhaps a metre wide. Back then, school holidays stretched from November to the end of January. Life revolved around football, strolls through the hills and games of table football.

At around three, Miguel left his house and crossed the road

to Mario's house. He whistled and Mario appeared at his door to tell him that his father had forbidden him to go out. Miguel said he didn't want to go out but to come in, so Mario let him in.

'My father says if things carry on like this, we're going to leave for Guatemala.'

'It's not going to last.'

'On the radio we heard that they're recruiting sixteen-year-old boys.'

'They're always saying they'll do stuff and nothing happens.'

'But now it's different. Now there's a war.'

'Well, maybe you're right. Maybe it's different. Fact is, it sucks. I thought this was going to be over in a day and now it looks like it's never going to stop. We can't even enjoy a game of table football.'

'Are you painting your new team in the colours of Naples?'

'Yes. It's going to be Naples against Milan. It's looking good.'

'OK, if things don't get worse, we can play again soon. By the way, they mentioned the ghost ship on the news.'

'Which news? On the TV?'

'Yes.'

'Really?'

'Yes, at the end of the news, they said a ship had run aground near Acajutla, although they didn't show pictures. With all that's going on, I was surprised they mentioned it.'

'Well, it's not a piece of news that they would skip over. It's not the sort of thing that happens every day.'

At that moment there was a different explosion to the previous ones and the boys huddled against a wall. They were at the side of the house where Miguel's father kept his car. The explosions had been very loud and when minutes later they looked out on to the street, they spotted a column of smoke in the distance. Mario's father thought the guerrillas must have shot down one of the helicopters.

'Things are getting worse by the day,' said Mario's father, who was also called Mario. 'If this goes on, we'll have to go to Guatemala or else you'll end up in the army or with the guerrilla forces.'

'But why Guatemala, Dad?' asked Mario.

'Because that's how it is,' said his father.

5

On Tuesday morning coffee was ready at six and over breakfast they discussed the possibility of going in search of Margarita. They also talked about some of the neighbours who were planning on leaving. Yesterday they had heard on the radio that the districts of Santa Marta and San Marcos had been captured by guerrilla forces; San Jacinto was right in the middle, surrounded by the war, but as yet untouched by it. Afraid of finding themselves trapped, some people were determined to get out while they still could. Three neighbouring families had left at dawn, minutes after the curfew ended. But Edith and her family were not making plans to run away. They had nowhere to go. And they couldn't leave until they'd heard from Margarita.

Miguel hardly tasted his food and Edith and Eunice only drank coffee. When they got up from the table they went to the bedroom to say the rosary again. They had prayed the evening before and in the afternoon; there wasn't much else they could do. Miguel thought of joining them, but they didn't ask him and he didn't feel like it. Eventually, he went to his room and carried on painting his wooden football players. As he did so, he kept thinking about his aunt, and the bombs going off in the distance. At about nine, he heard voices outside and opened his bedroom window, which overlooked the street. Just below him stood a soldier. He had left a huge backpack leaning against the wall and he was sitting on it. He was eating from a tin with a knife with which he cut something that looked like dog food. On the ground was a coffee cup. He was young, perhaps thirty years old, perhaps a bit less, and looked tired, his face red with exhaustion and his eyes bloodshot.

'What gives?' said the soldier when he spotted Miguel, who gave a nod in reply. The soldier sliced off another chunk from his tin and brought it to his mouth. Miguel observed him without saying anything and the soldier pointed to his food: 'Tastes like shit.'

'What is it?'

'It's supposed to be a chicken tamale, but it tastes of shit, not tamale.'

'Tinned tamale?'

'Well, yes, there's nothing else. There are tinned tamales, beans, pork meat, but they all taste the same.'

'Of shit?'

'Exactly: of shit.'

There were soldiers sitting all the way along the street, every six or seven metres, eating from tins or smoking or not doing anything. Miguel tried to count them, but stopped when he reached eleven. His mother joined him at the window.

'Hello,' said Edith.

'Hello,' answered the soldier.

'Are you passing through?'

'Yes, we've come from the Santa Marta district.'

'How's it going? Things seem to be getting worse. On the radio they said the situation was critical.'

'It is. But we've forced them back, at least in my zone. The bastards have retreated to the ravines and fled to the hills.'

'Did you kill any of them?' asked Miguel.

'That's not something you ask about,' interrupted his mother.

'I got separated from my unit for a while,' the soldier went on. 'At midnight, the order was given to fall back, but I was out looking for wounded comrades and didn't realise. I took shelter in a hut and a group of them saw me through a window. It was a miracle I got out.'

'They didn't get you?'

'No. I came under fire and there were a few near misses, but I wasn't hit. It's a horrible feeling when the bullets are flying. One almost took off my ear,' said the soldier, pointing to his left ear.

'Do you know what's going on in the north zone?' asked Edith.

The soldier shook his head. 'I only know about Santa Marta.'

'It's just that I have a sister there and haven't been able to reach her.'

The soldier started to put his things away. He tucked the cup in his backpack and said, 'I hope your sister is all right.'

'We're very worried.'

'There's no point worrying. If you're going to die, you die and that's all there is to it. Happens every day. I don't mean to suggest that something has happened to her – I'm sure she's fine – I'm only saying it's no use getting upset about it. She'll turn up.'

Edith thought he was an idiot, but she also thought he was right. She had an overwhelming urge to cry, but instead she stood there, mute, looking down into the street, as if by some miracle her sister would appear, but the street was deserted except for the soldiers sitting on the ground or loitering, and other curious onlookers, like themselves, who had stuck their heads out of windows to talk with the soldiers.

'Do you have any water, lady?' asked a soldier.

'In this house there's no fresh water,' said a voice from behind them. The soldier looked into the house and came face to face with Eunice. Edith stiffened with tension and Miguel didn't understand what was going on.

'What do you mean?' said the soldier, surprised. His voice had ceased to be friendly and he was glaring at Eunice.

'There isn't any,' repeated Eunice.

Edith cut in: 'Don't pay any attention to her, she's a bit senile. She gets so worried about the water bill that she won't even water the plants. Here, give me your water bottle.'

The soldier took a step forward, as if intending to come into the house and confront Eunice, but instead reached out his hand and gave his half-filled water bottle to Edith. Trying to hide her nerves, Edith took it and turned away from the window. She put a hand on Eunice's shoulder to steer her into the kitchen; to her relief, the old lady allowed herself to be led.

'She's ill,' said Miguel. 'She's my grandmother.'

The soldier said nothing, he just stared into the house. Miguel looked down the street and noticed that the soldiers were starting to move. One by one they stood up and joined the column heading towards his house. For a second he wondered whether it was because it was time for them to go or because they had been alerted by their comrade. When Edith came out with the water bottle she told him she had filled it with cold water.

'Thank you,' said the soldier, and he put on his backpack and set off along the pavement to join the others.

Edith and Miguel went into the kitchen, where Eunice was sitting at the table, gazing towards the patio with a lost expression. At first she said nothing, then:

'I don't know why I did that. I couldn't stop myself.'

'What happened?' asked Miguel.

'What do you mean, "what happened"?' replied Eunice in a whisper. 'Don't you understand? Those bastards killed your uncles, didn't you know that?'

'Yes, I know, but—'

'I understand,' said Edith, 'but that was a long time ago. You can't go saying things like that – those men are so wound up, it's madness to provoke them. Didn't you see the way he looked at you? Did you even notice? I thought he was going to shoot you. And he could have done it, too, and then walked away as if nothing had happened. You put us all in danger.'

'It wouldn't matter if a hundred years had gone by, to me it still feels as if it was only yesterday. Pain like that, you never forget.'

'I'll go and make some camomile tea,' said Edith.

'I want some too,' said Miguel. His mother lit the gas, filled a pan with water and took some tea bags out of a metal box, put them in the pan, waited for it to boil and sat next to Eunice.

'Do you think that praying does any good?'

'I don't know,' said Eunice. 'Right now, I just don't know . . .'

6

On Thursday morning, Miguel got up shortly after six and prepared a pot of coffee. While he waited for the water to boil, he leaned against the sink, thinking about the ghost ship. In the current situation, nobody could go and see it. The journalist who had written the article last Saturday might well be the only one who had seen it. Miguel was still very sleepy but didn't want to go back to bed.

The previous evening, his mother had sat for hours with the radio on low while his grandmother muttered unintelligible rosaries. At around ten the electricity went off. They'd spent the night huddled together in silence. In the darkness, Miguel realised that the usual noises from the neighbourhood cats had ceased, and he wondered if cats escaped a sinking ship the way rats did, running off to hide in the hills or in the drains. He tried to recall if he had seen cats during the day and was sure he hadn't. It is a possibility, he told himself. And he imagined one of the hilltop caves packed with cats, or a line of cats making their way down into the dark drains where they would wage their own war against rats, right below where they were sleeping, and the humans had no idea. He wanted to believe that animals lived their own lives when the humans weren't watching. Lost in his thoughts, he fell asleep and dreamed of cats pursuing rats. He woke up at around one. He could not get back to sleep until two, and woke again before six in the morning and forced himself to lie in bed, but quickly grew bored. He got up and decided to make coffee. With a bit of luck the offensive would end soon and then Mario's father would take them to the harbour. He crossed his fingers for the journalist to put some photos in the newspaper; it was too bad the paper hadn't included some with the original report.

How could they cover a story like that and not include a single photo? He did not understand it.

The water boiled and Miguel added a few spoonfuls of ground coffee, turned the heat off and put a lid on the saucepan. He had to wait a few minutes for the coffee to brew. He took out a cup and while he was doing this, he thought about yesterday's meeting with the soldier. He told himself that if any of the soldiers or guerrilla fighters could navigate, they could use the boat to escape. Then he got to wondering why nobody had thought of escaping. Several reasons came to mind. He supposed they were afraid of being caught and imprisoned as traitors, but even so it must be possible to head up into the San Jacinto hills and hide in a cave or take a boat and sail off along the coast as far as Patagonia. It would be possible. Especially from San Salvador, along the River Acelhuate. His grandmother had told him many times that half a century ago her brother-in-law, the husband of her sister, had sailed from the Chilean city of Valparaíso and then travelled upriver and moored under a bridge in the Candelaria district, almost by the front door of Eunice's mother. It is true that the river had been reduced to a trickle, everyone knew

76

this, but maybe you could still do it. Or that's what he wanted to believe.

An hour later, when his mother was serving breakfast, which consisted of spicy cheese, a roasted plantain and beans, Miguel was still walking along the river and only woke up from his daydreaming when Eunice started reproaching his mother:

'But for Christ's sake, Edith, how can you think about abandoning your son to go look for your sister? Would you run the risk of never seeing the boy again, all for the sake of your sister?'

'But, *señora* . . .'

'How are you planning to get there? On foot? While they're shooting in the streets? Are you mad?'

'What do you want me to do, wait here forever?'

'And how can you be sure she'll be there? If she was at home, don't you think she would have answered the phone? No, woman, don't do anything rash. It's too dangerous.'

'Has something happened, Mama?' asked Miguel.

'Nothing. Nothing's happened,' said Eunice, trying to restore calm. 'They said they have been evacuating people to safe locations. They said on the radio that people from San Antonio Abad are taking shelter in a school. That's what will have happened to your aunt: she'll be sheltering in a school somewhere.'

'If she's in one of those schools, she'll be all right, won't she?'

'They took people out of their homes and won't let them go back because it's too dangerous. That's what they said.'

'But nothing is going to happen to her.'

'That's what I'm telling you,' insisted Eunice.

'Yes, but we don't know for sure if she's there. We don't know anything,' protested Edith.

'What about us? How could we be sure that *you're* all right, that you've managed to reach her? Because if you manage to make it there, don't for a second believe they will let you leave to return home. This is not the time to play the heroine, especially when you have a fourteen-year-old son.'

'Sixteen,' Miguel corrected her.

'Whatever,' said Eunice.

Edith said nothing. She rubbed her eyes and took a sip of coffee and looked out of the open door to the patio. She was silently praying that her sister would phone when the phone started to ring. Her heart missed a beat and she ran to answer. It wasn't her sister. It was Luis, one of Miguel's friends, wanting to know if they could play table football.

Bored of spending his days shut up in his room, Luis had decided to phone his friends to arrange a game that very afternoon. He was tired of waiting for this situation to be over. Miguel was of the same opinion. He told his friend that the new teams were almost ready and if all went well, they could play that afternoon. They agreed to meet up after lunch.

As soon as he had finished his breakfast, Miguel shut himself in his room and set about painting his remaining players. He screwed each one to the board and by midday had wound black ribbon around the nails. That afternoon, they played several games. They played using sticks that were like miniature hockey sticks and hit the marble about. The dynamics of the game were simple: each player had the chance of launching a marble to try and score, and this was done again and again until they reached five goals. It wasn't easy. The nails stuck out all over the pitch, leaving only a few corridors.

You had to be a good shot to pass the marble between the nails and shoot past the goalies, screwed into the middle of the goalmouth.

It was a little after two and the score was Luis three and Mario two when they heard a bomb go off in the distance. Miguel leaned out of Mario's window and saw a fighter plane swooping in low and firing at some unseen target. He was so excited his hair stood on end. The luminous missiles disappeared among the buildings and then exploded. To Miguel, it seemed an amazing thing. A minute later, the three boys were on the roof watching two planes carry out identical manoeuvres over Santa Marta hill and then over the Zacamil district, to the north of the city. They came down off the roof nearly an hour later when the planes flew away. Miguel recalls that at that time he did not fully grasp what he was seeing; at the age of sixteen he was an idiot who thought only of the thrill. And he says it with a touch of shame.

'There were people dying below – not only enemy soldiers but civilians. Who knows how many died in those attacks. We didn't realise.'

'And your elders didn't say anything about this?'

'Not Mario's father. I think he was as excited as we were. Or at least, he was the following day when we got together to talk about the night bombings. Luminous missiles zipping across the night sky – as you can imagine, for us, this was something spectacular. We weren't even scared.'

Miguel had seen soldiers and war cripples all his life, because war was a part of everyday life. In those days, at least at the beginning, it didn't seem all that bad – that came later. That night he went to sleep listening to the din of distant explosions and regretting that his mother had forced him to stay inside his house when midnight struck. She would not even let him climb on to the roof, which at the time seemed to him completely unfair.

7

Only years later, as an adult, could Miguel grasp the true consequences of those things that had been no more than a source of excitement to him as a child. For two or three years he believed his aunt would appear one morning, large as life and smiling the way she had the last time he saw her. He used to think she would show up on his birthday or his mother's birthday and, smiling like an idiot, she would tell them how she had run off with a boyfriend, tired of living with the fear her husband might leave her for an American or Mexican girl, the way men who went to work in the United States so often did. But Margarita never turned up.

In June, on her birthday, his mother organised a Mass, which Miguel refused to attend. After that, every year on the same date, his mother organised a Mass for her sister. Many Masses were celebrated before Miguel finally agreed to attend. Even now, he prefers not to know nor speculate what could have happened to his Aunt Margarita. It doesn't interest him and he's convinced it's irrelevant. So far as he's concerned, only one thing matters: the awful truth that she never returned. He also tells me that many people have insinuated that Margarita must have been 'organised'; in other words, she belonged to some guerrilla army. They have no way of knowing whether this was the case, and he doesn't want to believe it, despite the rumour pursuing him like a niggling doubt. Not a day goes by that he doesn't wish he'd been more astute, that he had paid closer attention to what was going on around him. He didn't know who those men were who were assassinated on a Thursday morning, nor why everybody was talking about them when they came down from the roof after observing the planes dropping bombs.

One of his friends said that if the planes kept on bombing, the war would soon be over and they could go and see the grounded ship. The idea excited them. They sat side by side on the pavement outside Mario's house, and Miguel was telling them what his grandmother had said about ghost ships being a regular occurrence back when she lived on the beach as a girl. He was about to give them more details when Mario's father came out and told his son to go into the house.

'Mario – time you came indoors.'

'But nothing's happening, Dad.'

'Yes, but come in anyway. Can't you see: there's no one in the street.'

'Is something going on?'

'People are saying that they've killed the Jesuits of the UCA. This time they've gone way too far.'

'What happened?' Luis asked. 'Do they know who did it?'

'They claim the Jesuits betrayed the guerrilla fighters and that's why they were killed.'

'Were they part of the guerrilla forces?'

'That I don't know, but they claim they were. On the news it said those same guerrilla forces assassinated them; they felt betrayed and so they killed all of them. And that could be the case, Ellacuría was said to be close to Cristiani, so maybe they thought they had been betrayed. That could be it.'

Miguel knew that Alfredo Cristiani was president of the republic. He had seen Ignacio Ellacuría in the newspapers, but didn't even know he was a priest – he had always assumed he was a politician. As for the rest, he didn't know anything about them. They were not important to him, at least not at that time. A few years would have to pass for him to grasp the meaning of that terrifying news, almost the exact same number of years that he refused to attend the annual Mass commemorating Margarita's birthday.

When, some time later, Miguel went home, his mother and grandmother were discussing the assassination of the Jesuits. While she was talking, his mother was frying tortillas in oil. She had cut them into triangles and dropped them in a saucepan of boiling oil. Miguel loved eating tortilla chips with cheese, so he got close to his mother while she continued talking about the Fathers. She knew them all by sight, but Father Martín-Baró she knew well for he had been her teacher.

'May I?' asked Miguel, who wanted to help himself to the tortilla chips.

'There's cheese on the table,' said his mother, and the teenager saw that they had put fresh cheese out, so he took a plate and helped himself to some tortilla chips, cut a slice of cheese and began eating. His mother continued talking about the Jesuit. She had studied for a degree in Psychology for two and half years and although she never got her degree, she did have some good memories of that period, among them two courses she had taken with Father Baró.

'He was obviously a very intelligent man, and he was friendly too.'

82

'I once heard him give a Mass in Zacamil,' said Eunice. 'He explained things in a fun way. And made it seem easy. It's true that he seemed very friendly.'

'He was always laughing,' added Edith. 'Well, in class he was more serious, but that time he accompanied us on a trip to Jayaque he laughed a lot with everybody and was very affectionate.'

'He had the face of a good man,' added the grandmother. 'The face that good people have. Not like the others. Ellacuría had a serious face, that of an angry man. But Baró was more like Monsignor Romero, he had a sweet face, at least at Mass.'

'Yes, that's just how he was.'

Martín-Baró was born in November 1942 in Valladolid, Northern Spain. He arrived in San Salvador at the beginning of the sixties. He was a university man, an academic, through and through. Before he became a professor he had studied for a degree in Literature, another in Theology and had a doctorate in Social Psychology from the University of Chicago. But these academic degrees did not distract him from his spiritual duties. For many years, he busied himself with the Zacamil parish on the northern side of the city. And when he left that parish, he would travel on weekends to Jayaque, a village near San Salvador, where he looked after ordinary people, leaving behind his professorship at the university and becoming, once more, a priest. Everybody remembered him as very affectionate and friendly, like a little boy, always laughing.

'One day he told us that Chicago, where he had studied,' assured Edith, 'was colder than the village in Spain where he was born.'

'I don't know why I thought that it was far hotter in Spain,' said Eunice.

'Yes, in Europe it must get cold. But he said that in Chicago it got colder, far colder. That it was due to the lakes and a biting wind.'

'Just imagine it. To travel from Spain to study in the United States only to come and die here, and in that way. He deserved so much better. Poor man.'

'Yes, it's a real pity. I can't begin to put into words just how sad I feel. But sad, truly sad. And perhaps, a little ashamed. As a country we are a disgrace, we are savages.'

Miguel ate his last mouthful of tortilla with cheese, poured himself a glass of water and drank it down in a gulp. Leaving the glass on the table, he walked to his grandmother's room, hurled himself on to the mattress next to the wall and calculated how long he would have to wait before he could go to see the ghost ship. He tells me that he believed it would be a minimum of a week, but that his calculations turned out to be irrelevant because a few days later the newspaper carried another report on the ship that left him very disappointed. Apparently it had disappeared as mysteriously as it had arrived. One morning it was no longer there and nobody knew what had happened. The only explanation they could provide was a claim from some local fishermen that fog had dragged the boat out to sea, towards the ocean depths.

8

Miguel told me it was indescribable the way his mother aged in just one month. By Christmas she was thin as a rake, a shadow of her former self, with two grey half-moons under her eyes. Her voice changed and became soft, as if she could only talk in whispers. During the last days of November they went round the hospitals, the prisons, the police stations and even visited the lunatic asylum. But his aunt was not in any of them. When at last they entered her home, her belongings were intact. Her wedding photograph album, her blouses, her scents, a notebook full of unsent letters and pathetic poems, her sunglasses, her shoes – everything was in order. If she had run off, it could not have been premeditated. And not knowing what had become of her was the worst, at least for Edith.

By Christmas of that year, her hands were so fragile and feeble, she could not cook or wash clothes. The index finger on her right hand seemed to grow a few centimetres, enough for Miguel to recall the story of Hansel and Gretel, where the children show the witch a chicken bone instead of a hand.

It was unpleasant to look at, and in its way as strange and inexplicable as the disappearance of his aunt.

Over the following months things got worse. For some reason, the grass in the courtyard of Miguel's house dried up. By the beginning of March, it had been reduced to a patch of yellow dust. Moreover, ivy covered the front wall and the guava tree in the patio produced only rotten fruit. If that wasn't enough, rats moved in. There were so many of them that one morning Eunice discovered a nest they had made in clothes that she had left by the sink overnight. The house was falling to pieces, and according to Miguel's grandmother, this was all down to his mother. Edith's sadness affected everything, drying everything out, attracting pests and vermin. She even accused Edith of attracting the fog that for a day and a half covered the district where they lived. Miguel didn't pay any attention to his grandmother, but it was evident that during those days life was just one long series of disasters.

'And what happened next?' I asked Miguel.

'My mother remained in that state for years. I think everything changed around Christmas of 1993 or 94. And for no reason, or at least none that I could see.'

'She stopped being so sad?'

'She accepted that my aunt would not return. Gradually life returned to normal.'

'And what happened to the rats?'

'When my mother returned to her senses, not only did the rats vanish, but the grass in the patio began to grow and the ivy fell off the walls and the guava tree gave good fruit.'

Our conversation stops. We find ourselves in the Centro Monsignor Romero, in the hall where the martyrs' possessions are exhibited, not only the Jesuit ones, but also those of Monsignor Romero, of Elba and Celina Ramos and of the North American nuns assassinated in 1980. Miguel points out Ellacuría's bathrobe, Martín-Baró's dressing gown, the vests belonging to Father Lolo and Joaquín López y López. We comment on the simplicity of Father López's vest, with bullet holes in the back and blood stains all over. I can almost see the scene, the Jesuit on the ground, grabbing his assassin's leg, observing his face, which was the last thing he saw in his life.

'Do you know what I believe?' Miguel asks me. 'What I think about all this?'

'No.'

'That Ellacuría was a military target not because he was close to the left, but because he was helping the peace process. This became clear to me for two reasons. The first is that the military were getting rich with the war and they didn't want it to end. They were getting a million and a half dollars a day from the United States. And that's a lot of money.'

'It's true. It's known that they did not report the deaths of soldiers and kept claiming their wages. And I'm not talking about a few soldiers.'

'They didn't want peace. War was business.'

We leave the small hall, which has been turned into a museum, and walk towards a stall where Miguel stops to buy a magazine with an article by Jon Sobrino on the relationship between Romero and Ellacuría. They hand him the magazine, he pays and we walk towards the exit.

We leave the Centro Monsignor Romero behind and walk down to the chapel, which we enter. We go downhill to the pedestrian entrance to the university, where we say goodbye. The day suddenly clouds over, as if a storm is approaching. I say to Miguel that it's a pity there is so much darkness. Miguel wears a gloomy expression and when he talks about the war years, about his childhood and adolescence, nothing he says makes him smile. He assures me that there was nothing in his childhood that gave him joy. Perhaps there was, but he has forgotten it; his past is like a path that disappears in the mist under trees whose dense foliage forms a canopy that prevents even a shaft of light from passing through. Those who live in that cold are nothing more than silhouettes, their faces and bodies devoid of solidity and shape.

PART THREE

1

Jorge Cerna and his daughter walked along a tree-lined path through the university. The street lights were on, but there was no lighting in the administrative halls and the lecture theatres where the little girl liked to walk with her father when it got dark. Sometimes Jorge would tell her that when he was a child he had seen elves. He had seen them just once, in the evening. They were sitting on a stone by the riverbank smoking large pipes. They were tiny, he told her, no bigger than a one-year-old baby.

'We could have caught one.'

'What happened?' she asked, although she knew the answer, for it wasn't the first time she had heard the tale.

'I got scared and threw a stone at them. They escaped along the stream, jumping from stone to stone.'

It was the sort of conversation the two of them often engaged in on their strolls, because the girl enjoyed these tales enormously.

They weren't from San Salvador, but the district of Soyapango, where they had a house. But it had become a battlefield and they'd had to flee. Luckily, the Jesuits, for whom the little girl's mother worked, arranged for them to stay in a house near the campus, which was owned by the UCA. They had been allocated a room on the first floor, with some mattresses to sleep on.

The two of them walked between the buildings and climbed up to the library terrace, where they stopped to lie down under an enormous tree. That evening they saw a luminous swarm of fireflies that had gathered among the high branches. The little girl agreed with her father when he said it looked like a heavenly vault. After a few minutes, they climbed further up to the red-brick buildings where the teacher's offices are located and Jorge said to his daughter that the scent they could smell was jasmine, because up here those small white flowers grew all over the place. After a while they returned to the street that crosses the university and there they came across Father Amando López. The little girl thought that perhaps he was thinking about something important. The priest did not appear to be surprised by the meeting. He greeted them in a friendly way and stroked the little girl's head.

'Good evening, Father López,' they greeted him.

'Good evening. Are you taking a stroll?'

'Yes,' said Jorge. 'It's such a nice evening, and since dinner wasn't ready yet . . . '

'It certainly is a lovely time of day.'

'Father,' said the girl. 'Are there elves where you come from?'

'Elves?' exclaimed the priest with a smile. 'Well, when I was a boy I didn't see any, but in my village some said that they had seen them.'

'And where is your village?'

'I was born in a village called Cubo de Bureba, over in Burgos. A small village, but it was pretty good living there. If it's stories about elves and fairies you're after, Dublin's the place to go. It's on an island called Ireland.'

'Oh?' said the girl in surprise.

'Everybody there believes in elves.'

'I want to get to know that place,' she said. 'Is it far away?'

'Well, yes, it is far away, the other side of the ocean. When you're older, I'm sure you can go.'

It was in Dublin that Father Amado López had studied theology and been ordained as a Jesuit in 1965. He was born in 1936 and at the age of sixteen entered the Order of the Company of Jesus. He was sent to the Santa Tecla seminary a year later. Apart from studying in Dublin, he had also studied in Quito and Strasbourg, where he got his doctorate in 1970. Back in Central America, he spent some years in San Salvador as rector of the San José de la Montaña seminary, before travelling to Nicaragua in 1975. From 1979 to 1983 he was rector of Managua's UCA and in 1984 he finally returned to San Salvador. He was an affable man, with an excellent sense of humour, as capable of giving a class on philosophy as in helping the Red Cross take wounded men and women out of a conflict zone in the Nicaraguan civil war, or of speaking about elves with a little girl.

'But you yourself have never seen an elf, Father?'

'Never, but I haven't given up hope,' said the priest, smiling. The three of them walked together in the direction of the chapel.

'It may be dangerous, walking out here so late,' the Jesuit warned them. 'We have advised the guards to lock themselves in after curfew, which means anybody can enter the university.'

'Yes, they told us,' admitted Jorge Cerna.

'Well, you'd better get along. Your meal must be ready by now.'

'Thank you, Father.'

They reached the door in the side of the chapel that leads to the Jesuits' house and entered. Through this short walk, the girl hadn't stopped looking back or sideways, towards the bushes, as she always did when night fell.

Lucía, the girl's mother, was with Elba and her daughter, Celina, in the kitchen of the pastoral house. They had already served the priests and when the father and daughter arrived, they all sat down to eat. Over dinner, the adults discussed the dire situation in the country and it was mentioned that Ernesto Cardenal, a Nicaraguan Jesuit who lived in the house, had gone to spend the night at Santa Tecla. The other priests had suggested that he go because he had been feeling ill at ease and had not been able to sleep since the army carried out a search of the Jesuit house two days earlier. The four adults sitting at the table thought there was nothing to fear. They didn't believe that the army or the guerrilla forces would enter the university. But in the event that the guerrillas did seek refuge there, it would be best to leave at once rather than risk getting caught up in the fighting that would inevitably follow. Elba and Celina had already decided that they would escape through the house where Lucía and her husband and daughter were staying, because it had a door that led out on to the street that ran alongside the university.

'You shouldn't be so trusting,' Lucía told them.

'The Fathers say nothing is going to happen, that Father Ellacuría is a friend of the president,' said Elba.

'I'm not sure they are friends,' said Lucía. 'They might talk to each other, but . . .'

'He's even been to the university,' Elba cut in, 'so they are friends, and he says nothing is going to happen.'

'Father López is not so sure. When I went to serve him

coffee, he said they would be capable of doing it. That's why Father Cardenal left.'

'Well, I don't believe they will come to the university. Unless the guerrillas do. If that happens, things will get ugly. That's why it's best to leave in a hurry before the army comes and gets you.'

'I couldn't agree more.'

2

It was a little after seven when they got up from the table. Lucía, her husband and their child left by a side door that led to the chapel, then turned right and made their way towards the house where they were staying. At this hour, the university was in deep shadow; the street lights on campus had been turned out and everywhere you looked it was dark. At this time of year, night fell at six or a little earlier, and the night sky took on, at times, an intense and obscure blue like a canvas daubed with many layers of paint and not so much as a hint of white. The three walked slowly as they didn't have a torch or candle, and although the moon was out, it wasn't bright enough to light the way. There was no chirping of crickets, no rustling of the breeze in the leaves. No sound but bombs exploding in the distance. Jorge opened the door to let Lucía through, but she paused suddenly because, on looking behind her, she'd noticed that her daughter had taken a few steps in the opposite direction and was staring intently into the darkness. Her mother, a little alarmed, said:

'What are you doing? Come here.'

Jorge strode to the child's side and grabbed her arm, pulling her forcefully, with some haste, towards the door, while trying to see what she had been staring at. He had the sensation that somebody was observing them. As soon as he had lifted the girl up and pushed her into the house, he slammed the door shut. His nerves were on edge, it was a struggle to engage the lock.

'What's wrong with you?' Lucía asked her daughter. 'Standing out there like an idiot!'

'I wanted to see if there was anyone.'

'Who did you think might be there?'

'An elf, Mama.'

'But you didn't see anyone, did you?' asked her father.

'Not a thing. Nothing,' answered the girl.

'Are the guards out there?' Lucía asked her husband.

'They're all indoors. They lock themselves in at six. And they don't go out, not even for a cigarette. But our girl didn't see anything, so don't worry.'

'I didn't see anything, Mama.'

'Are you sure?'

'What could I see?' repeated the girl. 'Nothing. There was nothing there.'

Later, when they were getting ready to go to bed, Lucía opened the window that overlooked the inner campus. She wanted to be alert to any sounds of activity. Her husband asked her to shut it, complaining that mosquitoes would get in, but she paid no attention. They went to bed, said their prayers, though the husband refused to join in, and fell asleep while talking about their yearning to return home soon and their hope that Father Ellacuría was right and all this would soon be over. Some hours later, Lucía woke, clutching her hand to her breast.

She thought she'd heard a bomb explode, but she did not get up. Instead she lay there, listening in case something was happening outside. Hearing nothing, she thought she must have dreamt it, that it was just her imagination running wild, making her believe in things that did not exist. She tried breathing slowly, but could not rid herself of her anxiety, so she started murmuring the Lord's Prayer. Suddenly there was a burst of machine-gun fire. Lucía sat up, her hand over her mouth, because she knew the shots came from within the university. More gunfire followed, this time from M-16s and AK-47s, and shouts and someone hammering on a door: the Jesuits' house had become a battlefield. She got up to go to the window, but her husband, overcome by fear, tried to stop her, pleading with her to get down on the floor, take her daughter's hand and pray with him; still she dragged herself to the window and looked out. For a while she only saw shadows or the flashes of gunfire. Suddenly she heard one of the priests saying: *You are dead flesh.* A moment later, she could clearly hear whispering and knew that the Fathers were praying, and she wanted to pray too, but then further shots sounded and the voices fell silent and she knew that the end had come and started pleading with God to spare her daughter's life. She couldn't calculate how much time had passed from that first round of machine-gun fire, but she guessed about an hour. Lucía was still lying by the window when she saw flares light up the sky and watched a column of soldiers walking off, leaving the scene of the crime behind them.

When the clock struck six, Lucía dared leave the house and walked to the garden where she came upon the Jesuits' bodies. It was a cold, luminous and gentle morning and nothing seemed to be happening outside, but inside the garden lay the corpses of the priests and those of her friend Elba and her daughter Celina. Lucía cried bitterly. It was hard to make sense of what had happened. She hurried back to her husband and daughter and told them what she had seen. Later, she saw from her window that Obdulio, Elba's husband, was walking towards the pedestrian entrance. She said she had to go to the Fathers' house, she had to find Tojeira and the others and tell them what had taken place. So she left by the door that opened on to the street that runs alongside the university and walked to the end. In the Fathers' house she met Obdulio and Father Estrada. A little later Tojeira appeared.

'It was the military, Father, I saw them,' Lucía told him. And Tojeira asked her if she would testify to this. She was adamant that she would. Tojeira cautioned her to be discreet and said for the moment it was best to say nothing.

So she returned to the university, where she went unnoticed among the curious onlookers, who had come to find out happened. She realised most of those around her were journalists, none of whom suspected that this woman who did not say a word was the one person who had so much to say, because she was the sole witness to the crime.

That day there wasn't much to do except wait. Around midday she locked herself in with her husband and daughter and they ate some sandwiches. Halfway through the afternoon a priest came to tell her that they were negotiating a deal for her and her family to stay in the Spanish embassy. By this time the woman, who hadn't yielded to fear, had given some thought to what would best suit her and her family.

'Are you sure, Lucía?' asked the priest.

'I'm prepared to say what I saw, Father.'

'Our lawyers say that if you stand as a witness against the army, you'll have to leave the country. You would be risking your life.'

'My only concern is for my daughter, I'm not worried about myself, I assure you.'

'We will take you to the embassy and from there you'll leave for the airport. We can send you to Spain. There's no problem about that, we can arrange it.'

'Spain?'

'Yes.'

'So far away.'

'But you would be safe with your daughter and husband.'

'What about the United States?'

'The United States . . . Well, I suppose so, we have houses in many countries.'

'It's just that I have cousins in the United States.'

'I see. Well, we could do that. It's just a matter of trying to find a way.'

'Father . . .'

'Yes?'

'Do you think we are in danger? I mean, today and tonight. Will they come for us too?'

'I won't lie to you, all I can tell you is that I don't know. So long as they have no idea you are here and that you saw them, they will not come after you. I don't think they're planning on wiping out all the neighbours, but at times like these, we are all at risk.'

'I'm going to pray to God and the Virgin, especially for my daughter.'

'When we have news, I'll come and tell you immediately, but you must be prepared to leave at once.'

'Very well, Father, whatever you say.'

The news when it came was not good. The embassy said that they couldn't give them asylum and not much else could be done that day. So when darkness fell, they shut all the house doors and waited. And while they were waiting, they held hands and prayed, because that was all they could do during the longest night ever.

3

The voices came from the internal street that crosses the university; though it was some metres away, she heard them clearly. She got up and walked to the window and observed silhouettes that cast large shadows on the walls, but could not distinguish if what she saw were men or not. She wondered whether it was priests walking through the university or soldiers who had returned to see if anyone was still alive or guerrilla forces visiting the campus to say their farewells. Although she would forget it, or rather would claim that she had forgotten what happened on that second day at dawn, at that instant, standing by the window, she saw a group of people approaching from the west. From the way they walked, they seemed to be elderly. She didn't show fear, even when she thought that perhaps they were not people but ghosts.

She crept along the dark hallway and down the stairs to the door, then turned the key in the lock. The dawn cold froze her arms and she stopped. She noticed there were fireflies in the bushes lining the edge of the street. The scent of jasmines mingled with the smoke left behind by the lanterns and she was grateful for this scent because it had dissipated another one that had been around the university all day.

During the morning, many people had come to see what had happened. The outpouring of grief over the death of the Fathers was too overwhelming for her, so she headed away from the chapel and walked until she came to a building housing classroms, entered one of them, stood in front of the blackboard and looked up at the rows of empty seats. She sat on the edge of a chair behind a desk and stayed there a while, contemplating the classroom, wondering if at any moment one or two students would appear and mistake her for a teacher. That is when she understood, in a moment of lucidity, that the aroma she had detected from that morning at breakfast was blood. That thought exploded inside her brain, leaving her appalled. The smell of blood was in the wind like a stain on the wall, and there was gunpowder too, and she realised that the trees smelled different and were no longer fresh, that earthy, metallic smell was spreading everywhere, clinging to the network of branches. Blood and gunpowder, that is what the university had smelled of all morning and into the afternoon and she found it abhorrent.

Hours later, as she made her way back to her house, she was happy when she realised that the smell of blood had vanished. The wind had shaken the trees like a woman shakes her hair on emerging from water, and the jasmines glowed in the dark, infusing the air with their scent. An enormous moon shone high in the sky and she knew it was about three in the morning.

Although she had forgotten what happened that night, it is a fact that she entered the house where she lived, climbed the stairs to her bedroom and walked to the window. In the distance she no longer heard shots but a barely audible and real song sung by a group of women. She got into bed and prayed.

At the end of her prayer she fell into a deep sleep and didn't wake until the next morning. It was a very cold morning. Tojeira called by and explained to them that he had not heard from the Spanish embassy and assumed the news would still be negative, but that he would personally negotiate with embassies from other countries. And although Tojeira assured them about this, anguish had taken over like a fever. That was the bad news. But at least there was one piece of good news: when she went out for a walk around the university, the smell of blood had definitely gone.

4

The old embassy of the United States was in a northern area of San Salvador, some two hundred metres from the National University. It was a large building, surrounded by a wall roughly four metres high. In November 1989, the ambassador was a man named William Walker. Men like Walker are just the tip of the iceberg, the visible part of a mountain of political and military interests, that began in a room of a closed office in San Salvador and ended, after several connections, in Washington, that looked after its own interests or what it thought were its interests for the whole region. The United States' sphere of interest lay not just in Central America, but in the whole of Latin America. They did not want another Cuba, or another Nicaragua, so that's why they invested in what they thought appropriate to prevent revolutionary forces seizing power. The ice that fed this iceberg was the Cold War. Because of this, during the war years, the Salvadorian army benefitted to the tune of hundreds of millions of dollars, and that's without counting logistical help that included food, weapons, training and medical treatment. This being so, what Walker may have said aloud to the press or to his equals in the diplomatic world was what he was obliged to say.

When Tojeira visited him, he was friendly, considerate and moved by what had happened and offered all his help to Lucía and her family to leave the country for the United States. They had a brief conversation in an amicable tone. When it was almost over, in a slightly lower voice, Walker confessed something to Tojeira that he has never forgotten.

'That was a unit over which we had no control.'

His words confirmed Tojeira's contention that the military had murdered his fellow Jesuits. He had outlined his theory and instead of denying it the ambassador had uttered that sentence.

But how could he say that to me? Tojeira remembers saying to himself. And he confirms that he felt elated because it corroborated all that they already knew. *I assumed it was a slip of the tongue, but with time I was not so sure*, he says in a wary manner, trying to find the right words. Perhaps he was searching for a sentence that would sum it all up, even if it could not be used in a trial for there was no recording to prove he said it, and no judge or journalist, nobody but the two of them.

In spite of what he said in that meeting, in statements to the press Ambassador Walker backed the government's position. And the government's position was that the assassinations were carried out by the guerrilla forces, who had entered the university and, after clashing with the army, had assassinated the priests before fleeing. They went on to say that it was irresponsible to accuse the army of such deeds. The government of the republic, the army's high command and the embassy of the United States supported this version.

On Tuesday 21 November, a judge named Ricardo Zamora, two public prosecutors and a secretary came to Tojeira's house to take a declaration. It was then that he felt for the first time the weight of what was to come in this case. Already in this first meeting the public prosecutors spoke as defenders of the military and it was obvious they were following orders that obliged them to behave in this way.

'I woke at about two in the morning,' Tojeira told Judge Zamora.

'How do you know it was at that time?' asked one of the public prosecutors.

'Around two. I'm not sure,' answered Tojeira.

'Put down that he didn't know what time it was.'

'But I do know what time it was. I'm not certain, but it was more or less the time I said. Shots woke me up. They were using high-calibre weapons.'

'And how do you know they were high-calibre weapons?'

'Well, let's see. It's something we all know. It's obvious. The sound of a pistol is not the same as that of a rifle. Or don't you know how to distinguish something like that?'

'You could have been confused. It's easy to get confused. It depends on how close it was.'

'Well, there was a bit of everything. You can tell that by looking at the walls of the pastoral house. They're full of bullet holes. Anyhow, it lasted about twenty minutes.'

'How do you know it lasted twenty minutes? Did you look at a clock?'

'We all, my companions and myself, calculated how long it took and that's why I say it lasted from twenty minutes to half an hour.'

'For goodness' sake, with those two men interrupting me,' Tojeira became angry and pointed to the public prosecutors with his finger, 'I refuse to continue giving a statement. Moreover, if they interrupt me again, they will be kicked out. This is my house and they cannot remain here if I do not allow it, all of you will leave and you will have to take me by force to the tribunal under police orders because I refuse to continue.'

'Gentlemen, come now, there's no reason we have to get so tense,' intervened Judge Zamora. 'The situation is difficult enough as it is, so please do not interrupt Father Tojeira while he's testifying.'

'We're doing our job,' one of the public prosecutors protested.

'Well, it doesn't seem like you are,' Tojeira continued, 'or rather, I do not understand who you are working for.' His protest had its effect and the public prosecutors apologised and kept quiet. So Tojeira went on with his statement, said what he had to say and on finishing, read the written version. They were all in agreement and signed it.

That afternoon, Tojeira understood that he was facing an impossible struggle. He was up against the authorities of a country. He knew the government's position and knew also that the United States ambassador's statement backed the government's. Of course, he never believed that Mr Walker would tell the press what he had told him, he was not so naive as to entertain the possibility of something like that happening. Neither did he think that the government would back his hypothesis about the military, but he did not expect such an aggressive attitude from the public prosecutors when he was giving a statement solely as an interested party.

He feared for Lucía. What would happen to this woman? Had it been a mistake to talk to Walker about her? They could not hide her without help from the embassies. That would be impossible, especially with the country at war. It did not feel right, entangling a woman like Lucía in that mess. But even if it wasn't right, it was necessary. Earlier, he had discussed the matter with Dr María Julia Hernández, Director of Legal Protection, an institution that came under the auspices of the

Salvadorian archbishopric. Legal Protection was founded by Monsignor Romero while he was archbishop and its task was to ensure that human rights in the country were respected. Thus for Tojeira whatever Dr Hernández said about the case was definitive, and that was why he asked her to talk with Lucía.

'I do not wish to risk the life of that woman and her family if it isn't necessary,' he said to María Julia.

'The proof you've put forward,' María Julia said to him, 'that the UCA was six hundred metres from the high command, and four hundred metres from military intelligence and two hundred metres from the Arce district may seem persuasive to you, but here, in this country, eyewitness testimony is paramount. *I saw this* or *I saw that* counts for more than all your logical analysis. It's crucial that she testifies if you want to go ahead with a trial.'

It was obvious that risks had to be taken. They were a group of priests against the political and military regime of a small country, which was backed by the most powerful country in the world. And he felt the desolation of that difference. And yet he knew there was no turning back, that he had to continue and fight.

5

'The Spanish embassy have agreed to grant you asylum,' said Tojeira, and Lucía felt enormously relieved, as if she had emerged, gasping for breath, after being submerged under water for too long.

'Thanks to God, Father.'

'Well yes, thanks to God. So now we can instal you in the embassy and on Tuesday they will come and take your statement. You will not have to leave the embassy for that. The other news is that we are arranging for you to travel to the United States.'

'And when will we know about that, Father?'

'Very soon. Maybe by Wednesday you'll be on your way there.'

'And where will we be going?'

'Miami. Some of our Jesuit companions who live there will pick you up from the airport and you'll stay with them while we sort out the next stage.'

'We are going to Miami first.'

'Yes. But don't worry, you'll go on to Los Angeles, we're

making arrangements. And there's no need to worry about the airport here as the Spanish ambassador and maybe even the French ambassador will see you off, so there will be no problems.'

'That's good, Father. Thank you so much.'

'No, thank you, Lucía. Thank you. You'd best collect your things together because this afternoon they're coming to fetch you and take you to the embassy.'

That afternoon, when she climbed into the Spanish embassy car, Lucía regretted having left her house in Soyapango. That had been her first flight. They had escaped at dawn, in a lull between one skirmish and the next, walking hunched up with white pillowcases tied to a broomstick as their improvised flag of truce, saying they were civilians. Some men from the Red Cross had accompanied them. Most of those who escaped were taken to shelters, but she had convinced her husband that it would be safer to walk to the UCA, even if it was risky because they had to cross the city. She was sure that they would be better off staying with the Fathers, who would not abandon her. And so it was, but she could never have predicted the events that would follow, forcing her to flee a second time, in the direction of an embassy. Once in the comfort of the car, memories overpowered her and she thought that, had she had the chance, she would have liked to pack certain things like portraits of her father or mother or grandmother, some blouses she liked, some sandals that fitted her comfortably . . .

She thought of many things and her thoughts made her realise something else: she had not only seen her house for the last time, but also most of the friends she knew. Not her cousins, for they could come and visit her, but friends and neighbours. She wanted to believe that if she had known it was the last time that she would see them, she would have hugged them all and it weighed on her to realise that perhaps this had happened too many times in her life and she had not been aware of it until that moment, sitting in the back seat of a car that would, perhaps, take her to the airport. Would she ever return to her homeland? She suspected she wouldn't. At that time, there was no way she could think anything else. But now she dare not look back and didn't want to. She owed it to the Fathers, to Segundo Montes and Father Amado and the rest, to Ellacuría, and Tojeira. She could not let them down. In her mind these were not just men but something more, like Romero. She had heard Romero many times on the radio and had seen him taking Mass in the cathedral and had cried when he died; she had considered him to be a saint, a real one because he had died denouncing injustice. And the Jesuits had died for the same cause. She had heard Ellacuría talk countless times on the radio or on television and always about injustice, and sometimes from the comfort of her home, she had heard him say that his place was not the land that he had come from, not Europe, not Spain and that he had much to do in this place, and she could not comprehend why he had chosen to stay in a country at war. Although she had never understood him before, she did now. In her eyes, they were martyrs.

'For me, they are like Monsignor Romero,' she had said, deeply moved, to her husband.

'But Monsignor was a saint. They killed him for standing up against the military.'

'And the Fathers too.'

'Well, perhaps, but I don't know. I don't see them that way because I knew them.'

'For me, they are like Romero. Saints like him.'

She was convinced of this, just as she was certain what she had to do. She was ready to travel her own journey and suffer her own sacrifice, even if that included not returning home and her life becoming an unending flight.

When the car started up and they left the UCA campus there was not much time to think about what she was leaving behind. She and her husband sat together and held hands while they were travelling. They both looked out on to the street. He gripped her hard when they stopped at a traffic light in front of the staff college after passing along the six hundred metres, about which Father Tojeira had so often spoken. The place was cordoned off by soldiers and protected by some tanks parked there. As they were travelling in a car with diplomatic number plates they were not stopped. A soldier or two stared at them in surprise. They were humble people and it was unusual to see their kind driven in such a car. Everybody in the car felt those looks. Perhaps they asked themselves who they were and what they were doing in that car. Perhaps one of them felt the urge to stop them. Lucía did not turn around or shut her eyes as she would have wanted. She only looked ahead. When the traffic lights changed to green and the car got going again, she felt a strange relief, as if she was completely safe. But that sensation left her when at night a security guard in the embassy told her not to approach any window in the building.

On Tuesday afternoon, Judge Zamora and the public prosecutors came to the embassy to see them. They were shown to a small room with a table in the middle. Lucía was accompanied by a Jesuit priest, Fermín Sainz. The interrogation lasted hours. As with Tojeira, the attitude of the public prosecutors was aggressive. It seemed that they were trying to confuse her, casting doubt on her statement. They wanted to know everything about Lucía, who she was, what was she doing in the Jesuit house that night, what time she woke up and why, and at what time she arrived at the scene of the crime. She was also asked if she knew what it meant to give witness against the army of her country and the government of her country, if she fully understood the consequences.

'You cannot distinguish the military from the guerrilla forces,' said one of the prosecutors, 'and even less so in the dark at that time of night.'

'There was a moon out and it shone like the sun,' she assured them.

'It's impossible to distinguish them.'

'They were soldiers like I've always seen in the street. There was no difference.'

Lucía was in no doubt, but then neither were the public prosecutors. So they carried on in the same way for ages until Sainz could no longer contain himself and intervened:

'Gentlemen, it seems to me you are destroying the witness instead of making use of her,' the Jesuit pointed out.

'We are not destroying anyone, but the law obliges us to find out everything.'

'The law does oblige you to find out everything, but not by coercion. And you are coercing. That's obvious.'

'We are investigating, which isn't the same thing.'

'You are coercing her. You are telling her that she cannot distinguish between one thing and another, when she assures you she can.'

'That's a matter of opinion.'

'If I tell you that what I saw was white you cannot tell me it was black because I'm the one who saw, not you.'

'And you cannot tell me how I should do my job. Don't you agree? Should I tell you how to take a Mass, Father?'

'That's enough. You must calm down, gentlemen,' said Judge Zamora. 'I'm asking this of all of you because this could drag on forever and we are close to curfew time.'

So they continued for a while longer and at five thirty the judge decided Lucía's testimony was over until the next day, early in the morning.

That night everybody in the embassy was nervous. It was clear that the public prosecutors were following orders and Tojeira had already alerted them to this. On the other hand, faced with such a situation, where everything had been turned upside down and all reasonable limits had been exceeded, the Spanish ambassador, Mr Cádiz, did not exactly feel safe with his charge. The embassy security had told him it was dangerous to continue protecting the witness; being the sole witness in a case like this one made her an obvious target for the assassins of the Jesuits, whoever they were. They had also reminded him that the country he found himself in was caught up in a full military offensive, which kept both sides in an extreme state of heightened nerves where they would stop at nothing to achieve their objectives. The ambassador heard them out, but he knew he had no option but to let the witness stay. He tried calming them down by reminding them the witness had to spend one night there, just one. Tojeira had informed him that the next day Lucía and her family would be boarding a plane bound for the United States. The second meeting with the judge and the public prosecutors would take place not in the Spanish embassy but in the French embassy, who would collect Lucía in an armoured vehicle, which, luckily for the Spanish, they did not possess. For one single night. The only thing to do was to wait and ask their guest to pray for them:

'As you have such a strong faith, Lucía, pray, pray hard for all of us because they are coming to kill us,' Mr Cádiz said more than once to his guest.

'Nothing is going to happen; the Lord and the Virgin are protecting us.'

'If they didn't protect the priests, who were priests, I do not know what chance we stand.'

'Nothing is going to happen, you will see.'

That's what Lucía said, comforting Ambassador Cádiz and praying and asking for protection for her daughter and husband, more than for herself. She wished that the hours until they could board their plane would pass in a flash, like when you wake up after a long sleep and realise many hours have passed without you noticing. Lucía, to her dismay, could not fall asleep as she would have liked. The hours of waiting are always the longest.

6

After one in the morning, someone knocked on his door.
'What's up? Has something happened?' asked Tojeira.

He had fallen asleep thanks to a pill that calmed his nerves and had been sleeping for more than an hour when that knock on his door woke him up. He could only raise his voice, searching for an answer that came to him in less than a few seconds, yet seemed to take ages.

'You have a phone call, Father.'

'A phone call? From who?'

'They're calling you from the embassy of the United States.'

'The embassy of the United States . . .'

'Yes . . .'

'The ambassador?' asked Tojeira, who had sat up in bed and was looking for his sandals before emerging. 'Is it a call from Mr Walker?'

'No. But he told me it was on behalf of the ambassador.'

Tojeira went to his door and opened it.

'I'll go and answer,' he said, and walked to the nearby office that his companion pointed out to him.

The caller announced himself as soon as Tojeira came on the line:

'I apologise for the late call, Father, I'm Richard Chidester, legal adviser at the embassy. We have an urgent matter to discuss with you concerning the case of Lucía Cerna.'

'Good evening. Yes, the late hour is a little inappropriate perhaps, but tell me what it's about.'

'It's regarding Mrs Cerna's impending journey. Ambassador Walker and I think that it would be helpful if someone from the embassy were to accompany Mrs Cerna on her journey to the United States.'

'Helpful? I don't know if it's helpful,' answered Tojeira. 'She's going with her family and in Miami she will be met by some Jesuits of the order.'

'It's no more than an act of goodwill, Father,' Chidester assured him. 'I myself will accompany Mrs Cerna to Miami and assist with all the immigration paperwork – these days, it's no simple matter and I can facilitate the process. We would not want her to run into any problems entering the country. Bear in mind that nobody knows who she is or her importance in this case. An immigration officer who knows nothing about Lucía's situation would not greatly care who she is.'

'Well, yes,' conceded Tojeira, 'we wouldn't want her to run into a problem and be forced to return here.'

Thousands of Salvadorian citizens travelled year after year to the United States hoping to stay, fleeing the war to seek out a dream of the good things in life that didn't exist in their country. From the end of the seventies, the exodus increased, and a decade later the population of Salvadorians or Central Americans in the USA was still on the rise. As a result, migration conditions had become more and more complicated. Nowadays, only a lucky few were granted a visa. Every day more and more people slipped into the country without visas. In this context, with immigration officials more vigilant than ever in checking for fake visas at airports or patrolling the land frontiers, Tojeira thought it would be best to agree to Chidester's offer.

The following morning, Lucía arrived at the French embassy to continue her testimony. The judge was asked not to carry on too long, because Lucía had to board a flight in a few hours. Lucía knew what she was facing, but tried to remain calm; she managed for the first few hours, but began to get nervous as the time for the flight approached with the public prosecutors carrying on with their questions, without any pause. The ambassadors were nervously waiting. Tojeira rang the airline and explained that there was an important person who was due to travel but was giving testimony to a judge. Someone in the company assured them that their plane would not take off without that person on board. They were relieved. But the court appearance lasted much longer than they had imagined and they barely had time to reach the airport.

Comalapa airport lies half an hour outside San Salvador. You reach it by a motorway that's the same one you take to travel to the west of the country. If you travel along it today, you will find places to eat, hotels, huge advertising hoardings and stalls selling coconuts and other fruit. Along the route you would see cars and buses and new districts springing up on each side of the motorway, but back then most of the journey was through the middle of nowhere. It was common to come across military reservists stopping cars they thought suspicious or making everyone get off a bus looking for weapons or anything they could find to incriminate the passengers.

When they got into the French embassy car, they asked the driver to accelerate and he did as he was asked. Though weighed down by its armour plating the car was fast, and thanks to the diplomatic number plates they were not stopped by the military; in less than twenty-five minutes they found themselves at the airport. Lucía, her daughter and husband went straight to the airline's reception desk, the only one open. When they saw there was no queue, somebody said: *Thank God*. But it didn't help them as the plane had already taken off.

'The plane has already left, madam,' the check-in clerk told them.

'But that can't be, they said they would wait.'

'I'm sorry, but you were over an hour late. An hour is a long time.'

'But they said they would wait,' said Father Sainz. 'Has the flight already taken off?'

'Yes, sir. I'm very sorry but it could not wait any longer as it was almost full.'

'But they said they would wait. This woman cannot remain in this country.'

'I'm sorry, sir, but there's nothing we can do.'

'Is there another flight today?'

'No, sir, the next one is in two days' time.'

'In two days ... two days. That can't be true, it just can't be.'

'I'm sorry, sir, but there's nothing we can do about it.'

Neither Lucía nor her husband said anything and their daughter stared outside at the soldiers spread around the place. She also saw an army lorry parked at the back with several soldiers milling around it, some leaning on the palm trees opposite the parking area. She stared at them for quite a while and hardly heard the discussion with the airline clerk taking place behind her. She was just looking at the milling soldiers laughing or smoking. It all seemed peaceful and the girl wondered if those she saw would really be likely to do something like assassinate priests or if some of them were, according to her mother, among those who had entered the university. It was then that she heard a word that she had seen in films that woke her from her lethargy: FBI.

7

Lucía and her family were accompanied to the airport by Ambassador Walker, as well as Ambassador Cádiz, the Jesuit Father Fermín Sainz, who had been present at all Judge Zamora's interrogations, and a man called Bernard Kouchner, minister of health and humanitarian aid in France. It was Kouchner who suggested a solution to Lucía's lost flight. Everybody was clear that it was too risky to let another day go by with her still in the country. Kouchner said he would call the French base in Belize, where there was a plane belonging to the French army, to check if it was available to fly to Miami. In the airport offices a phone was provided, and while he phoned, Lucía and her family and the rest of them got together with Mr Chidester and a man named Ed Sánchez, who was introduced as an FBI agent. Chidester told Sainz that he had been in touch with Tojeira and said they would accompany Lucía and her family and Sainz answered that he had already been informed about that conversation and as Father Tojeira had no objections, he hadn't either, although he didn't expect someone from the FBI to be involved in the journey and asked for an explanation. *You must understand this is not an easy situation and we must protect the witness*, Chidester assured him. He also told him that the journey was only the start and they were even thinking of providing Lucía and her family with false identities, given they didn't know exactly who was behind the assassination of the Jesuits. While they were chatting, Mr Kouchner came back and said that everything had been arranged and in a few hours the French plane would come and pick them up. Chidester told the diplomat that they were also accompanying Mrs Cerna.

'I don't think that will be necessary.'

'It certainly is,' said Chidester. 'There's much to be settled with US customs and the situation remains very complex.'

'I could understand that if she was travelling on a commercial flight, but she's flying in a French Air Force plane. That changes everything.'

'It might change in your mind, but she's a Salvadorian national, not a French woman and nobody in the migration offices will know the circumstances in this country and this woman's importance. We have a duty to protect her.'

'That's how it is, Mr Kouchner,' said Walker. 'Our job is only to protect the witness and guarantee her safe arrival in our country.'

'Nobody mentioned a word before about the FBI's involvement,' said Kouchner, 'and that makes me uneasy.'

'Uneasy? On the contrary, you ought to feel reassured,' said Chidester.

'Don't think me naive, Mr Chidester.'

'Our job is to guarantee the safety of the witness,' insisted Chidester, 'I can assure you as I assured Father Tojeira. This is a very important matter for us.'

'It is for all of us and I hope there will be no more problems.

This woman has already been through a very tense time these last few days.'

'We wish only for that tension to end so that she can enjoy her stay. Nothing more,' said the legal adviser to the United States embassy. The exchange went on for a few minutes until Kouchner accepted that Chidester and Sánchez would fly in the plane with Lucía. A couple of hours later, they all climbed aboard the French plane and had a pleasant flight. Lucía knew that in Miami she would be met by some Cuban Jesuits who would take her to their house for a few days, before flying to California where she would find a permanent home. That calmed her down.

Besides, Mr Chidester had assured her they would have no problems with the migration officials. She wanted to believe that she had managed finally to leave the shadows of the last few days behind.

As she had been promised, there were no problems with migration. On leaving the airport, she was met by the two Jesuits Tojeira had told her about. They were holding some cards with her name on it and she waved at them. They approached and greeted her warmly, with words that consoled a woman who seemed worn out by the tension she had endured, barely having slept the last nights. It was then that Mr Chidester interrupted them:

'Gentlemen, good day.'

'This is Mr Chidester from the embassy,' said Lucía. The Jesuits greeted him.

'There are very powerful forces, the same ones that killed the Fathers and want to kill this woman,' Chidester warned them. 'If you put her up in your house, we fear that there might be a repetition of what happened in the UCA, that they would kill all of you. It would be better if Agent Sánchez took them to a hotel for a few days so that we can evaluate the risk to the witness. You're welcome to visit her. But I am clear about what's best and what isn't.'

Tojeira says that those Cubans took the bait too easily.

'They were from Cuba,' he tells me, 'and when they were told of powerful forces that pursued citizens, they did not think twice. Moreover, as that man had flown with her on the plane, they assumed he must be trustworthy. So they let her go with the FBI and on returning to their house told me that Lucía had arrived safely, that they had no problems with Migration and nothing more. And we were relieved.'

'They didn't say anything else?'

'No. Nothing more. We only realised what was happening days later.'

Lucía and her family were taken to the FBI lodgings. They were given a narrow bedroom with a window that overlooked the street, but was sealed shut. There were two beds with old sheets and a bathroom with two towels, a roll of toilet paper and toothpaste, but no soap to wash themselves. The air conditioning was on all day and that first night they were cold. They slept in one bed, the mother hugging her daughter, under all the sheets they could find. They had breakfast without leaving their room. At around nine, Agent Sánchez came to fetch Lucía for what he called an *interview*. The interviews repeated themselves up to five times a day. There were also some interviews with her husband.

When she entered the interview room that Friday, Lucía was devastated to come face to face with one of her compatriots, Lieutenant Colonel Manuel Rivas Mejía, head of the executive unit of the Salvadorian armed forces. He was standing talking to Chidester. He looked at Lucía without greeting her. Lucía thought of her daughter; she'd heard too many stories about the types of torture carried out by the Salvadorian military and didn't want anyone to touch her daughter. What would she do if that happened? She knew she could do nothing. She couldn't help her escape. Or perhaps she could.

Lucía sat in her seat, the usual one, and Rivas in the interviewer's chair. A man entered and placed a glass of water next to Rivas and said it was cold. Rivas said it was fine and sipped it and indicated that he hadn't slept much, that the mess continued and the water was to his taste. He pulled out a handkerchief and mopped his forehead, although he did not appear to be sweating. And he began.

'Fine . . . So you will not admit that you are a liar?'

'I am not a liar,' said Lucía, barely able to make herself heard and she hated her voice that got so weak that all she could manage was a whisper.

'Your husband and your daughter are fucked up because of you. Don't you feel sorry for them? They could be happily walking the streets of Miami and instead they have to stay in here because you won't admit that you didn't see what you said you saw.'

'I've told you what I saw.'

'They told you to say that. Recognise the facts, woman.'

'And what do you want me to say, when I saw what I saw.'

'I just want you to tell the truth, that you admit you lied, that it was the Jesuits who told you to say that you had seen soldiers. If you don't admit this, you'll be deported. You are going to return to El Salvador. And you know what will happen if you go back. And not just to you, but to your family too. Because you do know what will happen when you go back to El Salvador, don't you?

'I can well imagine.'

'So, what are you going to say? You are going to say that you are a liar. Because that is what you are. If you do say that, it won't matter to us, nothing is going to happen to you and we'll let you go. Miami is a pretty place and you would rather be here. What an idiot you are.'

They did not go hungry because they were fed three times a day. They did not have to sleep on the floor so they could not say they were being kept in a jail, but they were prisoners. When her daughter asked her, Lucía assured her that soon they would be walking about the streets of Miami with Father Tojeira's friends, and the girl's father confirmed that was how it was going to be, but neither Lucía nor her husband believed a word that they said to their daughter. They didn't even know if anybody in San Salvador was aware they were prisoners, kidnapped by the FBI. Lucía asked herself what she should do: tell them what they wanted to hear, or stick to her version. She was riddled with doubts. She wasn't sure what would happen to them even if she said what they wanted to hear. They might well release them, but what if there were assassins in the streets?

Lucía had often heard that the best thing that could happen to you in a foreign country was to meet up with a compatriot, she had heard that from many who were living in the United States on a visit home, as well as from a cousin who lived in Canada and from a friend of Father Joaquín López who had arrived from France, but for her now to meet up with a compatriot was her worst nightmare. She had one certainty: it would soon end. And she knew this because she could not hold out any more.

8

'Do you know what priests are?' Rivas asked Lucía's husband. 'What are they?'

'They're randy bastards. Especially when it comes to the women who keep house for them, serve them coffee and make their beds. They've always had women, all that stuff about chastity is a lie. And the worst of the bunch are the Spanish priests. They say that Segundo Montes was a devil for the women. Didn't you know that?'

'I don't know anything about that.'

'Segundo Montes and the psychologist, that Baró. Everyone knows that they grabbed women and fucked them. Everyone knows about it. If not, they walked about hiding it. So now you know what happened to your wife. Because those men fucked your wife. And you know all about that.'

'And what do you want me to do?'

'I'm not telling you to do anything, just what happened. I'm sure that they seduced even the old women. Or don't you know how priests are? You're lucky if that daughter is actually yours. I don't see any resemblance to you at all.'

'I think that you lot are the shits.'

'No, the priests are the shits. I'm telling you this for a reason. Ah, my dear boy, my dear boy, don't be blind. They really did fuck all their servants, but now it seems only your wife was the exception. Do you seriously believe that?'

'I don't know anything.'

'Well, if you don't know anything, we do. Even the seminarians fucked them, and let's not forget the old ones. Those old Spaniards were potent. That's all I'm saying.'

Colonel Rivas kept his cool. He was able to remain calm because he had done this many times. Over and over again he tormented Jorge Cerna. On top of this, they accused him of belonging to the FMLN's urban guerrilla command and they told him they would be prepared to overlook this, as long as his wife spoke the truth. Although Cerna's attitude started off by being aggressive, with time his spirit and rage about the situation wasted away and soon he didn't respond to what was said to him. Confusion and doubt began to cloud his mind. Lucía noted that her husband was different and silent. She began to feel discouraged and lost.

'And you still didn't know anything, Father?' I ask Tojeira. 'Not even a suspicion?'

'To start with, nothing, but then we did. When the Jesuits who were going to receive her in California asked after her, we realised that she wasn't in her house in Miami. We began to move, make calls, denounce what had happened. Even Archbishop Rivera denounced that the FBI had kidnapped Lucía in the United States and that she was undergoing psychological torture.'

'And did someone respond to what the archbishop said?'

'Yes. The president himself answered, and at that time he was Bush Senior. Bush said that in the United States they respected human rights. And, of course, he said this as his reply to Monsignor Rivera.'

'And did anything happen?'

'Well, something did happen.'

A few days later, the North American authorities passed on to the press some information about the witness, a new statement made to the FBI. In this press release the witness said the following:

What I said before was said to me by María Julia Hernández of the Legal Protection department and she said to me to say something about the soldiers. She asked me to lie. I didn't see anything at all.

9

'Every time they made her take the lie-detector,' Tojeira tells me, 'it confirmed she was telling the truth. The only exception was when she swore she hadn't seen anyone. When she said she saw soldiers in the moonlight, it was true. When she said that she hadn't seen them, a lie. But the Americans didn't say a word about that and we heard about it later during the trial with the declassified documents.'

'But what happened to her? Did they let her go?'

'Fortunately, yes. They let her go. And we picked her up and tried to do everything for her.'

'And she lives somewhere far off?'

'Yes. She did not return to El Salvador. She made a life far away and I like to think that it has been a better life than the one she would have had here. With other opportunities, and more comforts. And that's how it should be. She is an admirable woman. Very brave. Now you see how hard her days were, but she didn't give in because she always held on to her original testimony, that she saw what she saw that night. That hasn't changed, except for that one time, when they forced her.'

'And that was the beginning.'

'Yes, it was the beginning of the fight to find justice. It wasn't going to be easy. Those forces that Chidester had talked about were real, real and fearsome. What happened to Lucía woke us up. We wanted to find those responsible and bring them to justice. That had never happened before. The military had always acted with total impunity in our country. They'd got away with the massacres at Mozote and El Sampul and even with the most dreadful of all of them when they killed those thousands and thousands of peasants in 1932.'

'That was in Martínez's time.'

'Yes, dictator Martínez. There was never justice. There was never anything. Not one person was found guilty. You couldn't touch the army – and we wanted to touch them.'

'And at that time the army's response was to deny everything?'

'Deny it all. Deny it vehemently and lay the blame on the guerrilla forces. So we had to fight them. But we did not show fear. We were determined to bring the guilty to justice. It was the least we could do.'

'And do you still talk with Lucía, Father?'

'Yes. We have always kept in contact. Two decades have passed by, two and a half decades, but every now and then I'll give her a call.'

'And she's well?'

'Yes. She's very well. Very well. She's a strong woman.'

'That's good to hear.'

'It is, indeed it is.'

'But tell me, Father, what happened next, what happened when December 1989 came round?'

'What happened was a film.'

'A horror film?'

'We'd moved on from the horror. Next came the spies. Something shady like when you find yourself under a storm cloud.'

PART FOUR

1

The child's name was Juan, named after his father, and his mother was called Sara. Juan was seven years old when the nuns visited his village and told him that in November Monsignor would arrive to celebrate Holy Communion. It did not matter that the church lay in ruins because Mass would be celebrated in an open field. That news reached them in October. The village where they lived was called Las Moras. It was small, with something like twenty huts strung along a river on the slope of El Pital, a mountain lying on the frontier between El Salvador and Honduras, where wild cats still roam and there's always mist in the pine woods at dawn and dusk throughout the year. It's a cold place and distant from almost everything because no highway goes that far. Just a minor dirt track not wider than a cart drawn by oxen. The huts were made of dried mud, mixed with reeds or bamboos. Their roofs could be made of any materials, but mainly tin sheets. During winter, when great storms are unleashed on the place and winds like small tornados, you had to protect these roofs by placing stones or whatever on top – bags filled with earth, bits of mud flower pots – for these roofs were not screwed in or hammered into anything. Many times the force of the wind dragged them off like handkerchiefs.

When November came, they heard that Monsignor would arrive on a Friday. They heard that news on Saturday, which was not in reality too complicated. Three families whose children were to take their first communion gave one hen each and another woman, whose grandchild would also take part, gave a duck. These four families between them organised a meal for the Monsignor. Children from villages nearby would also assist, but they could not shoulder the responsibility for organising such a big affair because they didn't have enough money or animals, so the lunch would be shared by the four families in the village, and not even all of them.

When the day arrived, Juan's mother went with her children very early in the morning to the river to take a bath and she made them wash their hair with a scented soap. Normally they would wash with soap made of pig's grease. The children detested the smell of that soap, but she did not mind because she was used to it. But for an occasion like a communion, especially one attended by the Monsignor, it was worthwhile buying sweet-smelling soap from the market. Juan had three older brothers, who were eighteen, sixteen and fourteen years old. His parents had lost two girls who would have been twelve and ten, and a boy who would have been nine; he died two days after being born, and everyone put it down to the evil eye, an illness caused by a man passing through who had stayed for a week in a neighbours' hut. That man had a ferocious look and had seen the baby during a visit to the hut to wish them luck with the boy. He had recommended them to take care with the mosquitoes because there was an epidemic of dengue fever. They should burn a branch of *ocote* and chase them away with its smoke. After saying that he left. All this had taken place before eight in the morning. By dawn the next day, the baby had died.

With the death of that child they decided they would not have more children, so when Juan was born they believed it was a miracle, not only because he had arrived in the world with life but also because he was born with a fever that lasted a week and he did not die.

After their trip to the river, Sara dressed Juan in a white shirt, also bought from the market, and although he didn't wear his new trousers or his shoes, and put on his usual sandals, the new white shirt made him stand out from the other children.

Monsignor was Monsignor Romero and at that time it wasn't necessary to say which Monsignor he was, for many people recognised him as the only one. He arrived at around eleven and gave an open-air Mass. They put up a table and a chair and that man talked about the blessedness and privileges of living in the country under starlight, because in the city nobody could see so many stars, as well as being near a river, because in the city there were rivers but all were polluted and nobody would dare bathe in them. Lastly, he said, you can see God in everything in the country, in the sound of the pines, in the mist that came down from the mountain, in the yellow beetles that walked on the leaves or in the fields of flowers. Everybody listened to him as you would listen to the advice of a truly loving father. After giving communion to the children, he kissed each one on the forehead. At the end of the Mass, he said his farewell with a blessing and chatted with the people who came up to him. Juan's father said to his wife that this Romero was not like the other priests who lived in San Salvador, who never stepped out of their cars, and his wife said that was true and that they were lucky that he could give communion to their child as she already knew that their son had been born blessed and that this was one more proof. When the people from the neighbouring areas walked off, Monsignor accompanied the others to the home of one of the families. They had placed tables and chairs under an enormous *ceiba* tree whose foliage was so extensive and its branches so thick that Monsignor said it seemed like an upside-down mountain or a hill placed on its head. They sat down, but Romero did not want to sit at the head of the table. They offered him a refreshing *horchata* and he asked if he could drink it out of a cup cut from the *morro* tree. Some women said that they had cups and glass made of mud and he thought a large glass would be fine. A little while later, they served chicken soup and they ate and chatted like old friends. Many asked him about San Salvador, others about his life at San Miguel and someone asked him if he had travelled to Rome. Monsignor answered all these questions and several times said that the soup was really delicious and the women were happy to hear this. Almost at the end, Juan asked him if he knew anything about the *Gringo*'s estate.

'What estate?' Monsignor asked.

'There's a gringo,' said the child's father, 'who owns an estate that keeps some stuffed monsters and charges five *centavos* to see them.'

'Monsters? What monsters?'

'Well, they are animals,' Juan, the father, answered, 'bizarre animals, and that hairy man too.'

'These things are not known where I live,' Monsignor said. 'Are they scary?'

'I don't know,' said the child, 'my mum said that after I had taken communion she would take me, so I am soon going to find out.'

After the meal, Monsignor went for a stroll with whoever wanted to accompany him, which was almost everybody at the meal. They walked to the river and sat on stones and he bent over to wet his hands. It wasn't a river with deep currents. Its waters were cold, for that region was in a mountainous zone. Monsignor said that when he reached old age, if he ever did, he wanted to live near a river and walk every morning as he prayed whilst listening to the sound of the water, which was like music.

Half an hour later, Monsignor announced he had to go and said goodbye, embracing everyone and again kissing the children on their heads. He said he would return, and although nobody believed him because no one returns to these kinds of forgotten places in the country, surrounded by mountains, that man did return every six months or every year. He returned to celebrate Mass and give communion to other children, and people became very attached to the man who each time he came ate with them and strolled with them down to the river and didn't mind taking off his shoes and walking barefoot among the stones or consoling some impertinent drunk who would come up to him or drink *horchata* or lemonade and talked to them naturally like an equal. They all thought he was a good man, and perhaps he was, because he didn't stop visiting them even after being nominated as Archbishop of San Salvador and he began to appear more frequently in newspapers or on the radio. But that happened years later, and that day, when Juan was seven years old, they could not even have guessed it.

2

The following Monday was a day of much bustle. The three older brothers would be travelling to the west of the country to work as coffee pickers. They lived in the north in Chalatenango, but the most productive coffee plantations were in Ahuachapán and for over three years they had been going to work on those mountains in a place called Apaneca where they earned better money. They left at four in the morning, with other young people from their village. Their parents saw them off from their houses after drinking coffee and breakfasting on plantains roasted on cinders. When Juan woke up it must have been a little after five and his mother said that his brothers had already left. The child asked her why they hadn't woken him up to say goodbye. His mother didn't answer. Later, when Juan was drinking his coffee sitting next to the fire where the stew was placed, he reminded his mother that she had promised to take him to the gringo's farm in the mountain and she said yes she had, that they were going that day, and he must go and wash himself and not dawdle because they had a long way to walk.

An hour later, he left with his mother in the direction of the farm where that strange man, a foreigner with a white moustache and white hair and almost transparent skin, let people into his museum for five centavos, which was a fortune. They walked along a dirt track. There were pebbles everywhere and scraps of mango skins on the ground and cow excrement. At the side of the road they found a cart and a man next to it who greeted them by raising his hand. The cart was empty save for a dog dozing inside and the man was sitting under a mango tree, lying back against the roots, drinking water from a gourd. Sara asked him which was the way to the La Gloria farm.

'Straight on,' answered the man.

'That's good,' said the woman,

'Are you going to see the three-metre-tall giant?' asked the man.

'Yes, that's where we're going,' answered the child.

'I saw one once, one of those tall ones, but he was still living. I saw him as I reached Honduras.'

'Three metres tall?'

'They had him in a cage,' explained the man.

'Could he talk?'

'Yes, he could talk. But when I saw him he was dying, someone had shot him. He had attacked the wife of the plantation owner where he worked.'

'But he's dead now.'

'Better for us,' said the man and turned his face to the right and spat.

'But what had he done to the owner's wife?' asked the boy.

'He ripped an arm off. That's what they told me.'

'Had he bitten her?'

'Yes. And they had to shoot him twice to let her go. They were waiting for the owner to come and kill him.'

'And did he arrive?'

'Yes, on the next day, and then he killed him with blows from his machete. I saw that with my own eyes.'

They had stopped by the cart and when the man said that bit about blows from the machete, Sara thought soon they would have to return and better to get on, so they said goodbye to the man and went on. After some three kilometres of track they found the farm. The entrance had a *ceiba* tree on each side. Nailed to one of the trees was a sign in white letters that said *La Gloria* and nailed between the trees was an iron grille without paint that wasn't locked. They opened it and continued under foliage as if walking through a city. They walked for some time along a path with thick bushes of no more than a metre high on the sides. Between them, at every two or three metres, hung gas lights. Soon they reached a place without trees or bushes, a patch of land covered with grass with goats and cows and sheep eating or lying down. His mother noticed there were no dogs and that was lucky but unusual because normally dogs lived in sites like these in the country. There was a bend in the path and they came across a wooden bridge with a low river running under it and beyond an extension of land with sharp-pointed pines. The breeze there was gentle and under the pines the morning was dying out and becoming dark and seemed as if it was about to rain.

Soon they reached the main house built of stone. It didn't seem as if anybody was there for all was silent and without the buzz of life. Then they saw a dog. It was lying down but it stood up on all fours when it sensed them and barked, but didn't move from where it stood by the house door. She wasn't sure whether to approach or stay quietly by the edge of the path. They saw a man looming at the window and above his shoulder a woman appeared, and the man left the window and came out. He was old, with a white moustache and white hair and almost transparent skin.

'Good day,' he greeted them. 'The dog is tame.'

'Good afternoon,' Sara answered him, 'we have come to see the museum.'

The boy remained behind his mother, almost hiding himself.

'That's fine, but today is Monday and it's closed.'

'But we have the ten *centavos*,' the boy burst out, barely sticking his head out.

'Yes,' added Sara, 'that's right, we have the ten centavos.'

The man smiled.

'Well, the date doesn't matter,' he said. 'Come this way, come.'

He led them along a stone path about a metre wide that passed by the house. The dog had come forward and walked by the side of the man with a big moustache.

'My name is Helmut,' he introduced himself while walking, turning round to say that and shaking their hands.

Helmut took them up to a cabin at the end of the stone path and opened a door. He stopped under the door frame and before entering, told them:

'These are my treasures. What I collected over many years of life in Alaska. Do you know where Alaska is, boy?'

'No,' the boy said and his mother answered exactly the same thing, for they did not know where it was.

'It lies next to the North Pole,' Helmut pointed out. 'It's a land full of marvels and great monsters and now you are going to see some of them.'

The museum was in a wide room made of stone, with a wooden roof in the shape of a mountain ridge. Its main treasure lay in the middle, in a kind of rectangular pool with the body of an enormous, hairy man inside it. When the mother and boy drew up to it, they were impressed. And it was worth it for he measured three metres and two centimetres and was very similar to a gorilla, but neither the mother nor her son had even seen a gorilla. They stared at it for quite some time, with its thick fingers, its closed eyes, and cheekbones with little pimples forming a half moon under the eyes. The flat nose with round naval cavities was shaped like five-*centavo* coins and covered in hairs. A wide forehead was ploughed with furrows and a wide mouth, as if inflamed, had lips that had lost their colour and were almost transparent. Helmut assured them he had hunted it himself, like all the treasures in his museum.

Apart from the giant, they saw a bear, which had been placed standing up and was also enormous. It had a large snout and sharp teeth and claws thirty centimetres wide. On the wall was hung a great elk's head. Mr Helmut told them stories about how he had hunted these animals. He assured them that with some of these animals he had not even made an effort because he had found them while exploring in spring, completely petrified, scattered about the countryside.

'I mean by petrified, that they were stiff and very dead,' Helmut explained to the boy. He also told them that the man in the middle wasn't an animal but a prehistoric man, and that these men still inhabited those desolate regions in caves in the midst of frozen mountains.

The boy was fascinated and did not want to leave that place of marvels. Apart from the animals, there was also a two-thousand-year-old map where you could see the world as it was as well as a harpoon which the Alaskan natives used to kill whales and a ceremonial suit and crown of feathers and a bear's heart, which, according to Mr Helmut, belonged to a man called Taimanini, an old hero of the wars between the men of the North and the Vikings.

'Did they have hearts of gold?' asked the boy.

'Pure gold,' Helmut replied.

Two hours later they left the place. His mother gave Mr Helmut the two five-centavo coins, but he insisted it was not necessary for that day the museum was closed. The mother and her son thanked him. Helmut sat on a wooden bench by the entrance and said that by the time night fell it would be cold. They agreed. He began telling them that in Alaska it was cold all the year and that it was his favourite place in the world and the most beautiful, but he could no longer live in a frozen land because his wife was ill and they had been forced to come to a warmer country. By this time, they had been living here for ten years and as they did not have any children, they were overjoyed that people brought their children to visit the museum.

They stayed a few more minutes with the man and when Sara thought that was enough, they again thanked him for letting them see his animals and other treasures. He shook their hands and Mr Helmut invited them to return whenever they felt like it. They nodded and began to walk and as they walked they turned round again and waved goodbye to Mr Helmut and his wife who were leaning out of a window. After a while they stopped doing this and stepped up the pace because it was getting dark and at this time of the year night fell earlier.

The child would remember that day as the happiest in his life and would never forget that man from a very strange place: Alaska.

3

When Juan woke up on 1 January, almost four years had passed since his eldest brother had departed for the United States. He had left on 29 February, a day that almost never existed, so that he was not able to recall it as he would recall anything else. Half a year later, the brother who was next in line had taken the same journey north and had met up with the eldest in the city of Los Angeles. In no time at all he had got a job cleaning lavatories in a place that served hamburgers. Once or twice each month he sent a letter in which he told them working in a hamburger place was far better than picking coffee beans in the farms in Apaneca because you earned dollars and earning dollars was really something, whereas what he had got picking coffee or sowing beans and maize was nothing. His father earned in a year what he earned in two months and his elder brother was far better off mowing grass on a golf course in a hotel where Robert de Niro had stayed. Who is this De Niro? his mother had asked. A man who features in films, answered her son. In the village of Las Moras there were no cinemas, nor were there any in neighbouring villages, cantons or towns, but there was one in Chalatenango and his father had once seen a poster with De Niro's name on it and a friend had said to him: that one in the poster is a friend to your son. That very one.

These letters, packed with good tidings, ensured that the third of their sons took the same journey. And this journey began with a man who owned a lorry and took charge of bringing people to the United States. When he tried it, it went badly. Frontiers were not the same as when his brothers had travelled, the flow of immigrants without documents had so multiplied that the authorities had become more severe. At one of the controls, the lorry the third brother was travelling in was discovered to be a carrying a cargo of immigrants, so he had to spend a few months in a prison in El Paso, Texas before being deported. For some unknown reason, they deported him to Mexico, to the frontier city of Ciudad Juárez, and they heard nothing from him for over two years until one morning they received a letter from the eldest brother telling them that he had appeared in the hotel where he worked, that he was well, that he had gone through very bad times but was all right now and once he had recuperated the eldest would get him a job. In this letter they hardly mentioned how this third brother had suffered, but stories about dead immigrants had become common in the cantons, villages, towns and cities of El Salvador. This was the reason Juan had no interest in taking the same route as his brothers. All that and also that his mother begged him please don't go so far away, she couldn't bear it. Juan paid attention to what his mother said so did not take that route when the first of January came round; in the darkness of early morning as he heard the sound of logs burning in the kitchen, the same ones on which his mother would place the griddle to make the morning's tortillas, he thought he did not want to dedicate himself to sowing crops, for you earned nothing doing that, and that it was time to go to the barracks. He would follow in the steps of the son of Señora Lina, a neighbour, who was already a lieutenant and was respected by all when he came on visits to the village. He held this very clearly in his head and that morning told his father and his father said as far as he was concerned it was fine, that his mother would not like it because the situation was getting dangerous and already there were rumours of war all over the country, but he need not always pay attention to her.

And just as his father had predicted, his mother hated the idea, but it was always better to go to a barracks nearby than to travel far and join his brothers. Juan was sixteen years old and didn't join the military until he was eighteen. That was in 1979 and the civil war lay in the future. He joined the barracks and the first six months did not get a permit for leave and his mother used to walk to the nearby town each Sunday, some twenty kilometres by the tar road, to call him on the telephone. She asked him how he was and her son answered tired, but fine. Every Sunday, Sara wanted to know if he was going to be sent to the war and he said he wasn't, that it was too soon, but not to get worried, that things were going well for him, that the captain in charge said he didn't know anybody with an aim as good as his, that he was going to be sent on a special course.

'A course on how to shoot?'

'I've no idea . . . '

'Didn't you say you had a good aim?'

'Yes, but it can't just be that. It must be more, about other things too.'

'May the Virgin protect you, my son.'

'And how's my father?'

'Your father is fine. I left him sleeping in the hammock.'

'Tell him when he comes we'll go hunting for deer.'

'And they will let you carry a rifle?'

'I don't know, but a pistol, yes.'

'Look after yourself, child. Did you hear me? Look after yourself.'

'What could ever happen to me, Mum? Nothing ever happens here.'

'You look after yourself.'

'Yes, Mum, yes.'

4

Sara had heard church bells at dawn crossing the silence of the hills and had a sombre premonition. Because of this she told her husband that she was going to call Juan, although it wasn't a Sunday but a Tuesday. She left when the sun cleared the air and walked to the usual neighbouring town, called and whoever answered at the barracks said her son was not there, that he had been sent to San Salvador. She asked if something had happened.

'You don't know what happened?'

'I don't know anything,' she answered, already upset by the man's question.

'They killed your Monsignor,' he said.

'Romero?'

'That's him.'

'And where is my son?'

'This business with the guerrilla faction, those sons of bitches, has turned nasty and they sent a unit to, well, look after things.'

It was March 1980 and the morning had turned cold and Sara did not know if the cold came from outside or from inside, but she wished she had a sweater or at least a shawl to warm herself. She understood why she heard church bells so early, what they were announcing, and she feared for her son. What did he have to do in San Salvador? She feared a clash was getting closer and her fear turned her into a shadow.

When she returned to the village, her neighbours were sitting around a small radio. The women were crying without making a show of it and the men listened to the news looking down at the ground, but without daring to cry. They all had respect for Monsignor, he had given communion to their sons and daughters, he had bathed in the river and drunk *horchata* and had lunched with them many times, although the last time was now some years back. When he was appointed archbishop in San Salvador he no longer had time to visit the village, although the nuns who continued visiting them sent them his greetings. The nuns said that he usually called them on the phone and when he did, always asked them to send his respects to the people of Las Moras and they received these greetings with genuine happiness, as if being greeted by a cousin who lives too far away to make the effort to visit them.

They wept tears as they would for a family member. Romero had become someone important not only to the community that knew him but to everyone in the country. A figure who, with each homily, denounced repression and poverty in the country and stood up to the military and political factions. That man had undergone a transformation. Or suffered one each time he spoke at Mass in the San Salvador cathedral, when he turned his back on the sweet, peaceful man and became the defender of what he called his *people*. He had announced that he was under threat. He said he would be reborn among the people if assassinated. And all his speeches were listened to by hundreds and thousands of people, glued to their radios every Sunday. That day was a Tuesday and Romero was assassinated on a Monday, while lifting up the chalice for Mass. A deadly shot through his heart had finished off his life as a man and turned him into a saint.

5

The following day, Sara returned to the village to call her son, but she was told he had not returned. A day later she didn't want to phone again, but it was Monsignor's funeral and she couldn't sleep all night. During the Mass with his body in the cathedral, attended by thousands of faithful followers, so many that most of them had to remain outside the building, the army unleashed an attack. Marksmen on roofs of neighbouring buildings shot into the crowd. Dozens of people fled into nearby streets and dozens more were hit by bullets. From below there was an insignificant counter-attack from guerrilla forces who, dressed as civilians, blended with the crowd. You can still see local television images of people lying on the ground, behind cars or trying to protect themselves along the narrow edges of the streets. That day the whole country was silent. Fear of what had been seen and heard would sink the population into a darkness unlike any they had known before.

In Las Moras, the villagers heard on the radio what had happened in the capital. That day nobody spoke. Children were forbidden to go to the river to bathe and as night fell they locked their doors. Few lit oil lamps.

A day later Sara called her son again. Nothing. They did not give her much hope that he would be back soon. As the only thing she could do was to insist, she decided to walk to the neighbouring village every day. Ten days later that insistence would spare her life.

Every morning, Sara had walked to make the phone call.

'Don't you know anything?' she asked again.

'It's the same as yesterday, they have not returned, but we do have news,' said the soldier who answered her phone call in a tone that was meant to be friendly.

'You have news of him?'

'Yes, I asked about your boy.'

'Oh, you did?'

'As I've already said, he's fine, nothing's happened to your son. He's been doing target practice. They say he's good, that he shot everything that moved.'

'Target practice? And why did they take him to San Salvador for that?'

'He's been killing pigeons in the centre. Do you get me? There was a plague of pigeons, all those churches covered in pigeon shit, so you see what he's up to.'

'But you don't know when he's returning? Did you talk to him?'

'What would I talk to him about? I don't talk to anybody, but he's fine, as I've already told you, don't worry about anything.'

'That's something I can't stop doing, I'm even not sleeping.'

'If you want, call tomorrow. It's up to you, in the end I'm not the one walking every day.'

'It's my feet that walk.'

'And after today's first rainfall, the tracks will be covered in stones, but what do I care, it's your feet.'

'I'll call tomorrow.'

'Do as you please.'

It was a little after eleven when Sara walked back home, thinking that the man she talked to over the phone was right, the tracks were littered with pebbles and it made walking very uncomfortable. She was wearing rubber sandals and if she stepped on a sharp pebble she could feel it. But there was not much she could do except continue. It might have been an agreeable ramble if it wasn't for the nuisance of those stones, for there was a hint of rain in the breeze and the smell of damp earth. Some stretches of the walk were red because of clay and the morning rain had endowed it with a beautiful colour. On both sides there were pines with great roots and if there was a breeze, as there was, they whistled more than other trees. But she could only move slowly forward, taking care not to step on sharp-sided stones and not to stop thinking about her boy. She was so lost in her thoughts that it took her some time to realise there were explosions and shouts below her. They were still slight, hardly distinguishable. She then stopped trying to grasp what she heard quite clearly, she carried on going because she did not believe what she heard. She only knew that what she had heard was real when she saw some soldiers running towards her. They were running along the track, the three of them and one said as he passed:

'Where are you going?'

'What's happening?'

'The guerrilla forces are killing all the people they come across. Better hide in the woods . . .'

The soldiers continued running along the track and she watched them running until she lost them round a bend. Sara hesitated as to whether to go on or not. She was close to her village. She was in a terrible panic. She stood there, not moving, telling herself she must react, that she could not stand there like a fool. As she did not dare go on, she turned to her right, left the dirt track and went into the pine wood which was a hundred metres thick and the ground sloped gently down. She walked through the dark wood, stepping on the soft, damp, yellow pine needles while she prayed as best she could. She hadn't eaten since breakfast but did not feel hungry. She did feel thirsty, but soon heard the sound of a stream and approached it. The sky above the trees was grey like the belly of an old wild mountain cat. It felt like rain, the wind was shaking the branches until they almost broke and she had to walk very carefully to escape being hit by the longer branches, for they were like whips. The stream was in an open field lower down and Sara walked there without noticing where she was walking. When she was two or three metres away she discovered that the water was not transparent. She found that slightly brown colour odd. Her first thought was that the rain had stirred up mud. She stopped at the edge of the stream and its cold water soaked her feet and she stared at the mossy rocks in the deeper water and realised that if she followed it she would reach the river which ran a few metres from her community and then realised that it wasn't mud that the stream was carrying down but blood.

She took a step back and returned to the shelter of the trees. She was so weary that she sat down on a bed of leaves and prayed with her eyes shut. For a long time she couldn't bring herself to open her eyes. Without being aware of it, she fell asleep. When she woke up, the day had changed and a red twilight was spreading over the western sky. There was no wind and nothing but silence around her. Patches of darkness hovered above the distant maintains and under the now motionless pine branches. She walked in the direction of the dirt track, aiming to find her way home. A few metres from Las Moras, she came across the first bodies. They were soldiers, most of them as young as her son. It seemed that they had wanted to flee as they lay face down with bullet wounds in their backs or calves or heads. Maps of blood spread out from them or filled the path and Sara had to walk round them to avoid getting stained. After a while in the dark, she reached the village and saw nobody outside the huts. They were inside. She heard sobbing from the hut of a woman called Jesusa and found ten men, including her husband, strewn on the ground.

'They killed all the men,' says Sara later, many years later. 'Not the old men nor the children, but all the men who were of fighting age.'

'And was it the army or the guerrilla groups?'

'The guerrilla groups. Sometimes it was the army and other times, perhaps less so, the guerrilla groups. But for my kin, it was the guerrilla groups that killed them.'

'But you said you saw three soldiers.'

'They could have been guerrilla fighters. I don't know.'

'You don't know?'

'No. It's all very confusing. They killed my husband and the father of my children, you don't know what that's like. It was very hard. And it's all very confusing, for at that time everything was. One brother was with the guerrilla groups, another was a soldier. Everyone knows that. They could kill each other and it's difficult to tell who was who. It was a war.'

'I know. But please, tell me, what did you do next?'

'I left that place. We could no longer stay in the village, we just couldn't, they warned us not to stay, that they would return.'

'I suppose you don't know why they asked you to leave the place?'

'Nobody knew anything and they did not tell us.'

'Where did you go?'

'To a camp where they brought refugees, people like myself who had been left with nothing. And at the camp there were some nuns and that's where I met Father Segundo Montes.'

'Was he in charge?'

'Father Montes went there every weekend from the community, sometimes even weekdays, but that was less common. If you want me to tell you the truth, if it hadn't been for that Father I perhaps wouldn't be here. I would have put a bullet through my head. He got me to grasp that I had three sons and couldn't die.'

Sara smiles and stays quiet and it seems that a memory floats back to her. She tells me that the Father explained to them that their suffering had been suffered by many before them. That they had had the luck of remaining in our country because thousands had had to flee beyond the frontiers and had survived jungle and mountain camps in Honduras.

'He was a tough man, but, I can't explain it, he was also sweet. Do you understand me?'

'I believe I do.'

'He was a good man.'

Segundo Montes had been born in Valladolid in the same land as Martín-Baró. At the age of seventeen he had entered the Order of the Company of Jesus and a little later was sent to Quito, Ecuador, to study at the Papal University. It was his first encounter with Latin America. After Quito, he travelled to San Salvador around 1970 and worked for a long time with the boys at the Jesuit college in the capital, San José College. He gave classes there every now and then, because for years he undertook long journeys to complete his studies further afield. When he was established in the country, there came a time when his ties with UCA pulled him away from the college and by the 1980s his visits had stopped. University activities took up all his time and these activities could not be reduced to the classrooms. At that time, he became interested in refugees and migrants and his main research efforts turned in that direction. He visited refugee camps in El Salvador and in Honduras and founded the Institute of Human Rights of the University and directed it until his death. It was perhaps that kind of effort that led to Father Montes being considered as someone who broke the law, a religious man close to left-wing thinking; along with Ellacuría and Martín-Baró, he headed the list of dangerous Jesuits in the minds of the Salvadorian extreme right. Their sights were trained on them.

'And how long did you stay in the refugee camp?'

'Until the day my son arrived and took me off to a house in San Salvador. My other sons, those in the United States, said to him that they would pay the rent of a house in San Salvador and so I went there. That's from 1981 onwards, if I remember rightly.'

'I understand. And, let's see, why are you barefooted?

'It's my penitence.'

'But why on earth do you punish yourself that way?'

'Because I left my husband alone.'

'And have you asked yourself what difference it would have made had you remained with him?'

'Perhaps none.'

'So?'

'It's all the same to me. It is my punishment for leaving him alone.'

'And has this been going on for years?'

'I put shoes on again in December 1989.'

'And why did the penitence come to an end?'

'Because I felt elated. It was when my son returned after the offensive. I was frightened he would be killed – you know what I mean, they killed many soldiers. It was terrible. When he came home alive I cooked a meal for him and told him he could take me to buy some shoes. It was such a relief, you cannot imagine. He was my son. There's nothing worse than losing a son, everybody knows that.'

'Was he your favourite?'

'If you want the truth, perhaps he was. He was the last one. And the one who stayed at home the longest. It doesn't matter that I say this now. The other sons send me money for the house, but I never see them. This one lived with me. The other sons did not turn up when they killed their father, and this one always came to see me. Always. Do you understand?'

6

On Saturday 11 November, 1989, a little after midday, a helicopter landed at the barracks that served as the headquarters of the Atlacatl Battalion. Some soldiers saw the vice president of the republic, a man called Francisco Merino, step down from the helicopter. At that time, it was known that Mr Merino was close to the army's high command, but it was an unusual visit. For nearly four hours, Merino met with Colonel León Linares, the battalion commander.

The Atlacatl Battalion was the best in the army. It had been created at the start of the war as a special forces unit, trained by United States commandos in North American installations and under the most severe conditions. Much has been said about what those men were capable of, and they have been the subject of talk, oscillating between pride and dread. They have been accused of massacring the civilian population and praised for acts of true heroism, but the fact is the battalion was renowned for its ability to carry out missions. On the day after Merino's visit, the staff college asked for a group from Atlacatl, the most outstanding soldiers available, to travel to San Salvador to give them support. And so the chosen ones prepared their combat gear. Juan says he called his mother very early, before six in the morning, to tell her not to leave her hut. They had warned them that the clashes about to take place were not isolated events, that guerrilla forces had prepared an offensive throughout the land. But he also told her not to worry, that he was not going into combat, but just making specific installations safe. When his mother asked him what installations, he told her that he was not authorised to say. But despite everything, she was quite calm. Since the 1980s, Sara had been living in the house that her sons paid for in a suburb of San Salvador. There she had a telephone next to her bed on a wooden chair. Juan said he would call again when he could and put the phone down. Minutes later he left for the city with his comrades. It was not an ordinary expedition. They could hear clashes everywhere so they moved with their weapons ready, sitting along the sides of the lorry carrying them, alert for any sign of the enemy.

At the staff college they didn't do much that day except wait or carry out inspections in the area. Being a unit, they could not understand why they were not fighting, but not one of their members would query something like that, they would not demand an explanation.

They did not do anything early Monday morning. Juan would have liked to phone his mother, but nobody else called their family so he decided not to. Besides, he didn't want to answer her questions or pretend that all was well. There was a constant tension in the air and the news that reached them was not encouraging. Even their staying where they were made the situation more tense, so he did not feel like being put under pressure by his mother and end up shouting at her.

By the afternoon of that same day they were asked to join

the installations of the military school as part of a commando unit that protected that whole zone. They would remain under the command of Colonel Benavides, director of the school. At the end of the afternoon they were asked to carry out a straightforward mission, a reconnaissance of the nearby university, the university of the Jesuits known as UCA, where they would also check the house where the priests lived. They walked to the university, which was only six hundred metres distant, using the pedestrian entry near the Jardines de Guadalupe district. Juan says the priests did not object to being searched and collaborated with the soldiers and opened doors so they didn't have to break in and that they did their work without discovering anything incriminating.

He also says that at one point he recognised one of the priests, a man his mother had known from the community where she had gone when she fled her hut. He himself had seen him more than once.

'Do you often go to San Miguel, Father?'

'Less and less,' said the priest, 'with age you do less and less. Are you from there?'

'From Chalate,' answered the soldier, 'but I once saw you there.'

'Well, it happens.'

Juan did not say any more and carried on with his work and when they finished inspecting the house of the priests they left the university campus without checking much else, glancing into some of the classrooms.

'Who was that, Father?'

'Segundo Montes,' Juan tells me.

'And did you feel any gratitude towards him?'

'Gratitude? Let's see. Yes, he treated my mother well, but that's another story. It was not a moment for that.'

'What do you mean, "that"?'

'Gratitude, compassion, consideration. I was doing my job and nothing more. And yes, I did feel grateful because my mother spoke well of him, saying he had helped her, but what could I do about it?

On Wednesday morning they were ordered to check the Centro Loyola, a house where the Jesuits held spiritual retreats. Like the one at the UCA, the search was carried out without incident. It did not take long, but they received an order not to move from the place, so they remained there until further orders. It was a good place to be. It was peaceful and silent, with a small chapel and wide rooms and a panoramic view over the city. A little to the left they could see the San Salvador volcano and to the right, looking south, the San Jacinto mountains and opposite, the Guazapa mountains, where it was known that the guerrilla camps were situated, and further off in a blur of distance, the strange silhouettes of the northern range. In the far distance they saw a plume of smoke, and another one in Mexicanos to the north-east. But nothing that worried them unduly. They were relaxed, taking it easy all afternoon. A woman who worked there gave them sugared buns and coffee. There were more than forty men, but she served all of them. It was an agreeable afternoon in the midst of chaos. Everything changed at seven that night when they were given an order to leave the place. By that time they already knew they had a mission. They had been sent to San Salvador for a reason.

They returned to the military school's headquarters. A little later they were asked to prepare themselves because they had to leave again. They had to eliminate a few of the leaders of the guerrilla forces. They were given instructions to wipe out the enemy and to fake a confrontation. Juan says they were divided into three groups. Two would provide back-up and give them security and the third would eliminate the enemy. They would have to be precise and aim to kill. That's what they had been trained to do. That night not one witness would remain alive.

The streets around the university were empty. There was a large white moon on the horizon and the stars were not visible. They walked, sticking to the shadows, protected in the half-light and wary about what was going on from either side. They needed to act decisively. When they entered the university they walked along an inner street and stopped after reaching the chapel, to reorganise themselves.

'What do you think in moments like those?'

'About carrying out the mission.'

'And what was yours?'

'To provide security.'

'Did you remain outside?'

'Yes. In the second circle of security.'

'And were you grateful for that?'

'Not then. At that moment you think of nothing but carrying out your mission.'

'And now?'

'Yes. Now I would be grateful. It could have been worse.'

'What could have been worse?'

'The anguish. The regret. The truth is, I don't know, I don't know what to call this thing I have inside me.'

Those in the first circle of security shot at the Fathers' house or at the Monsignor Romero Centre. Their objective was to promote a fake confrontation. After a while, a flare was fired. It was the sign that the mission had been successful and they had to abandon the place. A little later, another flare lit up the night. It simply emphasised the first one. When they left, Juan knew that the Fathers they had seen during the search had been eliminated, including Father Montes. He couldn't get his face out of his head, with his deep blue eyes looking at him while he talked, while he was saying *with age you do less of everything*. And while he was meditating on these matters, the night persisted in being cold and the moon persisted in being enormous and white in the night sky.

7

A few weeks passed until Sara could meet up with her son. When the doorbell rang that Saturday, she knew who it was because nobody else visited her and especially so early on a Saturday. They had not talked since the start of the offensive. On finding him at the door, she hugged him for a long time and cried with emotion. She had spent weeks waiting for that visit, many hours praying, pleading with God to ensure that nothing would happen to her lad, that he would return safe, that the bullets would not strike him, although she had heard so many shots she did not know how that would be possible, but she took some hope from words that Archbishop Rivera once said over the radio: *What's impossible for men, is possible for God*. Sara hung on to that line taken from the gospel and repeated it during her prayers. She trusted in God, believed in miracles and confided in the Virgin of Fátima, whose picture she had above her bed. So when her son turned up without a scratch, she thought her prayers had been heard and thanked God and the Virgin and made her son pray with her and give thanks.

'It has been terrible,' he repeated later, while his breakfast was being prepared.

'I've been beside myself with worry.'

'It got very ugly. The truth was, nobody expected it.'

'And did you see what happened? I felt such shame when Father Segundo was killed.'

'Yes, I know,' said Juan. 'We found out about it.'

'I cried over his death for a long time because he was a good man. That poor man. Do you really think he was a member of the guerrilla forces?'

'What would I know, Mama?'

'Poor man. I don't think he was. I remember when he came to see us. Do you remember?'

'Yes I do, Mama.'

'I'm going to put on the shoes you gave me for my birthday and we can go and eat at Pollo Campero. I've got what your brothers sent me, so we can eat well.'

'You're going to put shoes on?'

'Yes, I am.'

'That's good, Mama.'

'Well, we have to celebrate. And tomorrow we'll get up early to go to Mass.'

'To Mass?'

'We have to give thanks to God that you came home in one piece.'

'I've got to get back early tomorrow, at five in the morning.'

'But, Son, that would mean we cannot thank God.'

'You thank him, Mama.'

'It's not the same.'

'I'm sure it will be better.'

'Not another word – we have to go. We have to go gratefully. If not tomorrow, we go today, to the afternoon Mass.'

'All right, Mama . . .'

At midday, Sara put on her shoes and though they hurt her feet a great deal, she did not complain. They went out to have lunch and Juan remembers it was a fine afternoon, that he liked seeing his mother in such a happy mood. He also tells me that that night he thought about his childhood, about the day he was taken to the farm to meet a man nearly three metres tall, and he remembered that this man, the owner of the farm, had come from Alaska. That was when he had the idea of leaving home. Before that, he already knew he did not want to stay on any more, that he could not stand to remain, not even in his country or near his mother, and the best way was to enlist in the battalion and go far off, to the north, the furthest north possible, to that region of ice where nobody would know of him. For a long time he was not able to enlist, but with the arrival of the peace treaties, some years later, he could and did. He asked his mother to travel with him to the United States, to Los Angeles, and visit one of his brothers. In that journey he told her that he wanted to go beyond the United States, further away. Everyone accepted it as normal, but it was not, and as the weeks moved on Juan did not call them on the phone or write to them telling them where he was and whether he was all right. Eight months had to pass before they had news of him. He told them he was in Alaska and had work in a coffee house, that he had never suffered such cold and asked them if they had ever seen bears, because in the town where he was living bears walked about at midnight and savaged rubbish containers. He also assured them that, despite the cold, it was a good place to live and he wasn't thinking of coming home.

'You're not planning on returning to San Salvador?'

'I don't think so. There's nothing there for me.'

'What's in your head, Juan, what's in your mind when night falls and you climb into bed, what memories?'

'A storm.'

'A snow storm or a rain storm?'

'However strange it might sound, it's never a snow storm. It's a storm of water, the kind that blows off the roofs of houses. Have you ever stood in a house with a corrugated tin roof during a storm?'

'No.'

'It sounds like a gunfight.'

'And that's what you recall?'

'Every night,' he tells me, 'every night.'

PART FIVE

The Twisting Road to Judgement

1

On 22 December, Tojeira and Father Francisco Estrada, the rector of UCA, were cited by the Investigative Commission for Crimes to attend a meeting where they would be informed of the latest developments in the investigation. The government's official position remained the same as in November: that the army had nothing to do with the assassination of the Jesuits, and everything pointed to the guerrilla forces. And although there was an international movement in favour of carrying out a rigorous investigation and the government, through President Cristiani, had committed itself to do so, and the Archbishop of San Salvador, Monsignor Rivera y Damas, had mentioned the case in every homily he made, the matter hardly advanced towards what the Company of Jesus thought to be the truth.

They were received in a wide room with a rectangular table and closed windows. The two Jesuits sat down and opposite them, on the other side of the table, sat three members of the investigating committee: Colonel Manuel Antonio Rivas Mejía, Colonel Carlos Armando Avilés and a man named López. Behind them sat ten or twelve researchers, all dressed in suits and ties with their hair cut in military style, but elegant and slicked back with Vaseline or gel. They looked clean-shaven and kept silent, although some took notes in notebooks. Others did not. They listened.

Tojeira, at a first glance, thought it odd that there were so many researchers and could not tell whether they were members of the military or police, nor where they had come from. Perhaps they were civilians, for at that time many men adopted the military look because it was socially acceptable and they hoped it would enable them to claim some of the privileges granted to serving members of the military corps, such as access to a store known as 'The Co-operative' where you could find all those items that could not be obtained from ordinary shops, for the state of war put limits on everything. Alcohol, video games, designer sports shoes and jars of peanut butter – products that came from the United States. There were other privileges too, depending on whether you were a captain, a colonel or even a lieutenant, such as living accommodation in protected city districts, and even immunity from prosecution, whether for committing atrocities or more mundane offences like failing to pay parking tickets. If you were fined for some misdemeanour and you had the good luck to know someone whose father was in the army, you made a phone call and everything would be sorted. Because it was possible. You feared them and respected them, but above all you feared them. They earned a fortune, and protected the fatherland's security, and it was highly unusual if they limited themselves to just one woman, or even one family. When Christmas or New Year's Eve came round, they took out their rifles and fired them into the air as it struck twelve, and although there was always someone who got hurt or even hospitalised after being hit by a stray bullet, those boys who had a brother or cousin or father in the army lined up to shoot knowing no one would punish them.

'Good day, Fathers,' said Rivas Mejía, who seemed to be in charge. 'We have asked you here today so we can bring you up to date on how our investigations are coming along.'

'Good day,' Tojeira replied. 'Father Estrada is the university rector, as I think you already know.'

'We are aware of that,' said Rivas Mejía.

'Good day,' said Estrada.

'So, here we are. Now tell us how you are getting on.'

'Well, very well. We have made exhaustive inquiries. As you can see, we have a large team of investigators and we are doing all that is within our power and even a little more.'

'And we are very grateful,' said Father Estrada.

'It's our duty,' said Rivas Mejía. 'As I was saying, we have been diligent and I must inform you that everything is pointing towards the FMLN.'

'I see,' Tojeira butted in. 'And what is it exactly that's pointing in that direction? What have you found and why do you continue insisting on that conclusion?'

'As you know, Father, rewards are very effective and many people who normally would not have come forward have been enticed to do so by the money on offer. And many of these people have passed lie-detector tests.'

'I see,' repeated Tojeira.

Rivas Mejía was referring to the fact that they had offered a reward to anyone who came forward with information relating to the case of the Jesuit Fathers. Informants were promised money and discretion.

'The most interesting testimony is that of a homosexual lover of Commander Dimas. Do you know who this man is, Father?'

'No, I don't know,' said Tojeira.

'Dimas was a guerrilla commander who fought on San Salvador's volcano and died in combat during the offensive. His lover confessed that, the night before Dimas died, the two of them slept together and in an intimate moment the commander told him that his men had killed the Jesuits. He confessed it all as I'm telling it to you. When he heard about the reward we were offering, this character came and confessed. He took the lie-detector test and passed.'

Tojeira assures me that they told it to him as he told it to me. This was the best the investigating commission could come up with in the way of evidence: this man's lie-detector result and what he had told them about his supposed relationship with Commander Dimas.

'What was your response, Father?'

'I didn't have a chance to respond, because Chidester turned up.'

While Rivas Mejía was recounting these matters to the Jesuit father, the door to the office where they were sitting opened and Richard Chidester walked in. He sat down in a chair next to the Jesuits. He did it without greeting them. In fact, he entered the room without even knocking on the door.

'What's this gentleman doing here?' asked Tojeira when Chidester sat down.

'He's our friend,' one of the three colonels answered.

'If this man stays, then we are leaving,' warned Tojeira, raising his voice. 'This individual is a liar. He deceived us. If he is to be present, I refuse to take any further part in this meeting.'

'What, how can you say that? I've never ever lied,' insisted Chidester. 'I was trying to help.'

'That's a lie. You are a liar. You abused my confidence and the confidence of the diplomats in doing what you did.'

'My intention was to protect the witness. You cannot accuse me of anything.'

'Your intention was to deceive us, mock us in the most vile way and manipulate that woman. I know your game.'

'As I've said, Father, my intention was to help. But you can believe what you want to believe.'

'If this gentleman is to remain, we will leave,' Tojeira reiterated, pointing his finger at Chidester and shouting angrily, out of control.

While this was going on, Colonel López rose from his seat and approached Chidester. He whispered something in his ear that nobody could hear and Chidester got up and left. His final words were *Believe what you want*.

'He's a liar, a man with no scruples,' insisted Tojeira.

'Forgive us, Fathers,' said López. 'He's a friend of ours and has our complete confidence, but he came here uninvited.'

'Some friend,' added Tojeira.

'He was not invited by us, he has merely collaborated in certain matters. Do you understand? Right, let us continue.'

'Look, Colonel,' Tojeira went on, 'you have already given us your proof, but the truth is your evidence is weak. I do not trust lie-detector tests, especially when we don't know the circumstances in which they were carried out or who operated the polygraph. And another thing: all this stuff about someone having a lover and the lover saying . . . This is not some TV soap opera. We need detailed evidence and in order to obtain that you need to take this investigation to another level. The inspection of the pastoral house, we know from the judge who issued the search warrant that this was carried out by the Atlacatl Battalion. They are the ones you need to investigate instead of wasting your time on people who will say anything in return for a reward. If those men from the Atlacatl Battalion were there on Monday, they could have been there on Thursday. Have you investigated that?'

'No. Not really, no.'

'Then I suggest you investigate them instead of looking into such nonsense as who slept with who.'

After Tojeira threw out that sentence, a dense, cold, immovable silence engulfed the room. Tojeira stood with his eyes fixed on the table, nervously drumming his fingers, while he thought about what he had just said and tried to calm himself. He realised that he had lost control, enraged by the gall of Chidester in showing up here. It seemed to him they had been summoned here to be treated like idiots. The whole thing was a mockery, and he refused to put up with it. He was going over all this in his mind when Estrada, the other Jesuit, who was prudent and far more diplomatic than Tojeira, asked if he could speak.

'Look,' said Father Estrada, 'I want to speak as a Salvadorian. First of all, I approve of everything said by my colleague, but as a Salvadorian I want to say one thing to you: you make me want to vomit, you make me sick, you bring shame on our country, you sell yourself to the *gringos*, and one of these *gringos* enters as if he owns you and you lick his boots . . . What's more, you are liars, everything you have just said is a pack of lies, you're an embarrassment to the military, not fit to be Salvadorians.'

Colonel Armando Avilés, who had been Estrada's pupil in the day school, the Jesuit College of San Salvador, intervened:

'All right, Father, maybe it would be better if we calmed down a little, eh? Can I offer you something to drink – a coffee, perhaps?'

'I don't want anything,' replied Estrada. 'I'm fine as I am and I've said all I have to say.'

'Father?' Avilés asked Tojeira.

'Water. A glass of water.'

The meeting did not last much longer. The two sides made a token effort at reconciling their differences, Tojeira handed over some physical evidence found at the scene of the crime, and a moment later the priests took their leave and left the room.

It was a fresh morning and in the nearby offices there were small Christmas trees on some of the secretaries' tables and a crib in the entrance with clay figures representing Christ's birth. Neither of the Jesuits noticed it. Both were deep in thought. They made their way out to the car park in silence, oblivious to the beauty of the huge *ceiba* with its canopy of branches; it wasn't the moment to think of such things. The soft white December light floated on a sweet breeze and the sound of cars came up from the street.

'Why did you ask for water?' asked Estrada.

'Because they offered it. I chose the drink with the least flavour.'

'Well, that was a bad decision. I read that there are pills they drop in water that don't taste of anything and three hours later you have a heart attack.'

'Thanks for the encouragement,' said Tojeira.

He assures me he thought of that glass of water for the rest of the day.

2

'This is the Santa Marta district, Father Kolvenbach. As you can see, the façades are marked by bullet holes. There were clashes throughout this zone. And that ruin over there was a house. At the height of the conflict the army shelled this neighbourhood; that is, warplanes dropped bombs on it.'

'I understand.'

'This district extends to Mount San Jacinto.'

'You can see it in the distance.'

'Yes, that's it. From here you can follow paved roads as far as the mountain zone and beyond that to San Marcos. As you can see, San Salvador is a valley surrounded by mountains that link many districts. No, not many, all of them.'

The car halted as it crossed a bridge and the priests got out. The street was no more than a dirt track and as soon as Kolvenbach put a foot down his shiny black shoes were stained white, but he did not seem to notice it, or if he did, he did not care. As he walked he listened intently to Tojeira. He stopped to observe a rivulet that had almost dried up as it passed under the bridge. He smiled as he discovered a bunch of kids playing football among ruined houses and rubble. They ran about in bare feet and kicked a rubber ball. The goal was made up of stones set a few metres apart. The children looked out of the corner of their eyes at those tall men with chestnut-coloured hair and continued playing.

'And did the people here go to refugee camps?'

'Many did, when they could, but returned almost immediately. Once it was over, people returned to their homes and work.'

'And when did it end?'

'Well, we don't know exactly, there were isolated clashes that carried on until December, but the actual offensive lasted two or three weeks, no more.'

'I see.'

'So if you hear a firecracker, don't be alarmed.'

'What do you mean?'

'It's normal to set firecrackers off. They're harmless. People make them from newspapers, like the paper used to make cigars, but rolling it with gunpowder instead of tobacco. They attach a fuse and even children set them off. I'm warning you because you might think it's gunfire and it isn't.'

'And you can tell the difference?'

'Well, yes, I can. If it has a hollow sound, that's a firecracker. Gunfire sounds solid. It's hard to explain, but if you've lived here for any length of time, you learn.'

'I see,' said Kolvenbach, and continued walking along the dirt track.

A little later they returned to the car and drove to further districts in the city. On reaching the centre they passed in front of the cathedral and Tojeira explained that this was the site where Monsignor Romero was buried. They stopped but did not enter, looking at it from the outside. It was almost lunchtime and Kolvenbach had said to him that he wanted to address the Jesuit community before eating, so they returned to the Santa Tecla house.

Peter Hans Kolvenbach was the General of the Company of Jesus, the highest authority among the Jesuits. He had arrived in San Salvador a few days earlier to spend Christmas with the congregation and his intention was to console his fellow Jesuits and assure them that the university would endure. A few weeks before, he had written a letter that he had sent to all the members of the Company of Jesus. In that letter, he recounted what had happened in the UCA and asked for volunteers among the priests to fill the posts of the assassinated Fathers. During his visit to San Salvador, he showed Tojeira a list of candidates from whom he should choose six. He spoke at length with Tojeira on this topic, but when addressing the community he referred to the work of the Company of Jesus, told them how they worked in other communities, even in countries undergoing conflicts. He celebrated Christmas Mass and ate dinner with the priests and seminarians in a small party. Tojeira remembers this time as serene days, when hope returned to the community. Especially after what happened on 23 December, following their meeting with President Cristiani. The president had asked to meet Tojeira's superior when he learned that Kolvenbach planned to visit San Salvador. The meeting itself was not particularly productive. They said what is said in those circumstances: the president expressed his condolences, promised an investigation, said every effort would be made to apprehend those responsible and lamented what had happened in words that pretended to be sincere. Nothing out of the ordinary. After their visit to the president's office, they returned to the San Tecla house and just as they were about to enter, bumped into Colonel López y López.

'Father,' exclaimed the colonel, 'how good it is to see you, we were looking for you.'

'What has happened?'

'We need your prints,' López replied. 'Your fingerprints.'

'What on earth for?' asked Tojeira, who was taken aback by the request.

'Look, Father, we're collecting fingerprints – we need to be able to separate yours from those of the criminals. You touched some of the items that we now have in evidence and when we know your prints, these can be eliminated, and we can focus on identifying the others. It's all in the interests of efficiency.'

'OK. But tell me, Colonel, who else's fingerprints are you taking, apart from mine?'

'Look, Father, that information is confidential, so I must ask for complete discretion, but the fact is we've been fingerprinting members of the Atlacatl Battalion.'

'Now I understand. You're on the right track,' Tojeira said in a happier mood, trying not to sound surprised. 'That's the direction you should be looking in.'

He let himself have his fingerprints taken then returned to his superior and told him what had just taken place. And although this kindled a glimmer of hope in all of them, they remained conscious that the slope ahead was as steep as ever and climbing it would prove difficult.

3

One afternoon Tojeira received an unexpected invitation: a private audience with Colonel René Emilio Ponce, head of the joint headquarters of the armed forces. The meeting would take place in the house of Eduardo Tenorio, a lawyer with many years' experience in politics, having served several times as a minister with a variety of portfolios. Tojeira didn't think it was a trick of some sort, but decided that it would be best to inform his fellow Jesuits of that meeting. It would not be easy, it was not the best moment for this kind of meeting and especially with a man they considered to be one of the main suspects in the assassination. When the day came, he didn't feel nervous or anxious, but neither was he confident.

When Tojeira arrived at the meeting, Mr Tenorio came out to meet him and led him into a study where Colonel Ponce was waiting. They greeted each other amiably and even with a touch of familiarity, the way people greet each other when they are not friends but know each other by reputation and want to appear relaxed and keep up appearances.

'Hello, Father, how are you?'

'Colonel,' said Tojeira and extended his hand. 'I'm well, given the circumstances.'

'These have been difficult times for all of us.'

'It has been hard, yes.'

The study was a large room, with shelves packed with books, most of them to do with law. Low music could be heard from outside and Tojeira didn't know if it came from inside the house or was filtered through the wall of some neighbour's patio. When he entered, the lights were on, but he could not say if anyone else was around so that it appeared empty except for the three of them, though he could not be sure.

'The DT were reluctant to leave the party,' said Ponce, 'but it's over at last and here we are.'

Tojeira hadn't come across the term 'DT' before, and did not know what it meant. He acknowledged his ignorance and Ponce immediately explained that it stood for Delinquent Terrorists – in other words, members of the guerrilla forces.

Tenorio offered them something to drink and entertained them for a while with some small talk. Tojeira was calm, biding his time, and Ponce seemed self-assured, serene, almost callous. When Tenorio excused the use of the study so that they could talk in private, Ponce got straight to the point.

'Father, we have carried out a thorough investigation and we are convinced the DT carried out the murders.'

'I do not doubt that you have been thorough, Colonel, but we too have been thorough. Having carefully studied the evidence, we do not believe it possible that guerrilla forces could have crossed the security cordon undetected. We are very close to the staff college, some six hundred metres away, opposite the military district and four hundred metres from the military school.'

'We have established how they did it: your district is

attached to Old Cuscatlán, and there are many connecting corridors through which they could have gained access.' Tojeira stood his ground, insisting the guerrillas could not have breached the protected zone, while Ponce remained adamant they had circumvented it. Although they held opposing views, both remained calm. It was as if each of them knew beforehand how it would play out and they were just going through the motions.

'It was impossible to provide one hundred per cent protection for the entire area,' said Ponce. 'Our primary concern lay on the other side of the boulevard to the campus.' He then moved on to the subject of the search warrant issued two days before the assassination. 'I authorised the warrant at eight thirty in the evening.'

'I'm not disputing the time that you authorised the warrant,' said Tojeira cautiously. 'I would merely like to point out that the search was not executed at eight thirty, but before. At least an hour and a half before.'

'No, no, that's wrong. The search warrant was authorised by me at eight thirty.'

'I'm not accusing you of lying,' Tojeira maintained. 'I believe that somebody has deceived you. The warrant was authorised by you at eight thirty, yet it was carried out at six thirty in the evening. I'm certain of it.'

'How can you be certain? How can you be so sure that someone is lying or that I did not authorise the warrant at that hour?'

'I didn't mean to suggest that I was sure about either of those matters, but I can be certain about the hour the search was carried out, and I'll tell you why. At seven or just after, Martín-Baró called me to warn me about the warrant because he thought our house would be searched next, since we're right next to the university on the same street as the pedestrian entrance. And this call came through just after we had finished eating. I remember it well. Because of the curfew, we were all inside our house by six, celebrating Mass. Immediately afterwards we sat down to dinner and we'd just finished when the telephone rang. Mass lasted half an hour, so at seven at night we were finishing our meal and it was then Martín Baró told me they had executed the search warrant. That's why I'm asking you to investigate, because perhaps whoever deceived you about the search warrant is implicated in the crime.'

'No, no, no, it was at eight thirty, Father, I can assure you.'

And they continued in this manner for a while longer until Tenorio appeared, asking if they would like another drink. Both men declined. A little later, Father Tojeira announced he had to go, said goodbye and left.

'And why did you do that, Father?' I ask.

'They'd arranged that meeting for one reason,' says Tojeira. 'They wanted to find out how much we knew. This was confirmed in two ways, and the first of these occurred only two days later.'

Two days after the first meeting, Tojeira was called to another meeting, this time with Colonel Juan Orlando Zepeda, deputy minister of national defence. Zepeda's approach was more serpentine. At this stage no accusation had been levelled against the high command of the armed forces, although everyone knew that an attack of this nature would have needed approval from someone higher up the chain of command than a captain in charge of a company of soldiers. There had been no specific mention of Ponce and Zepeda and their comrades in the high command; the accusation was generic, against the armed forces or against the Atlacatl Battalion. In fact, it would not be the Jesuits who would publicly name the brains behind the crime, but Major Eric Buckland of the United States Army, who was an adviser to the Salvadorian high command – but that came a few months later.

'So the first confirmation was the meeting with Zepeda. What was the second?' I asked.

'The second came about in the strangest way. I met a man whose name I never learned, nor asked about nor was told, and that meeting took place during a trip to Nicaragua.'

4

Tojeira was sitting in the waiting room at Comalapa Airport on the outskirts of San Salvador, waiting for the flight that would take him to Managua, Nicaragua. It was early in the morning and he was drinking coffee and trying to read a newspaper. The room was empty aside from a handful of passengers waiting to board the flight. At this time rarely a day went by without some story in the news about the assassinated Jesuits. These articles never contained anything new or interesting, but Tojeira read it all anyway, feeling that he had an obligation not to let any small detail slip by. As he was reading, a man in a suit and tie entered the waiting area and took a seat next to him. He looked to be in his thirties and reeked of aftershave.

'Father,' the man greeted him, 'I know you, although you do not know me, but don't worry and don't be surprised by what I am going to tell you. I work in military intelligence and I want to tell you something once we're on board the plane, provided there's nobody around who might make it awkward for us. I know who they are, and if I see someone suspicious I won't approach you. The plane is flying practically empty, about fifteen passengers, no more, so once the plane takes off you will see me walking down the aisle. If I consider it safe to do so, I will sit next to you and explain things.'

'Agreed,' Tojeira replied, not knowing what else to say.

'And now I'm going because anybody could turn up and see us. I just wanted to explain myself so you won't be surprised on the plane.'

The man stood up and left the room. When, about an hour later, passengers were told to board the plane, the man appeared as if out of nowhere and went to the back of the short queue of passengers. He never so much as glanced at Tojeira, although the latter couldn't help watching him out of the corner of his eye, while trying to pretend he wasn't. It seemed like some sort of bizarre joke. What was someone who worked in military intelligence doing on this plane? Why did he want to talk to him? Who'd ordered him to do this? Tojeira couldn't believe he'd be acting under his own volition. The man's presence disturbed him. Right up to the last moment, he was hoping that he would not sit down in his row.

When the seat-belt sign was turned off and the passengers could get up, the man in suit and tie strolled down the aisle towards the toilets at the rear of the plane, then came back and sat next to Tojeira.

'Good morning, Father,' the man said in a serene and firm voice. For some reason this greeting instilled confidence in Tojeira.

'Good morning.'

'Well, as I said, I'm a member of military intelligence and I will prove that. I know you had an interview with Colonel Ponce, and two days later a meeting with Colonel Zepeda. Both meetings took place in Mr Eduardo Tenorio's house. I'm going to recount Zepeda's version of that meeting, because he sent us his report.'

'OK, I'm listening,' said Tojeira. The man then gave a detailed account of the conversation he'd had with Zepeda: they'd talked for an hour and a half, little more, and they'd started by chatting about General Zepeda's childhood, before entering into the matter of the assassination of the Jesuits.

'And you might ask yourself why a deputy minister would send us his report. The answer is because the case is highly sensitive. The chief of staff isn't accountable to anyone, least of all us, which is why Ponce wasn't required to report. But deputy minister is an administrative post, so the army can ask someone like Zepeda what he's doing, having a meeting with you, and he, to justify himself, sends us his report telling us he wanted to assess how dangerous you were.'

'I see,' said Tojeira, who was impressed but at the same time couldn't help wondering what the man's agenda was in telling him all this.

'Do you want to know what Zepeda thought of you, Father?'

'Of course I do. Tell me.'

'Zepeda states in his report that he believes you can be manipulated, that you are not firm in your convictions and that we should carry on insisting our version of events is correct. Insisting on our version of the facts. And I'm telling you this so that you know I am who I say I am.'

'Given that you know more about the interview than I do, I have no option but to believe you.'

'I have one thing to tell you: Ponce and Zepeda are behind something very big. Do you get my drift?'

'I think so.'

'An operation like the assassination of the Fathers cannot go ahead without the support of the high command, and Ponce in particular. Zepeda arranged to meet you because he's also implicated in the decision-making process and wanted to find out how much you know. What you know and what you don't know. Because they are scared, Father. Here in this country they do as they like, but this case goes beyond our borders, there are outside interests involved – and this has made them nervous.'

'Why are you telling me this? That is, I am grateful that you've come forward to tell me these things, things that we have suspected but had no way of confirming until now. But why do you take this risk?'

'I am a Catholic, Father. I'm not idealistic or naive, that's not why I've come to you. I came because, despite the line of work I'm in, I didn't harbour any animosity towards the Fathers. I believe that you are trying to do what's best for our country. In fact it's not that I *believe* it, I know it to be true. People like us know certain things. And as proof of what I know, one day I am going to give you a gift of something that you will appreciate. You'll see what I mean in due course.'

'Well, I thank you in advance.'

Tojeira affirms that he was convinced that the man's motives in taking such a risk were genuine; that in those days you could never be sure who would support you and who would betray you, and sometimes support came from unexpected quarters. There might have been other reasons why this man came forward: resentment, vengeance, or some hidden agenda. He had not told Tojeira much that he hadn't already considered; it was more a case of having a mathematical hypothesis proven by some occurrence in everyday life – it is good to have it confirmed that you are right.

Whatever his motives, Tojeira remembers this man with esteem, and amazement at the situation that led to the meeting. Despite its brevity, it has lasted in his mind through the years. A flight between San Salvador and Managua takes between thirty and thirty-five minutes. Sometimes a little more, but not much more. So their chat was brief and when it was over the man stood up, shook Tojeira's hand and wished him good luck, urging him to stand firm and to resist pressure.

Sometime later, Tojeira received a phone call in his office and it was that same voice.

'Father, good afternoon. Don't worry, I've taken the opportunity to call you because there is no surveillance on your office at the moment. If it's OK with you, I'd like to drop by and give you the gift I told you about.'

'Good, good,' said Tojeira.

A few minutes later the man entered Tojeira's office. He was wearing the same suit as the first time they had met. Even the shirt seemed the same, and the smell of aftershave was very strong, as if he had just applied it, even though it was obvious he hadn't shaved for two or three days. They greeted each other and immediately he handed over a small yellow envelope with a cassette inside.

'As a memento of our chat,' he said, ' I want you to have this recording of a conversation between Father Ellacuría and Fabio Castillo, when he was rector of the university.'

'Well, well!' exclaimed Tojeira, sincerely impressed. 'But how did you come by it? Where did you get it from?'

'Years ago, I was asked to analyse that conversation. I delivered the report to my superior but accidentally left out the tape. When I came across it a day later, I stuck it in a drawer and forgot all about it until months later. I didn't hand it back but kept it as a souvenir, then I thought, best give it to you. It took place years ago. There's nothing in it.'

'Do you recall what was said?'

'Something very simple. They say that they have to talk to the Cousins to see if that would lead to a greater dialogue and some concrete steps in the peace process.'

Fabio Castillo had, for many years, been rector of the University of El Salvador. He was a well-respected intellectual in political and academic circles and it was known that he had some kind of link with the guerrilla forces. Those they called the Cousins were the political heads of FMLN, people like Guillermo Ungo and Rubén Zamora who, years later, when the peace agreement was signed, became very active in the country's political life, even reaching the presidency or later, as in the case of Zamora, assuming diplomatic posts like ambassador to India.

'Did you ever see this man again, Father?' I ask Tojeira.

'Never,' he responded, 'two decades have passed and I never heard from him again. At times it feels as though I was talking to a ghost, someone who doesn't really exist or exists only in the shadows. And yet, despite not existing, is omnipresent. Because people like that are everywhere and know everything. I wouldn't be surprised if he knew about this conversation at this very moment.'

'Do you recall his name, Father?'

'Like I said, I have no idea. And I suppose I never will. It has been lost forever.'

5

December mornings in San Salvador tend to be, if not cool, at least not too hot. But in that season a wave of cold had arrived from the north, so that for a few days you had to put sweaters and scarves on. Tojeira had taken a very early bath and was having breakfast in the company of other priests in the dining room at Santa Tecla. He was wearing a dark sweater, more blue than black, and a shirt with a wide collar underneath. Every now and then he rubbed his hands to warm them up while drinking a cup of hot chocolate. The chat was about everyday matters like the New Year's Eve feast, what they would eat that day, what sort of occasion it would be. After the sad and turbulent year they had been through, they needed some respite and it was agreed the celebration should be something they could enjoy.

Since November, they had endured day after day of tension and the Masses and prayers were insufficient to keep the darkness at bay. Sitting at that table, drinking, eating, talking and planning the celebration with his companions, Tojeira enjoyed a moment of light relief. The cold mornings made him feel more alive with the pure air, a gentle breeze, and the luminous, gentle sunlight. But the serenity was broken when one of the companions entered the dining room and announced that Monsignor Rivera was on the phone. It wasn't even seven o'clock, so for the Monsignor to call at that hour meant something had happened or was about to happen.

'OK,' said Tojeira, getting up from the table, 'we'll continue with this topic later. I'd best go find out what's happened.'

He left the dining room and went to his office to take the call. As he entered the room, a cloud passed over the sun. The timing of this sudden darkness was so precise and strange that Tojeira looked out of his window. Above him, a grey cloud threatened rain, although it does not usually rain in December.

When he picked up the telephone, he apologised to the Monsignor for his delay. Monsignor Rivera told him it was not a problem; on the contrary, he apologised for calling so early.

'Father,' said Monsignor, 'check your telex machine.'

Tojeira saw that there was a printed sheet in his telex machine. It had the heading of the Episcopal Conference, but no signature.

'I've got it,' answered Tojeira.

'Read it.'

'Right away.'

After a brief salutation, that telex read:

1. The government is carrying out an excellent investigation and everything points to the FMLN assassinating the Jesuit Fathers.

2. The Jesuits do not want to face up to the truth. As they are involved in politics, they

196

want to manipulate the case and use it
against the current government.

3. The archbishop does nothing but hinder
   police investigations, launching unfounded
   accusations against the armed forces.

'Tell me, Monsignor, what does this mean? Who sent you this?'

'It arrived this morning from the Vatican.'

Although he was wearing a sweater, the cold penetrated Tojeira's bones. His neck tensed and his hair stood on end and for a second he did not know what to think.

'My good friend Cardinal Echegaray, head of the Secretariat of Justice and Peace at the Vatican, sent it to me. He was indignant and surprised.'

'I understand.'

'It seems that Monsignor Tovar Astorga was handing it around to the cardinals.'

'Monsignor Tovar is in Rome?'

'So it appears. We'll have to put a stop to this as best we can. Can you come to my office?'

'Of course.'

'I'll expect you in an hour. And don't worry, we have reason and truth on our side. We'll come out on top.'

'I don't doubt it, Monsignor. I don't doubt it for a minute.'

In December 1989, the government created three high-ranking commissioners to look at three strategic points. One would travel to Washington. Another to Madrid. And the third to the Vatican. Their objective was to inform on what was happening in the case of the Jesuit Fathers. These were the three key places in the events that would unfold in the following days. The government sent politicians belonging to parties of the right to Madrid and Washington. They were told what had been repeated as the official version in San Salvador, but with many more details claiming to incriminate the guerrilla forces.

The most interesting was the commission sent to the Vatican. The Episcopal Conference is the assembly of church bishops from each nation, a permanent body that includes the highest representatives of the Church in each country. The delegation to the Vatican was made up of Monsignor Tovar Astorga, president of the Episcopal Conference, Monsignor Revelo, the second in command, and a priest called Manuel Barreiro, secretary to the Conference. The impression they wanted to give to the Vatican was that the bishops of the republic were completely behind the version of events these three men would give.

The morning continued to be grey, but it didn't seem as if even a light drizzle would fall when Tojeira arrived at Monsignor's office.

'I've sent a copy of the telex to the General of the Jesuits,' announced Tojeira. 'He said a copy was sent to him two hours earlier. He told me not to worry, but nothing else.'

'He must have things under control then.'

'I don't know. There's no way of judging – the Vatican is a very long way from San Salvador.'

'I take it you're not just referring to geographical distance.'

'Precisely.'

'But you must also trust in what the General told you.'

'It was too abrupt. He said nothing more and offered no explanations.'

'I've been wondering what to do and the first thing I came up with was that we should write a communiqué. Something

198

to counter the impression that this is the bishops' position. It's a delicate matter, drawing attention to the existence of a divided Church, a Church of the left and another of the right, but we must do it.'

'There's no alternative.'

'We must be firm, we cannot give the impression that we are weary or soft. The government is firm in its position. They are lobbying hard. They won't be budged, or at least they won't easily be swayed.'

'A few days ago Colonel López of the Investigating Committee told me he's investigating the Atlacatl Battalion.'

'If they really are doing so, it's a huge step forward. But I don't trust them. They tell us one thing while telling Washington and Madrid they had nothing to do with it. Look what's happening in the Vatican. Our own curia. Those on the government's side are playing a double game.'

'I know that. It's not that I trust them, it's just what that man said to me. They know who it was. Well, how could they not know, if they did it.'

The conversation was interrupted by a call from Rome. The archbishop's secretary announced Cardinal Silvestrini.

'Put him through to me immediately,' Monsignor demanded.

Rivera launched into a conversation while Tojeira stared at him and didn't move from his seat. Silvestrini's intention was for Rivera to travel to Rome and explain the facts.

'Come over here,' Silvestrini said to him. 'I've got you an appointment to see the pope. You must refute the charge in person.'

'Very well,' Monsignor answered, 'I'll start preparing for the journey.' As he hung up, Monsignor Rivera said:

'I'm going to talk to the pope.'

'That I understood,' Tojeira replied.

'I must thoroughly prepare all that I will tell him. We are going to fight for our views in Rome and before the pope. As I said earlier, we must remain calm in the knowledge that truth and reason are on our side.'

'I am calm,' affirmed Tojeira.

6

Monsignor Rivera looked out of the window of the plane and observed the black night dotted with stars. He remained almost without a thought in his mind, letting himself be lulled by the reality he found himself in above the Atlantic, suspended in the air, in a region where nothing happened, where there were no shots, no threats, no tensions, no fights and no plots. He pressed his forehead to the glass and, without planning to, fell asleep. He dreamt of Father Moreno. In his dream, he had first seen a man walking along from behind, and then this same man had turned around and looked at him. Then, he found himself in a garden and they were sitting next to each other on a metal bench. Father Moreno was holding a book titled *Jesús crucificado*. He had seen it clearly. Then Father Moreno smiled at him. He didn't say a word. Monsignor woke up deeply affected and his first thought was that Father Moreno looked younger. He also had a sense of utter powerlessness.

Over the last few days he had thought a lot about Father Moreno on account of the strange event that took place immediately after his death. His assassins had finished him off in the garden. However, for some inexplicable reason, they had dragged his lifeless body to the room he usually occupied with Father Jon Sobrino, who at that time was not at the university. This enigma had been the topic of conversation during a private dinner party at the archbishop's. He himself had spent quite a while trying to come up with an explanation. He wondered whether it had been intended as a message for Sobrino. It shocked him to imagine that scene with Father Moreno being dragged along the corridor; he thought he saw a message in the fact that when his body bumped against a bookcase, a copy of *Jesús crucificado* fell out and was later found to be stained with the priest's blood.

Father Moreno had been born in Villatuerta, Navarre, Spain in 1933. Like his companions, he had arrived at the Santa Tecla novitiate at a very young age, before he was twenty. He spent some time studying at the Catholic University in Quito. When he returned to San Salvador, he worked in the College of the Jesuits and later in the UCA. Then, in the mid-seventies, he spent some years in Panama, where he founded the Centro Ignaciano of Central America that was to promote Ignatius of Loyola's *Spiritual Exercises*. At the start of the 1980s he lived in Nicaragua, where he took part in activities of a humanitarian nature, but nothing political. He worked with enormous enthusiasm in literacy campaigns and directed spiritual retreats where he taught Saint Ignatius' *Exercises* to monks and nuns. His work was more spiritual than political. When he returned to San Salvador in 1985, he was put in charge of the UCA's Theology library, but his intention was to return to a rural area and become a parish priest. A village parish priest without further pretentions or desires. In the end, he couldn't manage something so simple.

Monsignor Rivera closed his eyes again and prayed for the souls of the Jesuits and also for Monsignor Romero's soul. And he remembered Rutilio Grande, a Jesuit who had been murdered a decade ago, at the end of the seventies. So many saints, he thought. And he asked himself if he was doing enough. Not that he wanted to become a martyr, it wasn't that, but he could not help wondering if he was doing enough. He asked God for wisdom and understanding and his prayer grew and lasted a long time, so much so that it was only interrupted when an air hostess tripped and dropped a tray. On hearing the smashing of glassware, Monsignor turned to look at her and watched her crouch and pick up the tray and some cups. He bent to look out of the window and discovered a gentle clarity spreading over the horizon and realised that he had completely lost track of time. His mission was drawing closer. He was going to the Vatican. The pope was expecting him. He knew his words had to be steady and wise and full of truth. He knew that Rome had wide corridors and he thought about them and suddenly felt terribly tired.

7

'Don't worry, I know the truth,' the pope said to Monsignor Rivera.

Although John Paul II spoke those very words, the Vatican did not issue an official statement favouring the Jesuit version of events.

Years later, sitting in his tiny office, next to a bookshelf filled with poetry books, I ask Tojeira:

'What did that sentence mean, Father? That he knew the truth about the case, or about what the Salvadorian bishops were up to, or what?'

'I think he was referring to all those truths, not just one.'

'Was that Monsignor Rivera's view?'

'Yes.'

'And what did it mean to you?'

'It gave us a sense of security that in the Vatican that letter was not received in the way the government wanted.'

'Wasn't it a disappointment, though? It doesn't appear there was any real communication with the pope.'

'Disappointing would have been if the Vatican had been in

favour of that note, but that was not the case. We could not give in to disappointment. The government were trying to let the army completely off the hook with their official version, but try as they might nobody believed them. So everything was working in our favour.'

'And yet, nothing was happening.'

'They would not give in easily, that's how it was.'

'I understand. What else happened in the Vatican? How was Monsignor received by the cardinals?'

'Very well, we felt we had a lot of support.'

Cardinal Silvestrini organised a Mass for Rivera that coincided with his arrival, led by himself. Later, on New Year's Day, Cardinal Echegaray arrived in San Salvador to offer his support to the archbishop and the Jesuits and a private Mass was held in the university chapel. Tojeira tells me that the atmosphere was tense and nobody felt at ease because they were arguing about matters that implied he was against all those who surrounded them. The sensation of vulnerability was real. During the Mass he spoke of a new beginning, in the literal sense because they were at the beginning of the year. He also said that they had to have hope, but then later, during the meal when they referred to recent events, anxiety and doubt dominated the conversations.

'Did you have doubts, Father?'

'We all had doubts.'

That same day, 1 January, the magazine *30 Giorni* – a publication that dealt with religious topics and was widely read in Rome, with interviews with cardinals and other Church dignitaries – published an interview with Monsignor Tovar Astorga. At that time, Monsignor Astorga was the favourite of the Salvadorian right to take over Monsignor Rivera's duties. Rivera had had to assume his duties as Archbishop of San

Salvador after Romero's assassination, and had faced the worst years of the war from his position in the archbishopric, speaking out against atrocities and a climate of fear. In this he was not unique because the ecclesiastical community had been supplying martyrs since the end of the seventies. Throughout he had remained strong and had steered the best possible course: never too close to extremist positions, yet not too far from them, without appearing naive. Nobody could afford to be naive on the battlefield. And he was in the middle of a battlefield. Whether he liked it or not, that is where he was. After years of this, his frailty became obvious. The years weighed on him and he was frequently ill. As a result, we had begun to think about his successor. The extreme right were in no doubt: Tovar Astorga had to be the next archbishop.

The interview in *30 Giorni* had a Latin title that translated as *To whoever benefits*, which was one of the questions used in Roman law to implicate someone, i.e. the individual who benefits most from a crime becomes the prime suspect. In the interview, Astorga alleged that the FMLN stood to benefit most. And he praised the national government for carrying out a thorough and very professional investigation that had uncovered incriminating evidence against the guerrillas.

'But the Archbishop of San Salvador thinks that it's the army,' said the interviewer.

'That's what he thinks, but he's wrong. He has no facts. It's just speculation with no foundation.'

The magazine, which is published on the first of every month, quoted Monsignor Astorga's categorical assertion in a headline:

The guerrilla army were guilty of assassinating the Jesuit Fathers.

And that was published on 1 January. Two days later, in a

press conference, President Cristiani recognised that the assassination of the Jesuit priests had been carried out by a group from the Salvadorian army and assured those present that the guilty would be brought to justice and punished.

The day Cristiani announced this news there was a small Mass of celebration in the Jesuit community. The case came to court months later. Monsignor Tovar was never appointed Archbishop of San Salvador.

PART SIX

PART SIX

1

Three people were travelling in a small Volkswagen along a dust road towards a canton called El Paisnal. A boy of sixteen called Nelson, an old man of seventy-two called Manuel Solórzano and a Jesuit, Father Rutilio Grande. It was March 1977, and the rains had arrived early; they could hear the loud chirping of cicadas in the bushes at the edge of the road. As they got into the car, Nelson said that he had been having a recurrent nightmare: he was in bed in the dark and heard a storm outside when suddenly the wind whipped off the roof of his hut and rain fell inside and flooded everything. He tried to open the door to get out, but he couldn't, and suddenly felt he was drowning. He had had this same dream four or five times in the last week, but with the arrival of the cicadas he had finally been able to sleep in peace.

'It's like a lullaby,' said Father Rutilio.

'Same with me, Father,' said Solórzano. 'That loud chirping makes me drowsy and I sleep well enough, although my head aches.'

'That's a pretty story,' said Nelson, 'very spiritual.'

'So it is,' considered Rutilio. 'It's like a lament, but one that makes you . . .'

He didn't finish his sentence. Ahead of them, blocking the road, were six or seven uniformed men from the National Guard. Father Rutilio braked until the car stopped.

'You stay here,' the priest indicated. 'I'll go and speak with them.'

'All right, Father,' said Solórzano. Nelson remained silent. Rutilio got down from the car and approached the guards.

'Good afternoon,' he greeted them.

'Where are you going, Father?' said the one who appeared to be in charge.

'We're bound for El Paisnal. To say Mass.'

'Mass, at this time of day?'

'Well, yes, it's not yet five.'

'Aren't masses held in the morning, Father?' asked the same man, spitting on the ground. He was sitting on a stone and after spitting, stood up and hung his rifle over his shoulder.

'Masses are held when they are necessary. There are even Masses at midnight.'

'Listen, Father, the truth is we believe you are going to join the communists. That's what they're saying around here. You know people say things. And that one has the look of a guerrilla fighter.'

'He's sixteen years old, man! And he's ill.'

'I mean the other one.'

'But he's frail and over seventy.'

'Then why are you taking them if they are so useless?'

'They help me with Mass. That's why I am bringing them.'

'Are you organised, Father?'

'Oh, dear me. What I do is help the poor and my sole organisation is the Church.'

'You expect me to believe that? They say that the Jesuits are guerrilla fighters, that they are lefties.'

'I have no means of making you believe or not. But if you know so much about everything, you should know that I belong only to the Church, nothing else.'

'Get back in your Volkswagen, Father. Get in and go to hell.'

'You lot don't even respect priests.'

'Not guerrilla priests, no. There are others that I do.'

'Well, we are going to be late, so we'd better leave.'

Father Grande returned to the car and said: *That's it, we can go.* But the guards had surrounded them. Rutilio noticed this and leaned out of the car window:

'What is it now, man? What's the matter with you?'

Until that moment they had not murdered a single priest. It didn't seem possible that they would do such a thing. Neither Rutilio, nor Nelson, nor Solórzano would have believed it. At least not until that moment. Rutilio received eighteen bullet wounds in his body. Hours later, around midnight, one wound, the one in his head, was still bleeding.

2

Jon Sobrino tells me that nobody expected that much from
Monsignor Romero.

At that time, the majority of Jesuits did not see Romero in
a good light. He was thought to be weak. A good man, friend
to all, who could lunch with a group of peasants and dine at a
party with women from high society, befriending students
who had been captured and tortured by the army while at the
same time rubbing shoulders with the acting president, Colonel
Armando Molina. When he was named archbishop there was
no one within the curia who felt anything but a profound
disappointment. Back then, rumours of war were rife. The
situation was completely polarised. It was the setting for the
Cold War. The military had been in power for decades and
abuses against civilians were common. To be a university
student in San Salvador in the 1970s was almost equivalent to
being a guerrilla fighter. At least that was the case so far as the
army authorities and the National Guard were concerned.
Massacres, kidnappings and torture had become an everyday
occurrence. The National Guard's building was a grey pile that

stood for terror. Anybody could be accused of belonging to an organised group and could be captured and brought to the police basements to be tortured. Tension and horror gripped the country. Against this backdrop, the Church played a fundamental role, so when in February 1977 the Vatican announced that Monsignor Romero would be San Salvador's archbishop, many believed that a vacuum would ensue. They also believed that Romero was chosen because he was a friend to the government. Someone who could be manipulated. A weak man. A tea drinker in gatherings of landowners whose coffee and cotton plantations stretched across a land sunk in poverty and surrounded by fear.

The night that Father Rutilio was assassinated, Romero received a call from Colonel Armando Molina, promising a full investigation. Romero knew that Molina's offer was a false one. And Molina knew that Monsignor did not believe his words, but that was the game both played. So long as they both played their parts, everything would turn out for the best – at least for the president and the archbishop. To do otherwise, in that context, could mean only one thing. Father Rutilio was a perfect example: he was a man who lived in the countryside, who visited the cantons and preached a gospel based on equality and justice. Did he do this as a member of the left? No. But he was deemed to be in opposition to the government. And back then, that was enough to make you a target.

A little before midnight, Romero came to the place where they were holding a vigil for Father Rutilio. Sobrino says that Romero and Rutilio Grande were friends and that the arch-bishop looked sad, sombre and desolate; he talked with none of his usual animation, and it seemed that his voice had to pass through a filter to reach them and was barely distinguishable. His voice was one that conveyed long pauses of silence. He entered the place where the bodies of Rutilio, the boy and the old man lay and did not say much, at least not at the beginning, although he did greet the nuns who were there. He led a prayer. When it ended, and still with his head lowered, he opened his eyes. He observed the land lit with gas lights. It was earth, not asphalt, a black, volcanic earth, typical in Central America. He looked at the stones, the unkempt grass, with the smell of fallen fruits over hundreds and thousands of years, a smell that was part of the landscape and yet nearly always went unnoticed, but not that night.

He raised his eyes and saw the vast starless canopy, because there was not a single star out that night, and thought, as if he was a child, that somebody had turned out the stars, that a gigantic thumb and index finger had squeezed them one by one, turning them off for this one night. He felt insignificant. A cold tear rolled down his cheeks and Monsignor heard it fall with total clarity. *That's enough*, he said to himself. Enough. Then he crossed himself. He said the Lord's Prayer. And as the word *Amen* slipped from his lips, followed immediately by *So be it*, he resolved that he would no longer be a silhouette, a whisper. From now on he would be a voice that cried out in the desert. Or that is what he thought. And he knew he was filled with God's Grace.

'We must see what we can do,' said Monsignor, and he gathered together the priests and nuns who were at the wake and asked their advice.

Sobrino says that everyone gave their opinion and Monsignor listened to every one of them. And although he assented and told them he was going to make a statement, not many of them believed that he would do this. But he did. Days later he sent a letter to the president, reminding him of his promise to open an investigation into the affair and informing him that until it was cleared up, he would refuse to attend any official state occasions. He also announced that on Sunday the entire country would celebrate just one Mass: a Mass commemorating Father Rutilio Grande. And it took place. On Sunday at midday that one Mass was celebrated all over the country and church bells in all the churches were rung before midday announcing it. That was when Monsignor Romero began his apostolate. He became another man. And this did not pass unnoticed, least of all to Ellacuría.

Ellacuría was in Spain that March. He had gone into self-imposed exile following a series of threats. Months earlier, someone had warned him that he should take these threats seriously, for his name was on a blacklist and his life was in danger. He continued to be rector at the UCA, but from a distance. When he heard about what had happened, he wrote a moving letter to the Monsignor. Ellacuría did not have a relationship with the archbishop, they knew each other, but they were not friends. Romero had once written a review of a theology book by Ellacuría, and although it had been polite, as Monsignor's writings always were, his position had been the opposite of the one expressed by the Jesuit. So the two were not close. But that immediately changed. *I have seen God's hand in your acts*, Ellacuría would say in a letter. A sentence that was ripe with meaning.

'He didn't say that about me,' Jon Sobrino tells me, 'and I was his friend, nor did he say it to Rahner or to Zubiri. It was something he said to Monsignor Romero alone. And that language for Ellacuría was filled with the deepest meaning.'

'You have told me several times, Father, that for Ellacuría both Rahner and Zubiri were colleagues . . . '

'Yes,' says Sobrino, 'but Romero was the person he aspired to be. Rahner was his colleague, no better or worse than him, and Zubiri was the same, but Romero was the spiritual ideal, he was God passing through his town. And those words, for a religious man, held an even higher meaning.'

Monsignor Romero's story had hardly begun. Over the following years the archbishop denounced what was happening in his country, a story of blood with new atrocities every day and no end in sight, no limit to the violence. One day a bullet-riddled corpse thrown on a highway, the next a group of students kidnapped from the National University, and the next a politician's car machine-gunned. The death toll mounted day after day. And the stories about torture and kidnappings made people whisper within their own homes and remain silent in public. Rumours of war grew. As did the abuses of power. The dark period in our history was opening out and war seemed imminent.

'Did everything begin then?'

'No. It began much earlier.'

'In 1932?'

'In 1932 the dictator of the day crushed a revolt of peasants armed with clubs and machetes. He murdered thousands. And much was lost along with these lives: their land, their language, their costumes, their customs. The great landowners of the early twentieth century became rich thanks to their coffee plantations. They rubbed shoulders with the upper classes in Europe, built their theatres, their mansions, while the other ninety per cent of the population lived on beans and maize. Plantation employees were paid with tokens that could only be exchanged in shops run by the landowner. So they couldn't leave. They were trapped. They were slaves of a barbaric system. Nearly a hundred years later, everything was the same, or worse. For half a century power belonged to the army, who appointed and dismissed the presidents, all of them selected from the ranks of the army. Against this backdrop, guided by what happened first in Cuba and then in Nicaragua, guerrilla groups began to be organised, which led the political and military forces to deploy an unprecedented level of repression.'

'And this gave rise to new massacres, tortures, unjustified arrests and persecutions.'

'Yes, and if fate granted you a parish in the country, and you set about helping the poor, which was almost everybody, you were suspected of being left-wing, a member of the guerrilla forces, of threatening the establishment. That's why they killed Rutilio.'

'And Romero, too.'

'Yes.'

3

'It scares me,' said Señora Zaida.

'I think it's better we don't talk about that,' Monsignor begged her.

'I'm not going to tell you what to do, the only thing I'm going to do is to commend the Virgin to you, that's all. But I'm still afraid that something awful is going to happen to you.'

The house was divided into two parts. Zaida, Monsignor Romero's sister, lived in one. In the other, Regina, a friend. The house was situated in the first passage of the Santa Clara district, beneath San Jacinto. All the passages in the district were named after flowers: Chrysanthemums was the first, Sunflowers was the second, Lotus-flower is the third and so on until Dahlias. They looked like piers, only they stuck out from the mountain rather than into the sea. The house that Zaida and Regina shared was in the middle of the passage. Monsignor did not often visit his sister's house, he was too busy, but he knew she was worried and he wanted to reassure her.

Zaida went with her brother to the kitchen, took a saucepan

from the sink and filled it with water. She put it on the stove and lit it.

'Coffee will soon be ready. In this kitchen it doesn't take long.'

'I have a little time, there's no rush.'

'Well, as I was saying, I'm frightened. As is Regina. By haranguing the army you're signing your own death warrant. All I can do is keep entreating the Virgin. I don't want to think what might happen to you.'

'We have to die of something,' said Monsignor with a smile.

'You think it's all a joke.'

'No, I take it very seriously. But it's true that you, myself and Regina, we are all going to die.'

'I think I've run out of coffee,' Zaida said, looking among the empty tins. 'I'll go and ask Regina for some.'

'Don't worry about it.'

'It's no problem, she never refuses me anything.'

Zaida returned to the drawing room with her brother. To the left there was a closed door. She knocked a few times.

'Regina?'

'Yes,' said a voice from inside.

'Guess what, I've run out of coffee.'

Regina took a few seconds before opening her door. When she did, they saw that she too had a visitor, a neighbour called Tita.

'Oscar, my dear,' said Regina, and came out to greet Monsignor. She hugged and kissed him on the cheek.

'How are you, Regina?'

'I'm well. Tita, do you know Oscar?'

'How could I not know him? I never miss any of his homilies.'

'Good afternoon,' answered Romero.

'Good afternoon, Monsignor, Tita de Arévalo, at your service.' Monsignor greeted the woman.

'Do you have some coffee?' asked Zaida.

'Of course I do, woman,' said Regina and went to the back of the room to search among the tins scattered about the table.

'Would you like to have coffee with us?'

'We'd love to. Tita has brought some sweet bread.'

They spoke of the time when they were children and lived near a baker and the smell of bread in the early mornings would fill the air around them with a sweet mist. The chat had nothing to do with religion or politics. In fact, it was about everyday life. It was 24 March 1980. When Romero announced he had to be off, it was about four in the afternoon. He had spent an hour or more in the company of his sister and her friends. They stood up and walked to the door. Zaida went ahead of him to open the door. As they were walking away, Tita could not avoid recalling what had happened the day before.

'Your words, Monsignor, yesterday at the Mass, almost made me cry. Please excuse me for bringing it up, but that's how I felt. And the same goes for my husband too.'

'What he said to the army?' asked Regina.

'Yes,' said Tita. 'But I want to ask you, Monsignor, to be very careful, to look after yourself.'

'That's exactly what I've been saying,' said Zaida. 'I live in constant fear, given how many priests they have killed.'

'Don't say that. Don't say such things.'

'Well, I must leave you,' Romero said, 'and pray to God for me. Ask him to give me strength and more faith. Much faith is needed.'

'Never doubt it, Monsignor, you will be in my prayers.'

'And in mine,' concluded Regina.

When Monsignor got to the pavement, the women were following. Then they met a man and a woman with a baby.

'Well, and where did you come from?' asked Tita.

'From the shop,' said the woman, who was just over twenty years old. 'Good afternoon, Monsignor.'

'Good afternoon,' Romero greeted her.

'Afternoon,' said the man accompanying her, while stretching out his hand to greet the archbishop, who shook it warmly.

'This is my husband,' explained Tita.

'Roberto Celestino, at your service, Monsignor.'

Romero nodded with a smile and bent down to look closely at the baby.

'And this is my daughter Miriam and our grandchild.'

'What a sweet little girl,' said Monsignor, bending right down to the baby and stroking her head. 'Is she a year old yet?'

'She has just had her birthday,' replied Miriam.

The baby smiled and chatted away incomprehensibly.

'And look how she talks,' said Romero, still smiling.

'If you could see her, she never stops,' said the mother. 'She talks and talks and is never silent.'

'What's her name?'

'Roxanita,' said Zaida.

'Such a pretty baby,' said Monsignor and he bent over again and kissed the baby on the forehead, and stroked her hair and turned back to the adults and said: 'Well, I must be off.'

They all said goodbye to the archbishop with embraces, the last one being his sister, who asked him to be careful, to look after himself because the times were bad and were even worse for priests. He told her again not to worry and kissed her on the forehead just as he had done with the baby, and promised to pray for her and she said she promised to pray for him.

'You are always in my prayers, you know that,' said Zaida while embracing her brother and kissing him on his forehead.

At that time, people listened to what Archbishop Romero had to say. Every Sunday morning, hundreds of thousands listened on the radio to Monsignor's homily. His voice signified something. A consolation. A hope. Something palpable that could be touched with a hand. Three years had passed since Rutilio's assassination and at that time Romero had followed what he thought was his path. He had not abandoned his visits to local communities, and he had gone on being the same with all people, that is, friendly, close, affectionate, ready to listen to anybody that might need him, but when he stepped up to the altar and gave his homily he was transformed from a humble man to a tower of strength. The speech to which Tita referred had been given in San Salvador's cathedral the previous day, 23 March. Dozens heard it in the cathedral, but thousands, hundreds of thousands, heard it on the radio. During his homily, Monsignor said words which carried such weight it is difficult to comprehend: *In God's name, and in the name of this suffering people, whose laments, every day more tumultuous, rise to heaven, I beg you, I demand, I order you . . . to stop the repression.* He said these words without fear, in a voice that was not that of an ordinary man. Whether they were present or sitting in front of their radio, everyone who listened was moved by this speech, which was like a luminous bridge that united two parts of the history of a country, a bridge of light over two territories of darkness. At that moment, without realising it, Monsignor sealed his fate. But he said what he had to say. He had used the right words. Terrible ones. Brave ones. Perfect ones. He had become a prophet in his own country. He had left behind the little man who got together with his sister, a friendly man who blessed children in the cantons

224

and dived into rivers and bathed, like any other man, under the sun. He had left behind the man who talked with a quiet voice and consoled drunkards and old people or gave advice to love-sick young men. He had risen above all the others as he trans-formed himself.

The next day, 24 March 1980, Romero set out to give the late-afternoon Mass in a place known as the Little Hospital of Divine Providence in the Miramonte district. Monsignor lived in a room opposite the hospital's chapel. So that day, when he got home after visiting his sister, he rested a while in his room, said a prayer, put on his priest's cassock and left to give Mass. At the chapel door, he stopped to greet people and exchange a few words. The Mass was conducted like any other. He read from the gospel and gave a short speech. He said, as was usual, the Lord's Prayer, gave the peace sign and then it was time for communion. He took the chalice in one hand and the host in the other and said a prayer, asking for peace for his people, with his hands slightly raised. A moment later a shot rang out. Just one. It had come from the back, beyond the chapel door. It hit him right in the heart.

4

When he heard the telephone ring, Jon Sobrino dropped the book he was holding, got up and hurried to the drawing room. At that hour, around seven in the evening, the house was dark and silent. There was nobody there so all the lights were out. Sobrino lifted the receiver and said hello. At the other end of the line he heard a woman's voice. *What are you saying?* asked Sobrino. All he could make out was an incomprehensible mixture of words and weeping. She spoke again, stammering in her haste:

'They have shot the Monsignor.'

'Shot him? Where did they shoot him? Is he wounded?'

'They shot him.'

'Wait, wait . . . he's dead. Is that what you're trying to tell me?'

'They shot him,' sobbed the woman. 'They killed him.'

Sobrino hung up without saying any more. He was literally in absolute darkness.

He left his house immediately and went to the Jesuit Provincial's office, which at that time, March 1980, was run by a priest called Jerez. The office was just round the corner from his own house, the same one where, years later, Tojeira would receive the news of the death of the UCA Jesuits. At that hour, the Provincial's secretary had gone home, so Father Jerez himself opened the door.

'How are you, Jon?'

'Well, to tell you the truth, shocked. That's the word.'

'Why?'

'I've just received a phone call. I think it would be best if we listen to the news.'

'What's happened?'

'They've assassinated Monsignor Romero.'

They turned the radio on. Some of the stations carried reports of Monsignor's death. They did not have many details, but they announced that he had been killed by a single shot while holding a Mass in the hospital chapel. The two men listened again and again to what the journalists had to say, in silence. It was the thing they had all feared, although it had never been a topic of conversation, only mentioned secretly, if at all. Everyone had been aware that it could happen. Rutilio's death had been but the first of many; they had even coined a phrase: *Be a patriot, kill a priest*. It seemed like a macabre joke, one which, distressingly, was carried out too often.

Sobrino assumed that the news had spread all over the city, but he wanted to go to the university in case the rest of the Jesuits were unaware. He entered the campus and walked its entire length, from the pedestrian entry to the administrative offices. There were hardly any students about, as classes tended to end at seven or even before. So he walked alone in the dark. In the offices, he found many of his fellow Jesuits. Sobrino did not even have to ask if they had heard the news. The silence was unbearable. Each individual seemed like a shadow projected on to frozen ground. Like a scene that belonged to a painting rather than a film. Fixed, or moving in slow motion, very slowly. Desolation had gripped them all.

In many churches the bells rang all night. Thousands, hundreds of thousands, even millions of candles were lit, and soon none could be bought in the market or in shops. San Salvador woke up at dawn on the following day a little grey, as if a storm was about to break, but it did not rain, it was not the rainy season, it was something else, like a shirt washed so often that it suddenly loses its colour. They assumed that the smoke from the candles had blackened everything. It is known that many photographs taken that day had no colour and inexplicably showed images in black and white. For three days and nights mist hung around the peaks and volcanoes. Those who lived in those regions, and there were many of them, told stories of having seen a silhouette of Monsignor walking through the mist. Others said they heard him smile. Others said that he had granted them a miracle. In every Mass in every church in the country they talked about Monsignor Romero and asked for the repose of his soul. It is clear that the whole country joined in a long lament and a never-ending prayer. Very quickly, too, they turned to the subject of who was responsible. They talked about Roberto d'Aubuisson Arrieta, a man linked to the Death Squads, a paramilitary group whose reign of terror was at its height. Despite being implicated in crimes including kidnapping, torture and murder, d'Aubuisson – who later founded the Republican Nationalistic Alliance, the main political force of the right – was never brought to justice, even after witnesses from his own party accused him. He eventually died of cancer of the oesophagus. Few doubted that he was guilty of this crime; not the one who fired the weapon, but the one who gave the order. And yet the culprit was never brought to trial and there is no definitive answer to the question as to who murdered Romero.

As when Rutilio was assassinated, people were called to attend a special Mass, which would be celebrated in the metropolitan cathedral on the 30 March. Mourners came from all over the country. Thousands attended. A hundred thousand, a hundred and fifty thousand – there was no way to count the people who filled the church and the Plaza Gerardo Barrios, in front of the cathedral. People also gathered in the neighbouring streets. The plaza where they were concentrated is surrounded by buildings, with the cathedral on its north side, the National Palace to the west, the Library on the south face and to the east a series of offices that today are restaurants. Posted on every roof and terraces were members of the army and National Guard. For a while, everything unfolded calmly, but the peace was shattered when a bomb exploded at the corner of the National Palace. It was never known who threw that device, if it was someone from the army or from the guerrilla forces, who were mingling with the mourners. But what is certain is that soldiers stationed at the palace shot into the crowd. Many were killed by the bullets, but many others, perhaps even more, were crushed to death when the crowd burst into a stampede, hoping to find shelter in the cathedral. There were so many that there was not room for all of them. Through megaphones they were asked to keep calm. It was useless. Terror had led to chaos. Soldiers in what was then a bank and is now the National Library, also opened fire. There was no need to aim, they shot indiscriminately, hitting whoever was there: children, women, men and old people. Some returned fire with low-calibre weapons, mostly pistols. Some who escaped into the neighbouring streets were shot down by soldiers posted all around the perimeter. The city centre became the scene of a massacre. You can still see those terrible scenes in video footage taken at the time. People thrown on the ground, the living with the dead, or crawling away from the area, trying not to be an easy target. Later, you could pick out thousands of shoes lost in the street by those who tried to escape. Dozens died that day. That afternoon, San Salvador, desolate, in silence, cried not only for its archbishop, but for many others as well.

5

'There's a photograph,' says Sobrino, 'in which you can see Ellacuría carrying Monsignor's coffin that day in the cathedral.'

'I didn't know. I didn't know that he was there.'

'Well, yes, we were all there.'

'I've looked many times at images of that day. People running or dragging themselves and megaphones appealing for calm or the sound of shots, and the dead, it was sheer madness. And one thing that struck me: dozens of shoes strewn in the street after all that happened. I will never forget that image.'

'Well, that's what happened during those years.'

'But if it was like that, why did they stay? Didn't they think they could be killed?'

'They had killed many of us, civilians too, thousands of dead, and that's why I say that I'm convinced Ignacio knew he too might be killed.'

'And did the rest of you know it?'

'We knew, or rather, thought it,' said Sobrino. 'He had been on some of the army's blacklists, the ones they prepared in order to know who to kill first and who later, and that's why he left for exile. With everything that happened or had happened, we knew it could happen again. It's not that we talked about it, because those things were not talked about, but we knew. UCA had suffered attacks, four bombs exploded. It was obvious that danger was in the air and Ignacio knew this better than any of us.'

'Do you remember when he knew this?'

'When Ignacio knew?'

'Yes, Ellacuría.'

'I met him playing football. In the seminary, we organised a game between the seminarians and the priests, I'm sure it was at the end of the 1950s. Ignacio was a few years older than I am, so we played in different teams. He played on the inside.'

'Was he any good?'

'He was, actually,' says Sobrino.

'And was it then that you became close?'

'Close? That took place later.'

'But would it be fair to say that you knew him well, not necessarily at that time but over a period of time.'

'In some ways, yes, you can.'

'I'll ask you again, who was he? Why did he decide to stay on here? When did he know he wouldn't leave?'

'Nobody can answer those things exactly,' says Sobrino. 'Nobody can read the mind or the feelings of a person. If it was an act of love, well then, nobody would dare to assert that, and yet, I ask myself, what other reasons were there to stay?'

Sobrino's office is located in the Centro Monsignor Romero. It is not large or comfortable. A simple space with a desk, a computer and shelves of ordered books. A big window that looks towards the south reveals a small garden. If we could climb out of the window and walk west, a few paces beyond we would find a space planted with roses that bloom throughout the year. Twenty-five years ago, in that same space, the bodies of Ellacuría and his companions were found. But the windows cannot be opened to let us through nor was it our intention to do so. Our intention is to talk about Ignacio Ellacuría, to learn why he came here and why he became what he became. We have to go much further back in time, almost seventy-five years, and revisit a morning where a priest asked for a volunteer to travel to America. Sitting in their seats, the group of young men, none of them older than nineteen, listened to him in fascination. It was like listening to an adventure story. The man spoke of a place with cobbled streets in the foothills of a valley dominated by a volcano and surrounded by peaks, which were part of a mountain chain that stretched from Mexico into the heart of South America, interrupted only by the Panama Canal.

The seminar was held in a city called Santa Tecla, to the west of San Salvador. Ellacuría, who was barely nineteen years old, said he was ready to take that trip. He had entered as a Jesuit Noviciate in Tudela, Navarre, two years before. He was thin like a pine seen from far off and liked playing football, because in those days he was a supporter of Atlético de Bilbao on the radio.

Ellacuría had been born in 1939 in a village called Portugalete, in Vizcaya province in the Basque country. If he had been a very tall man and had stood in his village plaza, he could have seen the sea. If he had looked to his right he would have seen the city of San Sebastian and beyond it Pamplona and France. And yet he did not look to his right or to his left or ahead, where he would have seen enormous regions of ice; he looked elsewhere.

One afternoon, he visited his father in Portugalete to tell him the news. It was still a place with cobbled streets and houses with windows always open where you could just hear the screaming of gulls and smell the sea.

'Where is this place?' asked his father.

'El Salvador is in Central America.'

'And is it a good place to live?'

'It can't be too bad. There are many Jesuits there. They say it's a lively place full of gigantic trees, as in all America.'

'There will be diseases.'

'Like anywhere.'

'And you won't get tortilla de patatas. Or stew. Or ham.'

They were walking down a street and when they approached a fountain, his father led him there, bent down and drank from it. The water was fresh, almost sweet and you could catch the reflection of a man bent over, losing himself in the sunlight that fell on to the water at that moment. It was a round and simple stone fountain. The water flowed monotonously, imitating the sound of a stream.

'It'll be a short stay, perhaps two years.'

'Two years without tortilla de patatas.'

'Well, there must be potatoes in America.'

'And no more football.'

'They do have transistor radios.'

'Perhaps, but it won't be the same. It's never the same.'

Some weeks later Ellacuría found himself in a country he had not imagined. In the fifties, the doors of the houses in El Salvador were not locked and you could walk along the new pavements and not look behind you. In the street, carts pulled by horses or oxen mingled with Ford cars. In the early morning, in the mist, there were many days when you could hear the sound of whistles from the carts that came from the harbour on their way to the markets. Twenty or thirty carts. The driver of the front cart would sound his horn and would be answered by the last cart as they moved forward with agonising sluggishness along the black streets, under the glow of the gas lights through the five a.m. mist while church bells tolled for Mass. Life revolved around the downtown area, home to the post office, the few hotels, the cafés and the larger parks in whose bandstands, always situated in the middle of the park, orchestras played pieces from Vivaldi or Strauss as the sun set. Everything happened with a slowness that has been lost forever. People were dressed in suits, despite the heat, with thin ties, suits, trousers that were tied up above the waist, hats . . . and you could have lunch at a market stall or walk at ten at night or stay and study in the parks, guarded by owls that flew down from the mountains or volcanoes. And nothing happened. You did not have to always look behind you or several metres ahead of you, you did not have to remain on guard. This was the country the young Ellacuría arrived in, with its wide avenues and trees with canopies of foliage like hills suspended in the air, dense with yellow and white flowers. A city dominated by a volcano and surrounded by hills and mountains that formed a ring linked by slopes, like a colossal green roller-coaster that flourished all year round. The city was crossed by a river with shallow but navigable waters, as the locals would say. Santa Tecla kept its mild climate all year round and it was not hard to get used to it. And you could say that he lived a placid life and that he soon learned that the locals smiled easily and were very Catholic. They believed as much in St Antonio and St Ignacio as in the Virgin Mary, and also in fairies or in a woman who appeared on the banks of the rivers to grown-up men. He found it very easy to get to know these simple people and speak to them about the blessings of the Gospel.

'Did he stay for a long time?'

'No. Like all the Jesuits who arrived at that time, he left for Quito and the Catholic University. He returned and soon after left for Innsbruck in Austria, where he studied with Rahner.'

'Who is that?'

'Karl Rahner was a very important theologian, top of his field.'

'And he came back?'

'At the start of the sixties he studied in Madrid at the Complutense. He got close to Xavier Zubiri and became his favourite disciple.'

'That's well known.'

'Yes, everybody knows that. It's said that Zubiri would not publish anything without Ellacuría reading it first. Then, after graduating, he returned at the end of the sixties and joined the UCA. But by then everything had changed. It was no longer the same country, and there were rumours of war. Kidnapping was common and violence increased to the point where people started locking their doors and making their homes secure. Salvadorians changed, they became fearful, distrusting, speaking in low voices and always far from windows. There were *ears* everywhere. The Cold War between the United States and the Soviet Union had reached San Salvador.'

'Was that when it all started?'

'I'm not sure. Perhaps. Although, in my opinion, in Ellacuría's case it all began in 1976.'

'What happened?'

'At that time, UCA was a university outside the political arena. It received government funds and began to grow. The country's most important university was the National, which is where the movement that gave rise to the guerrilla groups is said to have started. The UCA was becoming an option for the young to study, although still without the prestige or respect that the National University had. But it was starting up and publishing important works like the *ECA* magazine, which was read everywhere.

'In 1976, the government of Colonel Molina, President of El Salvador, announced it would carry out agrarian reform. The plan was to provide several thousand peasant families with land taken from the large holdings of existing landowners. It got off to a promising start but very soon petered out. No more land was expropriated and the peasants received no more grants. Ellacuría responded with an angry editorial in the *ECA* magazine, where he said: 'The government has given up, the government has submitted, the government has obeyed. After so much fuss over previsions, forces and decisions, it has ended up saying, at your orders, my capital.' This led to the UCA having the government's financial funding withdrawn while the author of the editorial fell into disrepute in the eyes of the current military government.

'So by that time, the Jesuit had his role defined. He already had a voice. And it was a voice he used on behalf of those who didn't have one. Although it might appear to be a romantic gesture, it wasn't, not in 1976. They could have killed him for saying what he said. Assassinations and disappearances were counted by hundreds and, before long, by thousands.'

'Rutilio Grande, Monsignor Romero, and many more.'

'Yes, many many more. Nevertheless, he decided to remain. Why? Nobody really knows, but he assumed his responsibility. He only left the country for a few years when someone warned him that his life was in danger and that he was on a blacklist prepared by military intelligence. And he left, but never stopped being rector of the university. He was in charge of it from abroad and then, after a few years, perhaps two or three, returned and never left again. He exercised caution – didn't go and visit communities, didn't go the cinema or go out on an afternoon to eat a hamburger – but he did remain in the country. He stayed here and decided to say what he thought, to strengthen the UCA, to lend his voice to those who didn't have one, which was nearly everybody. His thinking prevailed and he became a lighthouse for many. He faced up to those who would later assassinate him, and did so with conviction and with faith. Who that man was, I cannot say. Just as I cannot say when he knew that he had to stay or what made him take that decision, whether naivety or love or the revelation of a divine mission. It doesn't matter. The fact is, whatever it was that made him take that decision, he had the faith and the courage to do what he thought was the right thing. And he did it until he paid the ultimate price.

6

Sobrino left the Jesuits' house at the UCA without taking his leave from his companions because it was very early. The morning of 8 November 1989 was strange due to mist that had come down from the mountains to the campus and had hung around in the high branches of the trees taking on the aspect of a gigantic cobweb woven around the branches. Sobrino did not notice this because he was in a hurry. He had to catch a plane. The first in a series of flights, for he was on his way to Thailand, where he had been invited to lead a spiritual retreat. In the car that was taking him to the airport, he was told about the rumours of the start of a military offensive. Sobrino says it was not the first time the guerrilla forces had announced an offensive; they had done so many times before and almost invariably it turned out to mean something like an incursion, or sporadic clashes with military positions near the capital, or even bombing a government institution or a high-ranking bureaucrat. But nothing of real importance. So it never occurred to him that this rumour might warrant changing his plans or cancelling the retreat.

In Thailand, everything happened as predicted. The retreat was given in a house by the sea and nothing interrupted Sobrino's serenity until the thirteenth day when news about the military offensive reached him and he realised that this was different from any campaign the guerrillas had launched in the past. He immediately called San Salvador and asked for details; he was told that, despite the clashes, everyone in the house was fine, that the only news was the search that had been carried out on Monday, but there had not been any further developments since then.

'Has Ignacio returned yet?'

'He got back last Monday afternoon. Chema called him when he was in Guatemala and tried to convince him to stay there, but it was useless.'

On Monday morning after breakfast, the UCA Jesuits discussed Ignacio's arrival. They had thought it would be better if he stayed in Guatemala and had asked Tojeira to telephone him. And Tojeira did that. He tried to convince Ignacio to stay in Guatemala, told him he need not return, but he rejected this. He was very confident that he could help bring the two sides together, to help stop the offensive. He wanted to return to negotiate for peace, idealistic as that might sound. There was no way of stopping him.

After the telephone call, Sobrino continued with his retreat and his days there passed without incident. Until, that is, he received a call not from San Salvador but from a friend in London.

'Are you sitting down, Jon?'

'What do you mean, "Are you sitting down"? OK, I am sitting down.'

'Jon . . . They've assassinated the Jesuits at the UCA. They have killed Ellacuría, Segundo Montes . . . '

Each name was like having a strip of skin pulled off. He was broken. It was a blow to his soul.

'Martín-Baró, Joaquín López y López, Amando López, Juan Ramón Moreno and two women, Elba and Celina Ramos.'

When he heard the two women's names he was filled with rage. That they had assassinated his fellow Jesuits was distressing, terrible, but he could understand it, or rather, assimilate it, for they were carrying out their duties. But that they had assassinated those women was an act that exceeded all limits.

After the telephone call, Jon Sobrino went out to walk along the beach. His guide and translator in that country accompanied him. It was a night without moonlight, a darkness with stars. The sea did not smell like it did on the coasts he knew in El Salvador. It was the Pacific Ocean, but had a different smell, without the crashing waves of the Salvadorian coastline, without the noise of seagulls, without the smell of salt. It appeared, perhaps, darker, an extensive patina under the stars, without ships on the horizon, without men on the beach, except for Sobrino and his companion. Far off, between the shadows of the mountains, the faint lights of a fishermen's village and beyond that, a lighthouse, very far off to the south. Sobrino remained silent for ages, feeling the sand, thinking of former times, trying not to imagine the death of his companions. He began to say a prayer and then it was interrupted by some memory, by a sentence, by the image of a face, a voice, many voices, the last meal, Ignacio's farewell when he left for his European trip. Why had he insisted on returning? Would they have assassinated the others if he had not been there? Too many questions and no answers.

After a while, his companion drew near and they exchanged a few polite phrases, then the other man asked him:

'Father Jon, why do you think you are not a martyr like them?'

'I am not worthy,' answered Sobrino, without meditating on it. 'Because I am not worthy.'

7

The next morning, after meeting with the people who had asked him to run the retreat, a Mass was held. They made an improvised altar and brought flowers to decorate it. At the end of the Mass, they asked Sobrino if he wanted to say something.

'I have bad news to give you: they have killed all my family. I have good news to give you: I have lived with very good people.'

Sobrino speaks about his companions the way Ellacuría did about Monsignor Romero, with the same devotion, using words that for a monk have great specific weight: *Good people*. And while he speaks that way, he himself has taken on a kind of levity. Days before, when I asked to interview him, he seemed to me like a stone without cracks, somewhat rigid, and yet, on the afternoon of this conversation, all that hardness has given way to levity. His words follow each other like in a piece of music. An intensity, a drama, with meaning and depth, his own words, not of an everyday conversation in a university office, but a work performed in an auditorium that narrates a tremendous story, that of a startling moment that defines what it means to be human.

'Why did they kill them, Father?' I ask him, even though I know that he has been asked this question too often before.

'They killed them because they spoke the truth,' says Sobrino.

'Do you believe that, Father? Is that the way it was? Is it as simple as saying *Because they spoke the truth*? Isn't your answer too naive?'

'When we think, we think only of ourselves, but those men no longer thought of themselves, as individuals they abandoned their egos and turned into a collective *We*. Whether that is acceptable or understandable to the rest of the world is of little consequence. That's why Romero said what he said every Sunday, denouncing what he was convinced needed denouncing, assuming leadership even though he accepted the risks in speaking that truth. The figure of a shepherd protecting his flock from a pack of wolves, armed only with his crook, would be a precise image. He was not given an opportunity to back away, but he wouldn't have done. Neither did the others back away. His faith did not allow it. Ellacuría could not stay silent.

What he had to say, he said. His final word was always guided by his faith. His faith was his ultimate truth. And that truth made people uncomfortable. That truth that was spoken embraced the masses, offered them a path to follow, showed them the how and explained the why. And that did not go down well, it disturbed many people.'

'And did that cause a reaction?'

'An irrational reaction. That's why they killed him. For that truth. For his faith. And because of that faith, Tojeira could not convince him to stay away. He had to return.'

'He had to return and mediate between the two parties. Or,

that's what he said. And it was known that he was close to both sides. Cristiani himself invited him to take part in an investigative commission on the Fenastras case.'

'Yes, the president had invited him. He received the invitation while on his trip.'

'Was Ellacuría close to Cristiani?'

'I can't say they were close, but they had become closer.'

'What was the reason for this?'

'The most obvious reason of all: he believed in a reasonable solution to the conflict. We had seen and suffered the threat for years. There had been innumerable atrocities, massacres, tortures, kidnappings and the nation was already tired and ill. Ellacuría wanted to build a bridge between both sides, and it wasn't easy. Some regarded him as idealistic, as naive. But he was convinced that only dialogue could lead to peace. And for that reason, he had to talk with the FMLN as much as with President Cristiani's government.'

'And that's what he did.'

'That's what he did.'

8

In 1989, the Presidential Palace was located in the foothills of the San Jacinto district. Behind it was the National Zoo. The zoo is still in the same location, but not the Presidential Palace, which was moved to the northern zone of San Salvador. But in September of that year, two months before the offensive was unleashed, you could still hear, at night, the roar of lions that came from the zoo next door or the chatter of birds whose cages could be found at the back of the house. In front of this house, some of the tallest and oldest pines in America grew in a garden that did not need gardeners because the grass never grew. The pines were separated by gaps of some three or four metres and it must have been pleasant to walk under their shade at any time of the year, but especially around Christmas, when they were decorated with coloured light bulbs. It was a lovely sight. There were no flowers in the garden. Nor benches to sit on. And often it was said that it had not been cultivated to entice people, but to isolate the house. Indeed, you never saw the tenants step on the grass. Apart from soldiers or workers who hung the lights in December, no one frequented the place.

The house had great windows and ample drawing rooms and it is said it also had secret passages, some of which reached the city centre, although nobody has ever confirmed this, not even former inhabitants. That September of 1989, a number of soldiers were stationed opposite the house, by the entrance, and more patrolled the garden, and there were many more at the rear of the property. Inside, however, everything seemed calm. A smell of roasting meat on a barbecue reached the dining room from a patio. In the dining room, President Alfredo Cristiani was sitting with Father Ellacuría.

'I must tell you, it's the first time I've been invited here,' said Ellacuría, as soon as he took his seat at the table.

It was not the first time that there had been a meeting between the politician and the priest. Months before, when Cristiani was president elect, he had asked for a meeting to discuss a topic that interested both of them: the peace process. Cristiani knew about the Jesuit, had read him and listened to him on numerous occasions, they had even coincided at some official events like a doctorate *Honoris Causa* given to the president of Costa Rica, Óscar Arias. However, they had never met in private. The president had come up with a proposal to launch the peace process and knew that Ellacuría would be a key player. Up to then, he did not know how the FMLN would react, faced with such a proposal, and he did not want to make a false move. That's why he telephoned Ellacuría and told him of his hopes, and the Jesuit offered to act as an intermediary with the leaders of the guerrilla forces and attempt to bring the two sides together. And that is what he did.

This had taken place months earlier and the peace process, after a decade of civil war, had started.

'You aren't a vegetarian, are you, Father?'

'No, you don't need to worry on that score. Where I come from, you learn to eat everything.'

'Good, because this meat is excellent.'

'Well, so it seems, and that's before even seeing it.'

They were eating a salad, but the smell of the meat advertised its imminent arrival. Cristiani tells me that that day they chatted about the witnesses to the peace process. The Episcopal Congress had been asked to nominate two representatives from the Catholic Church to be witnesses to the discussions. Ellacuría felt they also needed representatives from other sectors of society.

'I think it should be more inclusive. Businessmen, the evangelical churches – that would help establish credibility.'

'We could work on that,' said Cristiani.

They ate the meat and the rest of the lunch and drank coffee in the inner garden. It was a placid afternoon. In the distance, you could hear the sound of the zoo animals. While they were drinking, a man was pruning bushes and another was watering the flowerbeds by the side of the house. Cristiani and Ellacuría spoke a little more about the possibilities of the peace process and how to proceed in one or other situation. A few minutes later, the Jesuit left.

Cristiani assures me that that was the last time he met up with Father Ellacuría.

Almost two months later, on the morning of 16 November, Cristiani was drinking a cup of coffee when he received a telephone call telling him about the death of the Jesuit Fathers, among them Ignacio Ellacuría. After the initial explosive impact, this news took on denser and darker meanings. He had been at the staff college until late the previous night, but he claims nobody informed him of anything.

'How did you receive the news?'

'Badly, very badly,' Cristiani tells me. 'For many reasons it was the worst possible thing that could have happened at that time. Not only for the way they had been assassinated, a true act of barbarity, but also because we were in the middle of an offensive and trying as best we could to move beyond it, and this complicated everything. Moreover, they had eliminated a person who had been collaborating in the peace process, a person with contacts with the FMLN, and in our terms, a person of obvious significance because he was well respected by the guerrilla forces. Ignacio Ellacuría was a key person to bring the two sides together. As I saw it, it was a devastating blow that he had been killed.'

That's what he thought at first, but it turned out that the impact on the peace process was the reverse of what he had imagined. Assassinating the Jesuits so weakened the armed forces, particularly their international reputation, that it led ultimately to their defeat. Perhaps, without realising it, in murdering Ellacuría the army had struck a blow that gave the peace process new impetus.

Twenty-five years have passed. We are not in the Presidential House but in an office in San Salvador. The table is wide enough for meetings between many people, but it is just us. Cristiani is smoking a cigar and has left a coffee cup on the table, which he does not touch at all during our conversation. Next to me, a jug of some soft drink, which I do not touch either. There is no singing of birds outside, nor lions' roars, we are too far off, shut inside, isolated from the rest, invoking the names of people who are no longer with us, talking about the dead. The air conditioner purrs and the room is artificially cold, the light is clear but dim, even sterile. There is not one flower, not one plant in that place, not only in the office but in the whole building. It is September, the time when he had his last meeting with Father Ellacuría.

He takes a drag from his cigar. He seems calm. Serene. He is not making a fuss about anything. We talk while everything around us dies down because it seems as if there is nothing around us, except for our voices that blend together in a series of questions and answers that bring those terrible events that happened more than two decades ago back to the present. For their meaning is still relevant, as if the assassinations had all taken place only weeks ago.

We discuss his relationship with Ellacuría. He tells me how he got to know him, and how he received the news of his death and his decision to take part in his funeral. His voice is restrained, keeping his emotions contained, even when he assures me that he attended the burial service because that is what one does when someone that you appreciate dies.

'I knew that it wasn't going to cause a good impression in certain circles,' says Cristiani, 'but it was important to send a signal that this wasn't acceptable.'

'Were you ever frightened of these "circles"?'

'Twice we had information that there had been talks between groups of officers about a coup. One was at the start and the other was when the peace negotiations were fairly advanced. And one of the first actions by the guerrilla forces during the offensive was to try to assassinate the presidents of the three organs of the state. They came looking for me at home. Did I fear for my life? Well, yes I did. I was afraid. We had already seen too many coups where they arrested or killed or exiled the leader.'

We are sitting in office chairs and still talking and he is still smoking his cigar. You cannot hear any sounds from outside; it is as if everybody has abandoned the building. At some point, I ask him if the death of the Jesuit Fathers was a determining factor in the search for peace. He answers that when it was known that they had been assassinated by elements within the armed forces, the military fell into such disrepute that it could not stand in the way and had to permit reforms to be carried out which before had seemed improbable or impossible.

'They had to accept very hard things,' Cristiani continues. 'To discharge one hundred and two officers in a year was one of the hard things. And amongst the one hundred and two were the minister of defence, the commanders of all the barracks in the country, as well as some people high up in the staff college. Everybody expected that the famous group, that wasn't under anyone's control, would have been made public, as Walker said to Tojeira.'

Earlier I had mentioned to him that Ambassador Walker had told Tojeira who killed the Jesuits.

'Are we speaking of the Tandona?' I'm referring to the group of army officers known by that name, which included some of the highest officers in the army like Colonel René Emilio Ponce, head of the staff college of the armed forces, Inocente Orlando Montano, deputy minister of public security, Juan Orlando Zepeda, deputy minister of defence, Óscar León Linares, commander of the Atlacatl Battalion and Francisco Fuentes, commander of the First Infantry Brigade.

'Not necessarily,' says Cristiani. 'There were officers outside the Tandona, for example, General Bustillo. We had to struggle with him when he took the air force out on the first day, even when he was ordered not to. High command called him and made him listen to reason. There were people from everywhere, not just the Tandona.'

In its report on the case of the Jesuit Fathers, the Truth Commission accused six soldiers of being involved in the assassination, five of them belonging to the Tandona: Ponce, Montano, Zepeda, León Linares and Fuentes. The sixth military man was the then head of the air force, Colonel Bustillo. In spite of being accused, they were never brought to trial. When the case of the assassination of the Jesuits came up, the six actual perpetrators were judged and condemned, meaning Colonel Benavides and the members of the Atlacatl Battalion who took part in the assault, but not the brains behind them, nor those in the high command who were believed to have given the orders.

Cristiani leaves his cigar in the ashtray. He hasn't stubbed it out. He coughs a few times. I ask myself how long he has been smoking and if it will make him ill.

The office where we are sitting is located in a three-storey grey-and-white building with two guards at the door. They are not the military guards he had during his time as president, but civilian ones with little training, employed by security companies all over San Salvador. I greet them as I exit the building and leave them behind me. I set off through the bustle of a morning full of colours. There is nothing black and white in the day, except distant rain clouds. They have announced rain for the afternoon but soon it will be midday. Clouds of smoke emerge from kitchens. There is a rumble of cars, which at this time of day is unbearable. The day is warm. Windows in some offices fly blue-and-white flags, for this month the independence of the country is being celebrated. In a few days the celebrations will begin and on the fifteenth the armed forces will come out on the streets to take part in the usual parades. As a child of about six or seven, going home on the school bus one day, I shook my fist at a small group of soldiers who were standing on a street corner. I don't know what those soldiers were doing there and I don't know why I shook my fist, nor do I recall who on the school bus stopped me repeating the gesture. The thing I do remember with a terrible clarity is the fear my gesture provoked in my companions. The gesture of a boy of six or seven. They beat me about the head, called me an idiot and I don't know what else. It must have been in the mid-eighties. Fear was real. Fear was like the contents of an iron pan on the fire whose stew had been boiling for the last hundred years. I knew that we continued to feel fear, but its nature was different. Soldiers no longer provoked anything but indifference. The military parades excited young boys and very old men.

I walk down streets illuminated by the September sun, under tall trees of a nameless avenue. I am thinking about the conversation I have just had with a man who was a witness to a story written in blood. I try to grasp the weight of his words. Their meaning. I try to look through them to work out the gestures of six men walking through the mist of an early morning. I want to understand which is the path I should follow.

'We had no evidence against the people behind those events,' Cristiani had told me. 'How does one bring these cases to justice when there is no evidence to show who was the brains behind them? Whoever we tried to convict would have got off free. We'd never be able to prove anything. It was our responsibility to bring the guilty to justice. Benavides could have been the mastermind, but obviously he wasn't, other officers at the meeting must have given the order, but there is no proof. The recordings of the military school have disappeared. It's hard to explain what the atmosphere was like or the world we lived in at that time, whether certain things were viable or not, if we could have accomplished more.'

'Had you had evidence, would it have been possible to bring the brains behind the assassinations to justice?'

'If Benavides had said: this matter was decided at a meeting with X, Y and Z, and I was given an order and it was my duty to give the order to the Atlacatl Battalion, then X, Y and Z

253

would have shared their fate in a court of law, but he never said anything. He just repeated: *It was me and it was me.* There was nothing we could do.'

'That was how it was from the legal point of view, but what about the personal point of view, do you think there was something more? Or is it as simple as saying; *I decided this and I ordered them to carry out the assassination*?'

'If there were more people involved than Benavides and the other officers who took part in this directly? Yes,' says Cristiani. 'I'm inclined to believe there were more.'

I grow older as I walk up the street. It is not the usual temperature for September. The sun appears larger and I have the feeling that somehow it has got closer. It is enormous, like a full moon. I feel as if I'm suffocating, but continue to walk up the street. Suddenly I ask myself where X, Y and Z are. In what part of the world is the heat destroying them.

PART SEVEN

1

On Saturday 11 November, a little before midday, all army units were put on maximum alert. This meant that the clashes that began to take place in the outskirts of San Salvador were not isolated ones but part of something far bigger. Members of the army who were on leave had to return to barracks, and the lecturers at the military school had to prepare themselves to protect their students. Leave permits that had been granted for after midday were no longer valid.

That Saturday, Vice President Francisco Merino climbed aboard a helicopter at the staff college and flew to the headquarters of the Atlacatl Battalion, to the west of the capital. The Atlacatl was an infantry rapid-response unit, created at the suggestion of United States advisers and trained in North Carolina by the special forces of the United States Army. The model for this battalion was the Green Berets. Much has been said about their role in the civil war because they are remembered as the most effective and frightening unit as well as the most bloodthirsty. They have been accused of numerous atrocities, among them massacres of civilian populations. Their fame is black and sombre. During the war years, people spoke of those men with a mixture of pride and fear. Their training was unquestionably superior and they were extremely effective. No other battalion was better equipped to carry out a mission than those men. Vice President Merino visited them that Saturday afternoon and was in a meeting for more than four hours with their senior officers.

'Is it known what he talked about or what he did, what orders he carried and to who?'

'That has never been known,' said Tojeira, 'but it's safe to assume that he would have been dealing with Colonel Oscar Alberto León Linares, who at that time was commander of the Atlacatl Battalion.'

'Why is it safe to assume this?'

'President Duarte opened a period of amnesty during his time in power, around the mid-eighties, and the only military man who took up this amnesty was León Linares. He was a hard-line army man but he wasn't stupid; if you're the commander of the Atlacatl and you're asked to send a unit to San Salvador, a combat group that will not go into combat, because they did not go to fight, it's obvious that the mission was of another kind. So we think that this man asked for political guarantees, as he had done with Duarte. He couldn't ask the army for that because his comrades were there one minute and gone the next.'

'So he had to ask the government for them.'

'And who would he approach for those political guarantees? The president? Difficult to be sure he'd grant them. Or the vice president, who was a conservative and friend to those in the army? Merino was definitely the right man for the job. It was known that the army was very close to the vice president; indeed, it's said there were some who, over many years, tried to hatch a coup against President Cristiani and replace him with Merino.'

'And did León Linares know about the mission that his battalion was about to carry out?'

'We think he did. One of the members of the battalion testified that on the morning of Thursday, the sixteenth of November, they were going to join in the fight in Mexicanos district. And over the radio, León Linares asks him: "Have you already done it?" And he answers, "Yes, my colonel." And he was referring to the mission, without a shred of doubt. They always knew. At least, he knew. As for the troops, I'm not so sure. And it doesn't matter.'

At the end of Saturday afternoon, there were clashes between the FMLN forces and the army all around the capital and its outskirts. As evening fell, people stayed in their homes. By that time it was obvious that what was happening was far more serious than what had gone before. By the night, guerrilla forces attacked President Cristiani's residence. That was announced over the radio, but the transmission was cut at about eleven at night, when all the country's radio stations were forced to join Radio Cuscatlán, a chain of radio stations owned by the army. Radio Cuscatlán informed us that there were attacks all over the city, but they were under control and the guerrilla forces' advance would not last much longer. Near midnight, people contacted each other over the radio, some calls came on air and terrible things were said. Many of them asked if they could begin assassinating priests, who they considered to be communists and traitors, people close to the left.

'Was there a sense of panic, Father? Panic over those phone calls?'

'Yes, there was some. There were not many people who shared that dark thought, but it was true that many saw us that way. An unthinkable thing. I recall something that made a great impression on me. Someone called the radio station and said: "Why don't you take Monsignor Rivera to Parque Bolívar so that he can be killed by the people? Not by being stoned to death, but by being spat on until he died." I couldn't believe it. It was irrational. That night some people also asked for Ellacuría's head.'

On the following day, an elite unit from the Atlacatl Battalion, perhaps the most outstanding and well-prepared men in the army, travelled to San Salvador to provide support to the army's staff college. They were to follow Colonel Cerna Flores's orders. He was head of the staff college's operations, a position known as C-3. That Sunday the members of the Atlacatl did not do much, except safeguard the installations. On the next day, Monday, they were entrusted with the first part of their mission.

2

Ignacio Ellacuría arrived on Monday at around five in the evening at the International Airport of Comalapa on a flight from Guatemala City. There was an atmosphere of emergency in the place, with curfew at six. Everything had to be done speedily. Father Armando López and Father Francisco Estrada had gone to meet him. The car journey was for stretches silent, although they talked of the latest events, of how unexpected that offensive had been, of the attack on Cristiani's house and of the call for a sector of the society to assassinate the priests. Ellacuría was full of confidence and said he had arrived to mediate between the groups. He would have to make some phone calls, meet with the president and all would quickly end. In spite of his good spirits, he was soon affected by the strange desolation of the highway. You could not see the usual sellers of fruit. The villages on each side of the hills seemed abandoned, had even lost their colour and become grey. The Jesuit Fathers did not notice this, they were too focused on what they were talking about, but if they had paid attention, they would have noticed the change in colour, like a postcard from 1901, and the cold weather dusting the tips of the leaves with frost. Apart from a pack of four or five small dogs with leonine coats, they didn't see anyone at all until they reached San Marcos, which marks the city of San Salvador's boundary, where they noticed some soldiers crossing the street, some five hundred metres off. They slowed down but as they drew closer, they lost sight of them in a ditch among bushes and trees along the side of the highway.

It was twenty to six when they arrived at the entrance to the university car park. That day the gate was shut. On either side, flanking the gate, there were soldiers. When the car stopped outside the gate, some soldiers approached and one of them said: *It's the Father, let him through.* And he was referring to Father Ellacuría.

'Was it by chance that they knew who he was?' I ask him. Ellacuría was a celebrity and often appeared in the press or on television.

'I don't think so. We believe they were waiting for him. Besides, more or less half an hour later they searched the house where Ellacuría was living in the UCA. So we were sure they were waiting for him.'

Before six thirty, soldiers from the Atlacatl Battalion stormed the pedestrian entrance to the university. They entered the campus to search the Centro Monsignor Romero, and the Jesuit residence, which is found in the same building, although in a different wing and with its own entrance. The Fathers had no suspicions of the military presence until they were well inside the block.

'When they entered,' recounts Tojeira, 'Ellacuría, who kept his calm in such matters but never abandoned his steadfastness, warned the man who commanded the troop, Lieutenant Espinoza, José Ricardo Espinoza, that this house was not part of the university but belonged to the Company of Jesus, so he needed a warrant to make his searches.'

'And what did Espinoza say?'

'He pointed out, in a respectful manner, that there was a curfew in place from the day before and they could do what they considered necessary. And they were going to search the whole university. They said that they had come to carry out a search because they were looking for weapons, but nobody believed that.'

'Why not?'

'Because it was obvious to everyone that they had come to see if Ellacuría was there. To confirm he was at home and whoever else lived in that house.'

'And why was it obvious?'

'First, because they already knew that Espinoza called him by his name. And called Segundo Montes by his name as well. And besides, they did not behave as at other times. It wasn't the first time they had searched the university. They had always been interested in papers and things like that, there was much talk of searching, they asked for explanations for such and such a thing, but this time none of that happened. Also, it coincided with Ellacuría's arrival; it was very obvious.'

There was no aggression. The soldiers behaved with relative good will. In this search they did not find any military equipment, so a little over forty minutes later, the soldiers abandoned the place.

3

'This house is a mousetrap,' said Father Lolo, Joaquín López y López. 'If they come there's no possible escape.'

The dining room reeked of coffee. The Jesuits were chatting about the search and Father Lolo was not optimistic. He had stood up from his chair and walked slowly round the table. Despite it being so early in the morning, he seemed tired, and he was. Due to the pain of his cancer, he didn't sleep well. He had been ill for a year and at times the unbearable pain made him double up. That morning, however, despite his lack of sleep and the pain, he had got up and even strolled for a while around the chapel before breakfast.

Joaquín López was a Salvadorian. Born in 1918, he entered the Order of the Company of Jesus at the age of twenty. He was ordained as a priest in 1952 in Spain and returned to his country to join the Jesuit College of San Salvador. Although his vocation was more to do with educating the working classes, he was one of the founders of the university. He had fought in 1964 so that the Legislative Assembly of Salvador could approve a law to allow for private universities. Up to then, the sole university in the country was the National University, founded two centuries before. It was not easy, but nothing was in a country where everything arrived late. Although he wasn't the only one who took part in that struggle; two other Jesuits accompanied him, José Mafría Gondra and Florentino Idoate. He did assume the most active role in the legal battles that took place three and a half decades ago. During that time, he had also founded the organisation Faith and Happiness, which offered a basic education to the working classes with workshops in carpentry and dressmaking, and even primary schools. In 1989, despite his advanced cancer, Father López was the director of that organisation.

'I would not trust those people,' warned Father Lolo, 'I know them better than you do.'

'No one trusts them, Lolo,' said Segundo Montes. 'We all know the kind of country we're living in, but to say that they'd come for us – that might be taking it too far.'

The weight of the country's recent history was a dark backdrop to his words. He could not say to himself that he did not know his fellow citizens. He was fourteen years old when General Martínez's army was ordered to massacre thousands of peasants in 1932. He remembered the foul smell in the ditches where they had thrown the corpses, a stink that had spread for kilometres around and flooded almost the whole western zone of the country. And he also recalled the columns of smoke on the horizon, which the people said came from bonfires where they burnt the bodies. Nobody knew how many were killed, twenty thousand, thirty thousand, nobody kept a record of the massacre, but greater than the number of bodies was the fear. There had been countless murders that went unpunished. Father López knew, perhaps more than his companions, that there was a real possibility of it happening again.

'I don't think anything as bad as that will happen,' Ellacuría gave his opinion.

'I wouldn't be so sure,' said Father Cardenal. 'Lolo is right, we can't afford to be complacent.'

'It's war,' added Father López.

'Moreover,' Father Cardenal went on, 'that was not a search of the UCA. They said that there had been shooting around here, that there were weapons. That was a lie, and we all know it, them and us. They said they would check all the university and they only checked the place where we're living. Those soldiers came here to find out where we were and who we are, and I think they are going to deport us.'

Tojeira tells me that all morning and evening they didn't talk of anything but the search and offensive. He also says that the two Central American priests, López y López and Cardenal, originally from Nicaragua, were so unnerved by it all that their companions tried to convince them to spend a few days in the Santa Tecla house. Father López rejected that option, but Father Cardenal did not and left for the house, and that decision saved his life.

During Father Ellacuría's last stay in Barcelona, at the start of the year, he was asked in an interview what were the chances of being killed, as had happened to other priests, and Ellacuría responded: *They can always kill, but it would be irrational to do it, so I don't believe it will happen*. It is difficult to know if his confidence was real or only partly real. The fact is he had reason to be confident. In these last months Ellacuría and the government had drawn closer, especially with President Cristiani. Some time before, the university had awarded a doctorate *Honoris Causa* to Óscar Arias, the president of Costa Rica who was a Nobel Peace Prize laureate, and Cristiani had been invited to attend the ceremony, which he did. In his speech,

Father Ellacuría spoke about the steps that had to be taken in the peace process. He said that they were closer than ever, due to exhaustion on both sides, to the guerrilla forces' will and to president Cristiani's ethical tendencies. The president received this speech very well, as Ellacuría had wanted him to. He had not said those words on the spur of the moment as they were part of his idea of searching for a reconciliation.

A little before the offensive, a bomb exploded in the central office of the organisation Fenastras, the National Federation of Salvadorian Workers, in which nine people died, amongst them, the secretary general, a woman called Febe Elizabeth Velásquez. It was not a minor event. Fenastras was an important organisation in the national political field, close to the left. Because of this, it was a case in which the government had to show an interest and it did and created an investigative commission to which Cristiani invited Father Ellacuría. The bomb went off on 31 October. At the beginning of November they contacted Ellacuría, who was in Barcelona, to invite him in the name of the President. Ellacuría answered that before accepting he had to talk with the Jesuits in San Salvador, but in principle he was willing and inclined to accept that responsibility. When he returned to the country on that dark Monday, 13 November, Ellacuría was full of hope.

On Wednesday, after lunch, Tojeira arrived at the UCA house to have a coffee and chat. In that kind of situation, with the noise of battle heard nearby like a storm breaking somewhere and the tension that this imminent storm generated, it was an agreeable stroll from the house where he was living to the university, under the shade of trees and with the pavements deserted, except for groups of soldiers posted on the street corners.

The desolation of the university was something that Tojeira could not get used to. Had it been a normal day, the campus would have been packed with young people going about their business. In the chapel at this time, the choir would be rehearsing, and around the building there would be young men sitting against the wall or lying in the grass, reading, talking or eating hamburgers bought in the street. If the offensive had not existed, the very slight sound of the breeze would have passed unnoticed as everywhere the shouting of the young surged like a wave between the rooms and corridors and empty spaces. But there was nothing of that sort. Silence spread around the place, becoming dense, almost palpable, and allowed what was usually ignored, the breeze and the scent of flowers, to take on the shape of the man who was moving along the inner street of the university, opposite the chapel, as Tojeira was before entering the part where the priests' house stood, through a metal door that separates it from the chapel's side.

When he entered the drawing room next to the dining room, there was still a smell of meat stew in the air. Some of his companions were eating fruit and others were smoking. After greeting each one of them, he sat down in a wooden chair by the door and Elba, the woman who looked after them, offered him coffee. Tojeira said he would drink a cup. He listened to a friendly argument that separated Ellacuría from the others; Ellacuría thought the offensive would soon end, the others said they did not think so, that it would last days, even weeks.

'This is more serious, Ellacu, it's not something that is going to end soon.'

'Not at all, man. Why, in three days there will be nothing. You'll see how quickly it ends.'

'I wouldn't be surprised if what happened in Nicaragua happens here with the people taking to the streets. If the air force comes out, there would be a popular rising.'

'I don't believe the air force will come out. I don't believe that they would dare to bomb the capital. It would be a despicable act.'

The coffee got cold but they still drank it in great gulps and all stood up except for Ellacuría and Tojeira. It was an agreeable room to be in and chat. Tojeira hadn't talked much with Ellacuría up to then, but that afternoon the rector drew up to the Provincial and told him how Colonel Zepeda, who belonged to the staff college, had phoned to ask if his son could study at the university, to which Ellacuría answered he could, not to worry and on his return from Spain would call him.

'You see, Chema?' said Ellacuría. 'Now we have more chances to talk with the army, more access to the senior posts. Montes is in contact with Colonel Vargas as well. They are conservatives, but you can talk to them. Colonel Vargas has a brother who is a professor of sociology.'

'Yes, I know that,' said Tojeira.

'And through that relationship Montes could visit a refugee camp in Chalatenango. I am convinced that both Cristiani and the guerrilla forces need us.'

'Well, yes. It seems that what you're saying is right,' he conceded.

Tojeira admits that if Ellacuría told him to stay calm, that nothing would happen, he would believe him. He had complete confidence in the rector. He was sure that Ellacuría knew what he was talking about. More than once he had had to absent himself from the country, warned by some contact that he figured on a blacklist, that he was courting danger, that they were going to kill him. Ellacuría had lived through these kinds of situations before; nobody knew better than he what to expect or how much leeway he had or what action to take.

A little later, Tojeira took his leave from Ellacuría, and walked back the way he had come. The day continued to be luminous, the flowers beds smelt light and fresh, a rat ran between the bushes next to the block of offices of the philosophy lecturers, some autumn leaves rustled on the ground pushed by the breeze, and, far off, in the Western sky, a white, ghostly moon was rising above distant hills, but Tojeira did not take in any of that. His thoughts had led him far away to the phone call he had to make to some seminarians who found themselves in a conflict zone. Thus he walked without realising what was going on around him, without understanding what he was hearing, without knowing even that he had seen his companions alive for the last time.

4

Around nine p.m. on 15 November, a man emerged from the mist that had risen among the tyres of the armoured cars and the stunted trees that flanked the entrance to the Captain General Gerardo Barrios Military School in the south of San Salvador. That man was Colonel Guillermo Benavides, who was in charge of the school and, in the current situation, of the defence of the whole zone. The soldiers posted at the door saluted him and let him pass. In the entrance to the place there was a wide parking area with soldiers leaning against the walls. They spent the night there, awaiting orders, talking, playing cards or listening to the radio while poking about in tins of food. Benavides walked among them without saluting them, aiming for the school's old social club, a room that was used for meetings and parties, to see his subordinates. He had to pass on the orders he was bringing.

Colonel Benavides was the only man who took part in the meetings that were held in the staff college from the eleventh when the offensive began. Usually, the military school and its commander did not participate in acts of war, but the state of emergency in which they found themselves demanded new efforts. Since Monday, the zone included the staff college, the military school, the seat of military intelligence and the Arce district, where many army personnel and their families lived. It was protected by a series of command posts under Colonel Benavides. He was, thus, the man in charge.

There was a large table and his men were sitting around it. The aroma of coffee floated in the air as if they were in a government office in an afternoon of any old day.

'The situation is serious,' announced Benavides, 'more serious than we thought, and we must act.'

One of his men helped himself to a cup of coffee and another one, next to him, pointed with a finger to his cup so he could also pour him some. Whilst this was going on Benavides said nothing, but it did not seem to disturb him, his look was of sombre gravity and he was staring, not at the two men helping themselves to coffee, but off into infinity. After a few seconds of silence, he went on:

'Gentlemen, we have orders to eliminate the left's high command; we are going to eliminate all the leaders. We have been allocated the UCA, which is in our zone. We must eliminate Father Ellacuría. The unit from the Atlacatl Battalion has inspected the zone and it has everything under control.'

That night there were several meetings at the staff college. There were as many as twenty-four officers who met from seven in the evening up to eleven thirty at night. According to testimony from Colonel Ponce, head of the armed forces' staff college, and from Colonel Larios, Minister of Defence, during those meetings they evaluated the situation throughout the night and analysed the ways they could recover the positions they had lost since the eleventh. Moreover, they decided to take more energetic steps. The principal step would be for the air force to bomb some key positions. At the end of the meeting, they phoned President Cristiani so that he could sign the order. Everyone present at the meetings on that Wednesday night denied mentioning Ellacuría or the UCA Jesuits.

Colonel Larios went as far as saying *it was decided to expel members of the FMLN from the zones where they were still fighting* . . . On mentioning that declaration, Tojeira frowns and says nothing, though it is obvious that that sentence was incongruous. In a state of war like the one they were in, why take a decision to expel the aggressors? Isn't that an obvious and implicit decision?

Larios also declared that Cristiani managed to meet up with them from eleven at night to two in the morning. And Cristiani, in his turn, swore in a declaration to a judge that he was present from twelve thirty at night at the staff college, that at that time they talked about aerial bombardments but never once mentioned the Jesuits in general, nor Father Ellacuría in particular. According to Cristiani, there were two or three North American advisers at the meeting, but he did not speak with them. If that is right, the minister of defence, Colonel Larios, the deputy ministers Colonels Zepeda and Montano and the head of the staff college, Colonel Ponce, were with the president while the assassinations were being carried out.

Who gave the order that Benavides passed on to the members of the Atlacatl Battalion?

It has been affirmed that they themselves commented on the assassination of the Jesuits as they left the Centro Loyola at the end of the afternoon. They were heard mentioning the mission that they had been entrusted with. If that is so, the order reached them far earlier, not at night.

Whatever the case, if the order was given that night, that afternoon or on the morning of that day or a day before or a week before, the fact is that it was not a spontaneous action but part of a premeditated plan. We know that the order was handed out to Benavides that day and that this man left the staff college installations, walked deliberately to the military school's social club to meet his subordinates and inform them that they had to eliminate Father Ellacuría without leaving any witnesses.

A little after Benavides' meeting with his men, the Atlacatl Battalion unit was told that they had to get ready to leave.

5

'And what's the truth in this matter? Did they really feel threatened or was it an act of intolerance, of viciousness, of abuse, of scorn, of feeling superior to everyone?'

'An assassination like that is an act of utter vileness. And of ignorance. And of hate,' says Tojeira, with the assurance of someone certain about the case.

'But it happened in the middle of an offensive. Did that make it valid in the mind of a soldier? Was it what they really believed they should do, with conviction?'

'They knew everything, or almost everything, or at least they knew they were in contact with both sides, they had got close enough to think that they could understand Ellacuría and the others' good intentions had nothing to do with war, that their actions revealed that they were working towards a peaceful solution to the conflict. For that reason, it has no justification. The UCA Jesuits were not generals, were not a branch of military intelligence, they were priests, Christians, humanitarians. They always argued for understanding, to attain peace through dialogue, Ellacuría even more than the others. That's why he drew close to Cristiani. He was always building bridges.'

'And at that time, those bridges might not have been convenient?'

'Probably not.'

'It's known that the army did not want peace. Peace meant abandoning many privileges, money, power, that kind of thing. Could this be a more real motive than hate?'

'It might be that or it might not. It could be a motive and it's possible the FMLN's advance led them to take that final decision. But the truth is I haven't a clue what their motives were. I do know one thing though: hate was very great, an irrational hate that killed Rutilio Grande and Monsignor Romero and so many others.'

'Do you think that there will be a time when the true culprits of the assassinations will face a judge?'

'I don't know that either. Sometimes I think there won't. They all know who they were, they all know that that order could only come from above, from the staff college, and all of them know who the members of the staff college were. It's been told countless times. Why is nothing done about it? Because there are great influences that stop it, influences that plotted the assassination from the start. And that is part of the hate as well. From hate to the truth, to do the right thing once and for all.'

'And something can be done?'

'We will go on insisting.'

'Is it worth it, Father?'

'It's always worth it. Even if you know it won't lead anywhere.'

'I suppose you say it like it is.'

'And now you're going to ask me if the Jesuits died in vain?'

'The eternal question. The one in every interview.'

'Yes.'

'And did they die in vain?'

'No.'

6

The members of the Atlacatl Battalion who found themselves in the military school were drinking coffee sitting on the ground of an outer corridor, which gave on to the car park, leaning on their backpacks, which were propped up against the wall. Nobody slept, nobody could sleep, they were awaiting an order. The order arrived at around nine at night. They were asked to get themselves ready to leave. They stood up, tied their boots, and some camouflaged their faces using a kind of black felt-tipped pen, drawing stripes across their foreheads and cheekbones.

At one point somebody asked who of those present had experience of handling an AK-47. One of the burly soldiers called Óscar Amaya Grimaldi said he could handle one, that he had been trained in their use. He was given one of those rifles.

The AK-47 was the weapon that the guerrilla forces used, a rifle originally from Russia, thought up by a former soldier in the Second World War called Mijaíl Kaláshnikov. During the Salvadorian war, hundreds of these rifles were used by the FMLN forces, most of them sent out by Cuba. Nearly eighty million of these rifles were manufactured. One of them was handed over to the burly man.

The rest of them prepared their M-16 rifles, which were the ones used by the Salvadorian armed forces, and had been used before by the United States Army in the Vietnam war.

When they were ready, they climbed aboard two pick-ups and were driven towards some half-built flats to the east of the pedestrian entrance to the UCA and not towards the university. It was a gloomy site, stinking of dirty water that bubbled up from a drain, forming a small pool in the middle. In that place, protected by the darkness, were some of the outstanding troops of the zone. Not one of them knew what the mission of the Atlacatl unit was, although they had been informed that they were going to the place and were expected. Apart from some saluting between those in charge, the troops remained separate. The men from the Atlacatl unit met up in a site distant from the rest and were given the latest instructions for the operation. The command unit would divide into three groups: the first would make a cordon in a wide circle around the site, beyond the chapel and the street that passed opposite the Centro Monsignor Romero, reaching even the buildings housing the offices of the lecturers and the houses around the chapel. The second would provide security opposite the Centro Monsignor Romero. And the third would enter to carry out their mission. They were reminded that the Centre and the priests' house were in the same building, and although the entry façades were opposite each other, they were connected, but this they already knew because they themselves, days before, had carried out the search. They were also told that they had to burn whatever they found in the Centre and some were picked out to paint the walls with messages in support of the FMLN.

After this, they moved forward in the dark towards the university, which was about one hundred and fifty metres away. They did this without talking, walking fast. They entered via the pedestrian entry, which was easy to force because it was barely protected by a door with a hurricane mesh. They walked to the car park, just before you reach the chapel, in front of some ancient storerooms, which now serve as food stores for those who work there. That November, the university guards slept there. There were four of them, armed with pistols. The Jesuits had advised them, once curfew began at six, to lock themselves up and not leave until it was over. They were not members of the military nor had they been police-trained, but they were simply working for a security agency. These men were lying down in bunks and heard the arrival of the soldiers with dread.

'We listened to them talking and we knew there were many of them,' one of them tells me. He says he heard one of them ask: 'And are they priests or guerrilla fighters?' 'They are priests,' the other one answered. 'We heard them in silence, without moving, almost without breathing, because we knew if they discovered us, we could only expect death.'

After a brief time, the members of the Atlacatl Battalion moved on. They walked towards their objective and divided into the groups already described. They surrounded the zone and those who had to enter went towards the door and knocked on it. They shouted. They ordered the Jesuits to open up.

7

In his bedroom, Father López y López is saying his rosary when he is alerted by the soldiers' shouts. He gets up from his bed, opens the door and hears someone saying they must remain calm. Another of his companions is praying at his door, *Father, protect us in this hour, now and in the hour of our death,* and Father López y López locks himself in his room and sits down on his bed, but immediately gets up again, opens his door and hears two of his companions speaking, but he cannot understand what they are saying. He goes back into his room again and kneels by his bed, then lies down on the ground and rolls until he is lost in the shadows. He is tired and sick and frightened. And he does not want to feel frightened but to be brave and resigned. He had thought it might be another search, but immediately put it out of his mind. These men have not come here for that. He knows it. They have come to get them.

Father Ellacuría suddenly recalls a morning in a street in his village with his father, sitting next to a fountain. And that thought, for some reason, vanquishes his fear. He stands up, goes out into the corridor and begs his companions to keep calm. A little later, recognising that this situation cannot go on for much longer, he says that it would be better to go outside and face whatever they have to face. Ellacuría has his father in mind, sitting at the fountain, and that thought gets confused with a prayer where he talks with God as if talking to a brother or father, and without being aware, with firm steps, as if stepping on stones, he walks down the corridor to the door that separates him and the rest of the priests from the soldiers. It is like reaching the edge of a cliff, stopping there, looking down at the sea and discovering how the waves crash against the steep rocks.

'Don't destroy anything,' Ellacuría begs the soldiers. His voice is firm and does not tremble. 'I'm going to open up now, don't destroy anything.'

The soldiers observe him standing next to a hammock. He has a coffee-coloured dressing gown on. He seems serene. He has a face without wrinkles. He puts the key in the lock and opens the door. The soldiers immediately pass through. They do not treat him well like they did the previous Monday during the search. This time they push him, take him by the shoulders and drag him to a small garden by the house's façade, a garden devoid of flowers. They force him to lie down on the grass, and Ellacuría lies down on the grass, under the moon, under all the night stars, under creation. He thinks that in his village it will be daylight, that it will be chilly because it is November, that the mountains will begin to show snow, that perhaps there will be frost in the trees, that bells in the church will be announcing Mass, and in the side streets, on the hills, there will be goats and sheep grazing and from kitchens with their windows open there will rise smells of stews or recently made cheese or of coffee, and the light will be clear, as clear as the moonlight shining down on him, like that of all the stars above, in what has no end. He is thinking of all that when another of his companions arrives, Father Amado, and lies down on the same grass under the same stars. Then two more, Father Juan Ramón Moreno and Father Martín-Baró. When they were young, they had all arrived in El Salvador from Spain, still boys, in the sweet years of the 1950s and they had gone off to study but had always returned. Although they had left many times, after a brief spell abroad they had always returned. And now they are all there on the ground and that has to mean something.

'Stand up,' they order Martín-Baró. They grab his arm and violently raise him, but the priest doesn't complain. They force him to walk towards the side door that leads to the chapel and make him open it.

That door is very close to the window where Lucía Cerna is standing. Lucía can't see them because it is too dark, but she hears what Father Martín-Baró tells them:

'This is an injustice. You're rotten through and through.'

A few seconds later, a whisper can be heard. Not only does Lucía hear it, but other neighbours do too. It is a rhythmic whisper. The Fathers are praying on the grass. They are not fighting, not arguing, they do not ask for mercy, they pray. They pray to God. Their voices sound like the breeze. All together. They are joined in the same prayer. Faith has led them to this place. At this moment, their story is also the world's story.

In his bedroom, under the bed, in the dark, López y López is also praying. Although he does not know it, his prayer is the same one as his brothers'. He feels exhausted and sick. He rolls over and comes out from the darkness under his bed and stands up. He stands up with enormous difficulty but he does so with determination. He is scared but knows he cannot stay hidden, that he has to come out and join his companions. He begins to walk. His feet are heavy and his movements are agonisingly slow.

'When are you going to start?' one of the soldiers, Lieutenant Mendoza, asks Corporal Ávalos, who understands the time has come. He draws close to Amaya Grimaldi and says to him:

'Let's get on with it.'

The burly man, Amaya Grimaldi, raises his AK-47, one of the eighty million made, and points it at the man in the coffee-coloured dressing gown. He shoots. Ellacuría dreams of cobbled streets and listens to tolling bells. The day is luminous. And as his last thought comes to him, he is extinguished, and all his years culminate in this final instant.

Amaya Grimaldi shoots Segundo Montes. Then Martín-Baró, with one shot. Ávalos takes up his M-16 and shoots Father Amado and then Father Moreno.

At that moment, at the other end of the garden, thrown on the floor of their bedroom, Elba Ramos and her daughter Celina pray with hurried, desperate words, begging for this not to happen, for these soldiers to go away and leave them in peace. They are crying their eyes out. *Please*, sobs the daughter.

A scream comes from within the property, a *now* that Corporal Tomás Zarpate hears as he stands guarding the bedroom door, in charge of the two women. Elba knows that it is an order and rolls over her daughter in a pathetic attempt to protect her. The soldier raises his weapon and shoots until the sobbing stops.

Father López y López sees what is happening from the garden door and shouts:

'Don't kill me. I do not belong to any organisation.'

Amaya Grimaldi calls to him, but Father López does not turn around. *Come through, pal, come*, says the burly man. But Father López tries to flee. He tries to enter his bedroom. He manages to open his door, but from behind a corporal named Pérez Vásquez shoots him and Father López y López falls to the ground. The soldier moves forward and passes through the door to look into the bedroom, which is in the dark. At that moment, as he passes Father López, he feels a hand grab his foot. His eyes meet the priest's. Between them darkness grows in an instant that goes on for ages, but the soldier averts his eyes from the priest's and raises his rifle. He shoots one, two, three and four times. The hand that holds his foot falls to the ground.

And everything is over. The six are dead. They have been murdered in that house in the university that has taken decades to set up.

The soldiers set off a flare to signal that it was time to leave. The Atlacatl unit assembled outside the chapel. They threw a second flare and that was the moon that Lucía Cerna thought she saw, that moon that revealed the soldiers to her. They abandoned the campus and minutes later reached the staff college. The head of the mission found Colonel Benavides to inform him that everything had been carried out as ordered.

In the early morning mist, the unit from the Atlacatl Battalion left the military school to head for the Mexicanos district where finally they entered combat. There was an enormous silence in San Salvador, as if an unwanted truce was in force. A few birds were singing, they had not flown away, and had not emigrated to higher ground where nothing happens. Without anyone noticing, morning dew had fallen on to the silent city, on to the marching soldiers' bodies, on to the bodies of the assassinated Jesuits and on to the roofs of those still sleeping unaware of what had happened.

The sixteenth day dawns. It is November. Light suffuses men and beasts.

Epilogue

'Did you notice that the light is clearer?' said Francisco Andrés Escobar.

'To tell you the truth, I didn't.'

It was early in 1993. He knew little about the assassinated Jesuits at the UCA, although he saw on television the trial that had taken place years back against the actual perpetrators. It had been transmitted as a spectacle. And we all saw it day after day as if we were seeing the longest-running piece of theatre known.

'It's always like this in November. Always. Even that year.'

'What, 1989?'

'Yes . . .'

'How did you find out what had happened?'

'Over the radio. They announced it from early on. I rushed to the university as soon as I found out.'

'You were close to Ellacuría, right?'

'Yes, Ellacuría was like a father to me. He brought me to work here.'

Francisco Andrés was a professor of Essay Writing and

other topics in the Literature course. He was also a writer. More than once, he told me that Ellacuría appreciated him for that. In 1978 he had won the international poetry prize of the Guatemalan city of Quetzaltenango, which was prestigious in the region, and Ellacuría had written a prologue for those poems when the book was published. Professor Escobar was a pleasant man, about 1.70 metres tall, who always wore jeans and white cotton shirts. Already by that time, his hair had turned white, although he had not reached sixty years old.

'Guess what,' said Francisco Andrés, 'Ellacuría always told me he was convinced that he could avoid his own assassination by talking with his executioner. He believed he could convince anyone.'

'Did they think of that, that they were in danger?'

'One assumes so. At times, he forgot, other times he remembered and assumed it. It was a possibility. Well, so possible that in the end it happened.'

We were on the terrace of the Faculty of Communications building. In front of us stood a tree with immense branches, almost devoid of greenery. It was a little after five in the afternoon. Below, the corridors were crowded with students leaving their classes. That day, 16 November, they finished earlier than usual. In the evening there would be a procession, then Mass would be celebrated, with a wake commemorating the assassinated Jesuit Fathers. The gentle breeze brought a fragrance from somewhere. We were leaning on the cement ledge. Neither of us mentioned that fragrance.

'Do you harbour any rancour? I'm referring to what they say about Ellacuría being like a father; it must be hard, accepting that situation. If seeing some photos moves one, I dread to think what it must be like to have seen the actual event, seeing them lying about there.'

'When you come across something like that it's like a vision that is not part of reality. It's difficult to explain. It is very hard and immensely sad. But it also contains an enormous dose of unreality. I kept telling myself, I don't hold anything against those who killed them. Those who pulled the trigger, I mean. They were puppets. Do you understand me?'

'Yes, I do understand.'

'They couldn't say no. They couldn't exchange their lives for the priests' lives. They were mere soldiers. If they were told to go and kill priests, it would be the same as saying go and kill pigeons in the centre.'

'So, you've got nothing against them?'

'Against them? No. The truly guilty ones aren't the soldiers. And we all know that. Those that they judged and put into jail are circus lions that leap through hoops, but the owners of the circus are something else. The owners gave the orders. The staff college. Those, yes. Those are the true assassins. And they remain with peaceful minds. And for them, there's a different feeling. It's abominable that nothing has changed. They should be judged as they should have been from the start.'

'The truth is that it doesn't seem as if anything is going to change.'

'You never know, perhaps with the years.'

'Maybe.'

A few months before we talked, the peace deal was signed between the Salvadorian government and the guerrilla forces. But that peace did not bring any kind of justice, not for that crime nor for other massacres carried out by both sides.

Twenty years have passed since we had that conversation. Throughout that time, the Spanish government has tried to extradite those who were truly guilty of the massacre. The

Salvadorian government has turned down this request on every occasion. The names have been given. Different investigations have reached conclusions about those who are truly responsible. At times, it looks as if things are moving forward. At other times, it seems all is lost.

'I had been to the chapel before,' I said, 'but not to the museum. By the way, did I mention that I don't like the chapel's paintings?'

'Too strong?'

'Well, yes, they are very hard to take. Actually, more than hard to take, I think they're too sombre.'

'But they reflect that period.'

'OK. I don't mean to say they are bad. It's not that.'

'Yes, yes, I understand. Don't worry about it.'

'They're good paintings, or so I believe, but they are so hard to take, so sombre. They make the chapel appear not to be a chapel but something else. Something like a horror show. Those paintings, the crypts. Too much darkness.'

The paintings hang on the chapel walls and have been drawn with charcoal in black and white. They show scenes of tortured bodies, tied up with chains around their wrists, and thrown to the ground or kneeling. There are many hanging there. In a corner, to the left, you can see six niches in the wall and an always-burning candle facing them. I had visited the chapel a month before, when I attended a commemoration event for the aunt of my friend Miguel, who disappeared during the offensive of 1989. But even then with those sombre paintings and the images in the niches, that visit did not affect me as much as a visit to the museum of martyrs.

It had happened the same afternoon as my conversation with Escobar. A few hours before. I had it in mind from weeks back, but that day, after reading a novel in the library that I would leave unfinished forever, I took the walk that leads to the Centro Monsignor Romero, which is where the small museum lies. There was nobody in the room, despite it being 16 November. A moving silence reigned in the depths of that narrow room. At its centre there was a display case that divided the room into two. There were display cases on all the walls. What was being exhibited were the Jesuit Fathers' belongings, as well as Monsignor Romero's, Rutilio Grande's and those of the North American monks assassinated by the army at the start of the 1980s. Through the glass, I could see a coffee-coloured bathrobe with a crust of dried blood similar to a map, some sandals, also with bloodstains, shirts ripped open by bullets, notebooks, a Bible, some toys, magazines referring to the football team Atlético de Bilbao, dirty vests, belts, envelopes for letters, and in everything that I saw I could observe a life lived without luxuries, and at times, even sunk in poverty. I thought that those people had stayed and I couldn't understand the reason why. They seemed good people to me. I mean, I couldn't think any other way. Notable. Simple. They used to laugh. I asked myself if I would have remained in my country under those circumstances and I realised that whatever I could answer would be a lie.

I walked around the room before coming across a table on which rested a photo album. I opened it and found images of the Jesuits' bodies. On their backs. Some had their brains splattered on the ground, another hardly a little hole at the back of his head. I also saw photos of the two women, Elba and Celina. The mother covering her daughter, in the middle of the chaos that was the bedroom where they had spent the night. The scenes were terrible. So much so I could almost smell the blood. Or could feel it, but what I couldn't take was that it had been possible. I learnt that the specks of ash and particles of blood were imperceptible and would remain invisible all over the place. On the walls. On the ground. Not only in the canvas or in the leather of the sandals and shoes, but also stuck to the glass and on the walls and on the metal doorknobs.

When I left the Centro Monsignor Romero, it seemed like there wasn't anyone in the university. I walked without thinking downhill to the Communications building. I asked if my teacher Professor Escobar was in his office. They told me he was. I went through. As soon as I entered his office, I told him that I had just seen the horrors of the Fathers in the museum. I do not recall what he asked me or what I responded, and my following memory is that we were standing on the building's terrace and he was saying something about November's light, if I'd noticed it was clearer.

That day, at the end of the afternoon as it got dark, we went down to observe the procession that moved along from the car park to the chapel. From afar, we saw candles approaching. We listened to people's soft, almost silent singing and heard in the distance the church bells of the Ceiba de Guadalupe. The wind still brought fragrances of incense from somewhere. And I was still disturbed by the ghastly images of the massacre.

'When do you think that this story began?' I asked Professor Escobar, without knowing why I asked him that. 'I'm referring to the history of the massacres. Did it begin with Ellacuría's decision to come back from Barcelona? Or with the start of the offensive? Or before that? When was the destiny of these men decided?'

'I believe', Francisco Escobar told me, 'that this history did not start with the offensive, nor in 1989, nor with Romero's death, nor with Rutilio's. I truly believe it should begin in 1950 when a priest spoke to some seminarians about our country and asked them who wanted to come to the Santa Tecla seminary. And someone called Ignacio raised his hand.'

I'm not sure if the procession moved beyond us and left us behind or we walked away from it. The last thing I recall from that afternoon was the strange sound of a murmur that was dying out and a very far-off light that got smaller and smaller until it vanished.

Thanks

It is just and right that I thank those who are also protagonists in this novel and whose very valuable testimonies made this book possible:

To Father José María Tojeira, SJ; to Father Jon Sobrino, SJ; to José Simán and Márgara Zablah de Simán; to the lawyer Alfredo Cristiani, ex-president of the Republic of El Salvador, among many others who prefer to remain anonymous through the years of terror and threats. Many hours of interviews that we have shared together, have recreated the key points in this history during those sombre days. I want to also thank Teresa Whitfield and Marta Doggett for their valuable research that contributed so much to my own.